Crescent Beach
A Novel

Jaime R. Forth

This book is a work of fiction. All characters and events portrayed in the story are either products of the author's imagination, or are used unintentionally and/or fictitiously. The majority of locations are real, as they appeared or operated in the 1970s.

Copyright © 2020 Jaime R. Forth

Cover Photograph by Jaime R. Forth

ISBN: 9798655943896

All rights reserved.

For Robert,
who deserved better

Oh life is a glorious cycle of song,
A medley of extemporania;
And love is a thing that can never go wrong;
And I am Marie of Roumania.

Dorothy Parker
Comment

ACKNOWLEDGMENTS

An author's work is never just about imagination. The grittier side of writing is about researching, fact-checking, and proofreading. I'm very grateful to Renee Pond Harrington, Leilani Kelly, Paula Ryan, Priscilla Fitzgerald and Vicki Radmore for their assistance and support.

To Diana Ostrom, whose advice and encouragement never fail, a heartfelt thank you. And thank you also to Sheryl and Jim Cobb, whose friendship and generosity were so appreciated.

Chapter One

April - June 1978

The patchouli hit her before she rounded the corner. The earthy smell slowed her gait and by the time she saw him she already knew who she was dealing with.

"Tommy, I told you, you can't camp out at our back door like this. The next time I find you here, I'm gonna call Mike and he'll come and haul your lazy butt down to County. You hear me?"

The prone figure smiling up at her was deeply tanned, middle aged, and dressed in old fatigue pants and a torn black tee. His feet were bare. "Now, you wouldn't do that to me, Miz Birdie, would you?" he said. "You're too kind fer that."

She cocked her head. "We've talked about this before and you know me, Tommy. I've gotta do what I gotta do. You can't sleep here. I'll give you money if you need it, but you have to go." Her voice softened. "You want me to call your brother for you?"

His smile disappeared and he rose awkwardly from his makeshift bed. "Naw, I'll go, Miz Birdie." He looked at her hopefully. "Got a drink for me, then?"

She looked back at him, raised her brows.

"Alright," he said "I'm goin'."

She put the trash in the can and went back into the bar.

"Tommy's back," she said to Georgette, who was cutting limes at the other end of the bar.

"Yeah, I saw him. I knew you'd take care of it," said the younger woman.

There were no barbacks at the Crescent Club, they did their own setups and breakdowns which meant mostly nine and ten-hour shifts. Today, they were both covering the morning shift with four other bartenders handling overlapping afternoon and evening shifts. Birdie didn't have a preference but her tendonitis had flared up, and the day shift meant fewer mixed drinks.

"Lee is getting a promotion," said Georgette.

Birdie looked up from wiping down the sink wells and bar top. "Oh yeah? That's great! Another department, or still in utilities?"

"He'll be a day shift supervisor in utilities," said Georgette. "He's really excited."

"I'll bet. You guys doing anything special to celebrate?"

Georgette laid the knife on the pad and began to collect lime wedges, transferring them into glass caddies. "We were going to go out tonight," she said, "but something came up."

Birdie dressed carefully for her 27th birthday party. She didn't want to appear informed and too perfectly dressed, so she put on a short flowy cream chiffon dress with tiny coral flowers. After thinking a moment, she added her favorite brown cowboy boots. No one would suspect.

She was supposed to have been surprised, but Kiki, who hadn't the heart to ambush a friend, had given her a heads up a day in advance. When she arrived, there were thirty or so people - some of them she didn't know - packed into Kiki's small apartment at the Mira Mar, screaming Happy Birthday and blowing noisemakers. Birdie was genuinely touched at the trouble people had gone to to be there, and spent the first few minutes profusely thanking everyone until Kiki hauled her off to the kitchen and poured her a large martini just to shut her up.

The guests. Her boss, Charlie, had kindly shown up but departed soon afterward with excuses regarding another engagement. Georgette, of course, with her longtime boyfriend, Lee; Claire, Birdie's best friend and former sister in-law. Nicholas,

Claire's brother and Birdie's ex-husband was there, too, charming as ever, turning on his southern drawl for Diana, who cashiered at Siesta Market in the village. Kiki'd invited a date, a writer she'd recently met who leaned against the wall much of the night, watching everyone else, eyes occasionally flickering over to Birdie's, eyes that were knowing and amused.

They had one brief conversation, she and the writer. Kiki had an enlarged photo of the Eiffel Tower hanging in the hallway, visible from the living room. When she saw him studying it, Birdie turned to him. "She took that photo herself, did she tell you?"

"No, but it's very good."

"Have you been there yourself?"

He turned slightly, shoulder against the wall, and regarded her. "Yes. You?"

She shook her head. "But did you know the tower is named after the firm that designed it?"

He swallowed some of his drink and smiled. "Somehow that fact escaped me."

"It was called Eiffel et Campagnie. The man who did the design work was named Koechlin. It was constructed for the anniversary of the French Revolution. The people of Paris thought it was a monstrosity and intended to tear it down afterward but never did. Obviously."

"Are you an architect, by any chance?"

Her turn to smile. "No, my father was a builder, he studied those things. I somehow inherited that sort of useless information."

"Not so useless, you never know what you'll trigger when you pass along information like that."

His voice had a warm, low cadence. She looked at him closely, wondered about the accent.

He turned, Kiki was calling for him. "Victor, there's someone you have to meet, he has this bookstore over on Main . . ." she stopped, looked at Birdie. "Am I interrupting?"

Birdie waved her hand. "Absolutely not. Go."

There was the requisite cake soon afterward, and Nicholas came to give her a birthday kiss. "Totally unnecessary, Nicky," she said. She could tell he was already hammered.

"Baby. For old times' sake." He put an arm around her and she laughed uncomfortably, looked around for Claire.

Diana was her rescuer. "There you are!" she cooed, taking his arm. "Stinger is here now and you promised you'd do that Who's on First routine for me."

Birdie watched, relieved, as Diana led him away into the other room. They passed a small group where the writer was standing, talking. He turned toward Birdie. Their eyes met. He tilted his head, communicating something, she didn't know what. She looked the other way.

At the end of the night the core group that was left sat laughing and trading stories over breakfast prepared by Kiki, who earned her living as a sous chef at Pattigeorge's on Longboat Key. They perched on chairs and benches and, in the case of Georgette and Lee, in each other's laps, in the tiny living room feasting on omelettes aux herbes, and frittes, sausages, and toasted baguettes smothered with homemade jam. Kiki was an unabashed Francophile and everyone loved her big eyes and big heart. She also had a reputation for promiscuity and, casting glances at her date for the evening, they all knew who was slated to be the next recipient of her famous hospitality.

But he fooled them all and left just ahead of Birdie, kissing Kiki on the cheek and turning to Birdie to wish her Happy Birthday before closing the door behind him. He had, he said, an early appointment that couldn't be escaped. Watching him, Birdie wasn't so sure an escape wasn't happening before their eyes.

Home was a two-bedroom two-bath condominium on Ocean Boulevard, north of the village on Siesta Key. Birdie had lived there on and off for eight years, never grown tired of the heavily landscaped entryway, the thick banyans in front, scattered coconut palms in back that gave way to the Gulf of Mexico. Inside, an eclectic mix of English and French antiques with Chinese porcelains and Russian artifacts thrown in. It took only twenty minutes to drive there from Kiki's Palm Avenue apartment downtown.

She pulled off her boots and mixed a martini, opened the sliding glass doors and padded out to the lanai, put her feet up and looked over the flowing dark expanse. Her place, on the second floor, was purchased by her parents for its optimal view of Sarasota Big Pass.

Her father said it would give good resale value to the property. That was her father, always looking to the future.

Birdie had never cared much for being out on the water, she was happy just to look at it. Her cousin up north had lost his life in the Great Lakes, a song had been written about it a couple of years ago, the Edmund Fitzgerald. She never knew him, he'd traveled for a living working as a deckhand on freighters.

She felt the history of her family like a solid rock beneath her, knew the stories and the people and where they came from. It gave her a sense of self-assurance. She had roots, knew what her father had gone through to get to where he was, to give her and her mother the things they had. Her parents worked hard, remembered, saved.

Her mother's family hadn't thought much of the Russian immigrant from Petrograd who was her father, they wanted better things for the daughter who had been raised to marry a Virginia aristocrat. The daughter said no and stuck to her guns. She saw promise in a man who could look at buildings and know at a glance what made them great, a man whose arms encircled her under the moon and spoke with passion about his native city and the Neva River on which it stood, described the future he envisioned for himself and for her.

The girl from Virginia had wanted a dreamer and found one. When they married they produced a child, named her Bernadette, then turned their practical attentions to building up a construction business. It thrived.

The daughter thrived, too, under their warmth and affection. She emerged from their home prepared to stand on her own, fend for herself, deal with most of life's vagaries. What Birdie hadn't been adequately prepared for was men like Nicholas Noonan.

She met him a few months after starting at the Chicken Coop, the bar on Osprey Avenue behind the hospital. It was a hangout for construction workers and All American guys. Nicholas had stood at the bar, leaned on his elbow a little unsteadily and asked for a beer. His friend had put a hand on his shoulder and said, "Nicky, I don't think you wanna go there. Spare this pretty girl an argument and jus' come with me, nice an' easy now."

"Believe this guy?" Nicholas had looked at her and grinned, co-conspirators having a pleasant chat. "I'll have that beer now, Miss."

The friend had moved quickly, taken his hand and somehow twisted the arm up and behind the shoulder, turned him around so he was moving away from the bar. Nicholas had managed to look over his shoulder and grin again. "See you 'round," he'd said.

She saw him again a week later. She turned and he was seated on a stool at the point end of the bar, watching her.

"What I want is to take you out," he said, when she asked what he wanted.

She told him she didn't date customers. "Okay," he said, getting up to leave. "Forget the drink. What time do you get off? I'll pick you up then."

It was against her better judgment, he was cocky and handsome and she was relatively sure he was a jock, but she hadn't had a date in months and figured she was due.

The courtship was long. She didn't want to sleep with him on the first date, or be predictable and sleep with him on the third; she planned to make him wait until the fourth, but by then he'd figured it out and made her wait until the fifth. It was worth the wait. She found her perfect physical match in a professional baseball player, a first baseman for an American League baseball team.

Not so perfect in other ways. She'd never cared much for sports, didn't fit in well with the other wives who could cite performance stats in their sleep. Nicholas was injured two years into the marriage, in rehab for another six months. The rehab was unsuccessful and he was released from his contract.

He bought a motocross shop on the east side of town that specialized in Pentons, but dirt biking couldn't compare to his former glory and his drinking increased. The fan girls were still around and he spent too much time at the shop late at night.

Toward the end she spent too much energy trying to sort truth from half-truths, listening in vain for the key at the front door. She left him a note and moved back to her condo. The document from her attorney put an end to his attempts at reconciliation. Too little, too late.

Birdie finished her drink, slid the door closed, went and placed the glass in the kitchen sink. Maybe this year would be different, better. Happy Birthday to her.

Georgette stepped to the service bar and called out an order. "I've got five Harvey Wallbangers," she said.

Birdie looked at her and smirked. "Someone been out front doing that dance again, Georgette?"

It was a joke between them. Last year a couple of women, out celebrating a divorce, had done too much celebrating and stood between Midnight Pass Road and the front entrance to the bar waving down passersby and doing a dance that might have gotten them arrested if Georgette, driving into the parking lot for her evening shift, hadn't talked them away from the road and called a cab.

The inspired performance had brought in a group of tourists who stayed the rest of the afternoon ordering Harvey Wallbangers. They turned out to be a lot of fun, three couples from Tampa driving down to Key West for a long weekend who strayed onto Siesta Key for lunch, figured they'd found what they were looking for and ended up staying on Siesta instead.

"I'm serious," Georgette said, laughing. "And if you don't mind me saying so, you're kind of cranky, I think you've been too long without. Isn't it time you started dating again?"

She returned a few minutes later. "I think I can save you the trouble of looking," she whispered theatrically.

Birdie glared at her from beneath stitched brows. "Georgie, what the heck," she said.

"Table three, in the corner by the phone booth. Check him out, doesn't he look familiar? Isn't that the guy Kiki had at your birthday party a coupla weeks ago?"

Birdie said, "I'm not playing this game, Georgette. Go take his order and bring it to me."

"Too late. I need a break and I have to use the bathroom."

Birdie sighed.

Sunday breakfast at the Zolenkos was served on a Moroccan tiled terrace overlooking the Gulf of Mexico. Birdie would rise early, put on a nice dress, make the 30-minute drive from her condo on Siesta Key. She turned right at Highway 41, turned right again at Blackburn Point Road and made her way south through the seagrape and bougainvillea-lined lane that wound serenely through narrow little Casey Key. She enjoyed her parents' company, enjoyed, too, the food produced by her mother's hand, delicacies loved by her father. Blini with red caviar, buterbrody with doctorskaya, oladyi with sour cream and raspberry jam, all accompanied by cups of strong black tea.

Birdie helped her mother with the table setup, carrying plates and cutlery past bureaus crowded with family photos. Uncle Jack in a top hat laughing with Aunt Caroline in fur and a diamond tiara; mother and Fa on skis, posed on a mountaintop somewhere in Canada; Cousin Harry who had died in Lake Michigan, low gray ship riding in the background; Birdie with Nicky's arm around her, his wavy jet black hair and dark blue eyes a contrast to her fair skin, chin length strawberry blond hair and light blue eyes. "Mother," she called out. "I wish you would replace that wedding picture."

Conversation was always informal at these breakfasts, and kind, her parents never pressured or presumed. They made suggestions with presses of the hand, kisses, little nods of affirmation. "We know you'll do the right thing," her mother would say. Fa had hugged her when she announced her divorce a year ago, sadly patted her cheek. "It is the best," he had said. "Let us put it behind us. There will be another."

Another husband? Another error in judgment? Birdie wasn't entirely sure but she knew her father was behind her, and that meant something.

After eating they would go inside, pour vodka, listen to a recording of Rimsky-Korsakov's Scheherazade or The Tsar's Bride, talk about their week. It was how Birdie found out about important events, her cousin's death, another cousin's wedding, her parent's trip to Michigan. Lately her mother might take her hand, lead her to her dressing room where she would open the safe, extract a piece of jewelry. "This is for you, Birdie, I want you to have it. One day it will come to you anyway, it might as well be now."

At first, Birdie was distressed by the generosity. Was her mother *dying?* But her father had been reassuring. "Your mother is just getting older, Birdie. Let her enjoy this." And so, Birdie was amassing a nice cache of precious jewelry. She would add the pieces to her safe as soon as she reached home, make a mental note to call her insurance company.

She placed his bourbon on a coaster and lingered a moment, leaned on the bar. His eyes flowed slowly over her callipygian curves, rose to meet her gaze.

His smile was reserved. "How are you?"

"Not bad, smooth sailing."

He put a hand to his mouth, nodded, looked away. He seemed pensive, lost inside himself, she felt she was being dismissed.

She moved down toward the door, greeted a newcomer, returned to the tap and started pouring a beer, glass angled forty-five degrees.

"Anything new since I've been gone?" he said to her back.

She was already walking away. "Nope," she called out.

They'd been doing the dance for two or three weeks. He'd come in a couple times a week, always alone, sit at the bar or at a deuce, they'd chat for a few minutes, he'd give her the look, she'd go back to work.

He was hard to ignore. Trim, ruggedly good looking with slender cheekbones, ridged nose, auburn hair swept casually to the side, eyes that appraised her when she was speaking. *What was he thinking* when he looked into her with those cool, blue-green eyes? She'd glance in his direction now and then, sometimes catch him watching her. It felt like high school somehow. When they talked, it was about everyday things. How was your trip? Oh good, successful. How were things here? Busy, well, it's season, you know. You spoken to Kiki lately? No, been kind of busy. What about you, anything interesting? Me? Not much. *Well, if you wanted to take me to bed I wouldn't say no. Just kidding!*

She found Georgette doubled over in the stockroom, hands across her abdomen, and closed the door behind her hurriedly. "Georgie! What's going on?"

Georgette grimaced, said, "Having a little spasm, I'll be alright in a minute."

Birdie stood next to her, uncertain what to do. "What can I get you? Do you need a doctor?"

"No, I just need a few minutes."

"Georgie, you look like you're about to give birth. Here, let me help you sit down. Come on." She put out a hand and guided the woman to an empty stack of pallets, stooped and looked at her.

"I dunno, Birdie, I've been having these for a couple of weeks now, off and on, it's starting to scare me. I just haven't gotten around to making an appointment. First I was kind of nauseated, then tired all the time . . ."

Birdie lifted her brows.

"I know what you're thinking but it's not that. Look," Georgette straightened. "It's easing up a little. I think I'm better now."

The door opened and one of the bartenders poked his head in. Birdie waved her hand, met him at the opening. "Girl talk, we'll just be a minute," made a facial expression that explained everything, returned to Georgette. "Are you sure you'll be able to work?"

"Yeah, these always go away, I just need a couple of minutes. Really, I'll meet you back out on the floor."

Birdie reached for the jar of olives, looked at Georgette. "If you're not back out there in five, I'll be back here looking for you," she said.

She ran into Victor the following day in the village, she was crossing the parking lot after leaving Rexell's Drugs. The door to the Butcher's Block swung open and he stood in the sunshine holding a paper-encased package.

She stopped, waited for him. "Hi."

His eyes drifted over her. She was wearing short shorts and a tube top, normal attire for running errands on a day off, bangs swept up in a wide headband.

He said, "Hello. Where're you off to in such a hurry?"

She gestured. "Siesta Market. I have one more thing and then I'm done for the day. How are you?"

He smiled, waved the package. "Dinner." He looked across the street. "As it happens, I'm headed that way myself. Walk with you?"

"Sure."

It didn't take long and they lingered afterward in front of the market, not quite saying goodbye, not quite anything else either. He looked at his watch. "It's almost lunch. You, uh, feel like the Wildflower?"

She thought quickly, almost said yes, then gestured. "What about dinner?"

He was nonchalant, "Oh, they'll put it in their fridge for me."

She hesitated, surprised herself, was rewarded with a smile.

Did they talk? It was more an interview than a conversation, he wanted to know things. How long had she been tending bar, did she like it, where had she learned it. Where did she live on the key? At this, he listened more intently, leaning forward as though hard of hearing. "And your father, does he live there as well?"

"Victor. I hope you're not some sort of axe murderer, setting me up for a fall."

He grinned. "Axe murderers don't usually announce their deeds beforehand, do they? I think they fall into the acts-of-passion category."

She grimaced. "Grisly thought. But no, my parents are down on Casey Key. When my father retired he built a house there." She looked at him. "What about you? What do you write that gives you the sort of schedule where you can travel and come into the bar at odd hours?"

He shrugged. "I'm doing a lot of research right now. That's why I'm here, I needed to take a day off from the library."

She searched his face, assessing him. "Not my idea of fun."

"Sometimes it is."

He was being deliberately vague but she didn't call him on it.

She glanced outside, clouds were gathering low in the sky. "This was nice, Victor, thank you, but I'd better go. It looks like rain and I don't have the umbrella."

He reached for the check and they slid out of the booth, parted ways in front of the drugstore. She looked over her shoulder as she got into her car but he had already disappeared.

Two days later, back at work. Georgette had left a note taped to the till. "Nicholas called, call him back. Important." The last word was underlined. Birdie sighed, put the note in her pocket. It was always important.

Customers filtered in slowly through the afternoon. Seasonal regulars were just starting to return, but the place had never been popular with tourists looking for something tropical, umbrellas in the drinks and Jimmy Buffet on the jukebox. It was a hangout for locals, a full-sized red English phone booth in the corner, loud rock 'n' roll, a smoky interior punctuated with red lighting, and Birdie, usually low-key and friendly, sometimes not.

Later in her shift she turned from the till and saw Victor leaning against the point end of the bar, waiting for a seat. She only had a moment to greet him, several others walked in at the same time.

A middle-aged man and woman, seated in front of the tap, grew silent as she approached.

"Hey, isn't that Victor Babel you were talking to, the novelist?" said the man to Birdie.

She looked at him blankly. "The who?"

"You know. *Last Train to Istanbul, Paris 1938.*"

"*Midnight in Munich,*" the woman chimed in. "I recognized him from his picture, I heard he was living around here now."

Birdie placed the filled glasses on coasters and reached for a check. "You want to start a tab?" she asked.

The man nodded. "Keep 'em coming. We've got some celebrating to do."

"We both retired last week," beamed his companion. "Just closed on our house, we're finally full-time residents."

Birdie smiled. "Congratulations."

He held out a hand. "Name's Will. This is my wife, Emily."

Birdie smiled again, introduced herself. "Hope you'll be happy here, hope to see you around." She caught a signal from another customer and excused herself.

She was steadily busy. When she glanced toward Victor he was turned away from her, talking to a new arrival. Young, thirtyish, pretty tanned face, swimmer's shoulders. The woman glanced at Birdie and gestured, her other hand rested on Victor's arm.

"Do you have any decent wines?" Spoken imperially.

"We don't serve bottled wine, by the glass only. White chablis or red burgundy." Birdie's tone was neutral, carefully professional.

Victor turned to look at Birdie as the woman hesitated. Their eyes met, his seemed to be saying something. She didn't speak the language.

The woman made her choice and Birdie went to fill the order, no backward looks. Men who went to certain lengths to conceal things, acted interested then showed up with other women, were harboring more than she wanted to deal with.

Georgette handled the bar while Birdie took a short break, she wasn't around when Victor left. She drove home from work with windows open so the fresh air could remove some of the smoke from her hair and clothing.

Her steps sounded unnaturally loud on the parquet floor as she moved through the entryway, tossing keys on the table by the door, heading back to her bedroom. Shower first, then something to eat. She deposited the smoke-infused clothes on the lanai, went to rummage through the refrigerator, a carton of leftover Chinese from the Golden Buddha, a container of borscht, two wrinkled apricots, the last piece of yesterday's quiche Lorraine. She settled on the quiche and ate it cold, accompanied by a glass of buttery chardonnay, thinking about the woman at the bar with Victor. She hadn't seemed his type. Birdie shrugged; what did she know, she had been wrong about his interest, maybe her skills at reading people were slipping.

She carried the dishes into the kitchen, brushed her teeth, went to bed.

A party two nights later. Kiki was in charge, they were dressing up, going to have fun, she was very determined. Birdie thought she might as well, she hadn't had much fun on her own lately and if you couldn't have fun around Kiki, something was wrong and it wasn't with Kiki.

The place was just around the corner from Birdie's, Kiki talking excitedly in the car, turning to smile over her shoulder, checking her lipstick in the mirror, really, as Nicky used to say, almost as nervous as a virgin at a prison rodeo.

"Here we are, turn left down here, on Anglin," Kiki waved her hand, and at the second house, too many cars so they parked down the street.

"Okay, I guess we're here," said Claire. "What do you know about this guy?" They crossed the lawn under a pale turquoise sky.

"Well, you met him once but you wouldn't remember," said Kiki, taking Claire's arm.

Birdie was puzzled. "We did? When?" They ascended the rounded steps, opened the first door. There was music and laughter inside, Robert Palmer gleefully Sneaking Sally Through the Alley.

Victor approached as she entered the room, took her hand. "What are you doing here?" He drew her close, eyes searching her face.

She slid her hand away. "Not much of a smooth operator, are you?" she said.

He laughed. "I'm just surprised, I wasn't expecting you."

"Me neither."

Kiki, scented and polished to satiny perfection, wasn't going to waste her energies on *this*. She stepped forward, took his arm and led him away, whispering in his ear, laughing.

Claire stood and looked after Kiki as they walked away. "Poor man doesn't stand a chance."

Birdie found the bar, ordered a martini, turned and surveyed the room. Older house, probably 1950s, fireplace, wood ceiling, configured for maximum airflow. He went for the old style Hawaiian pieces, thick cushions over bamboo and rattan, classic Polynesian with a little tiki. She thought it went along with the house, approved grudgingly.

Victor had interesting friends. A historian who held Claire's knee while he talked earnestly about the Indian wars out west and the tragedy at Wounded Knee. Claire turned to Birdie and burst out laughing, waved her hand, quickly blamed it on the alcohol, laughed some more.

Birdie wandered. A movie-star tall, dark and handsome man materialized, kissed her cheek, Victor's agent, he said. The party was to introduce his book locally, she was buying it, of course? She laughed, because Kiki had never said a thing. She took a couple of hits from the joint he offered before moving on.

A travel journalist on a spiritual pilgrimage to find himself said he had been to India, but of course who hadn't, and Vietnam, the most beautiful women in the world were there he said, and looked at her as if expecting an argument. He offered her what he was smoking but she shook her head, drifted toward the flirtatious look of a stranger across the room.

The accidental owner of a gay dance club downtown.

"Accidental?" said Birdie, taking a sip of the gin and vermouth, appraising him over the rim of the glass.

His blue eyes went slowly from the bottom of her glass to the top, settled there. He was amused.

"Let's sit down." He pointed, took her arm, led her to two chairs in a corner. His knees rested carelessly against hers.

"At first it was just a little hangout, you know, imported beer, sandwiches, lots of plants, friends meeting for backgammon, that sort of place."

She nodded, watched him talk, set her glass on the floor.

He leaned forward, lit a cigarette, made the offer but she declined. "It did alright, so I opened a second place downtown, this was a nightclub. It caught on, too. I guess it was the location, I don't know, next thing I knew it was attracting a gay crowd. So I went with the flow, everyone was happy, the money good," he shrugged, smiled into her eyes. She smiled, too.

A shadow fell, knelt beside her. "Hey John, how ya' doin'."

Her companion looked over, smiled. "Vic, how are ya'?"

She was observing her 'not looking at men that are interested in *other* women' policy. Instead, reached for her glass.

A warm hand gripped her arm. "Can we talk?"

She hesitated.

He placed his mouth against her ear, a shiver went up her spine. "Please."

She smiled apologetically toward John, rose from the chair.

He took her hand and pulled her swiftly through the rooms and out the back door to a place where the music was muted, nothing around them but open space and faint overhead stars.

She jumped and swore at him when he touched her waist and he laughed softly, caught her against him when she stumbled.

She shook off his hand. "What are we doing here?" she said.

"What do you think?"

She gestured impatiently. "I'm a little puzzled. You're a busy man."

"Why are you being like this, Birdie?"

She said, "Being like what?"

He tilted his head, eyes wandering her face. "Christine Granville," he said.

"What? Are we in the same conversation?"

He leaned unperturbedly against the house. "There's something about you that makes me think of her. She was a spy who volunteered her services to the Brits in World War Two, they sent her to Warsaw, then Hungary. She had a lot of nerve, was famous for skiing across the mountains into Poland to rescue POWs. She did a lot of other things too, but like I said—"

"Why didn't you tell me who you are?"

He studied her in the starlight. "You strike me as someone who likes to keep things private. Well I do, too. You going to fault me for that?"

She looked at him silently, assessing him, slowly shook her head. Neither of them spoke for a moment. He stepped forward, took hold of her arms but she jerked away angrily.

"What is this? Your date turn you down so now you come on to me?"

He gave a short laugh. "My date?"

She said impatiently, "Burgundy by the glass."

He paused, laughed again. "My sister? She was on an academic trip to Miami, passing through." He looked at her closely. "Is that what this is about? You thought —"

"Kiki," she said. "She's a friend, and I'm not inclined —"

"There's nothing there," he said. "I made that very clear."

She stepped away but he moved in front of her.

"Not so fast," he said.

She made a gesture of irritation. "You're drunk," she said.

He grinned. "Maybe just a little."

She didn't like it, he was too sure of himself. "You have the wrong idea about about me," she said.

His eyes washed slowly over her face, he shook his head. "No, I don't think so."

"We don't know each other well enough." She started to turn away.

He seized her wrist. "So let's change that."

She sighed, looked up into his face. "What do you want?"

He stepped closer, smiled slightly, took her chin in his hand and tilted her head back. "I want to kiss you so badly I'm willing to put up with your testiness. You have a nice mouth, Birdie. I've been thinking about it ever since we met."

She was silent, looked at him through half-closed eyes, felt his mouth rest on hers, the slow tilt of head, the sweet charcoal taste of bourbon, the whisper of the wind as it picked up around them. His hands were warm on her face and neck. They paused, kissed again, more slowly this time and she knew, as her hands clutched his arms, as she settled closer to his chest, that she was headed for trouble.

She didn't see him again for several days, he called her at the Crescent Club the fourth night. "I don't know your last name," he said by way of greeting.

"Noonan."

"Can I see you tomorrow night, Birdie Noonan?"

"I'll be here, working tomorrow night."

"Let me rephrase that. When can I see you? For an evening, not just a few kisses in the back yard."

"Monday. I'm off Mondays and Tuesdays."

There was a short silence. "I can't believe this. I'll be out of town Monday."

"Well," she said, "I'll be around."

"Sunday. Are you working all day Sunday?"

"No, but I have plans on Sunday morning."

"You go to *church*, is that it?" He sounded amused.

"No, I have breakfast with my parents on Sundays."

"Oh. How late are you there tonight?"

She looked at her watch. "For another hour."

When he came in and leaned against the wall by the phone booth, he didn't look at her the same way. He *observed* her. It made her feel awkward, heavy handed. She spilled a beer, added well rum to a daiquiri instead of the Mount Gay called for, and had to start all over again. Georgette looked at her oddly and she shrugged it off, *some days are like that.*

They walked out to her car and he followed her home so she could change first. She had thought about it beforehand and decided if she couldn't trust him, she had no business going out with him in the first place.

He made an appreciative sound when the front door closed behind them.

She turned. "What?"

"I was expecting, I don't know, surfboards, fishnets, conch shells. Not this."

She smiled briefly. "Sorry to disappoint."

"It's very nice."

She laid her keys on the table. "Have a seat, I won't be long."

When she went to find him he was out on the lanai, looking over the dark water. She could hear the hiss and boom of the surf, see the sky lights reflected on the waves moving toward the shoreline.

He turned, looked at her, raised his brows. "You're full of surprises."

"I think we've already established who's full of surprises," she said tartly.

He laughed. "Touché."

He drove to the Turtle Beach Marina at the south end of the key. Small restaurant on the bayside, not too fancy, quiet enough for good conversation. They both decided on grouper and set the menus aside.

"So." He looked at her. "Let's see. You're off every Monday, live in a ritzy condo, your parents are nearby, you look good and sexy in a dress, and get a little prickly when things turn personal." He leaned on his elbow, smiled. "Have I got that about right?"

"This is your idea of charming?" she said. "You must not get out much."

He laughed. "As a matter of fact, I don't," he said.

The waitress returned and took their orders. She wasn't much of a charmer, either.

Over dinner, they found things in common. Both liked to read into the wee hours of the morning, it was a start. From there, bits and pieces, music preferences, then history.

"What period, specifically?" he asked her, over dessert.

She picked up her fork, it was an easy answer. "Russia in any timeframe. My father came from the Soviet Union and I grew up on stories about the great Russian writers, the tsars, the generals, the rivers, the architecture."

"He sounds like a romantic, your father."

"Oh, I guess. He's very practical though." She licked whipped cream from the fork, looked up at him. "I think you would like each other."

"I would probably be tempted to interview him."

"No doubt," she said dryly.

After dinner they walked across the street to Turtle Beach, where they sat on the warm smooth sand for a while and watched the moon floating over the Gulf of Mexico, a perfect round sphere of milky white illumination. The water was dark, waves spilled onto the sand languidly, their slow rhythm restful. They were alone on the beach, most of the nightlife was concentrated on the mainland, just across Stickney Point Bridge, or in Siesta Village, but not here, at the residential south end of the key.

She told him about her first night at the Crescent Club. "There's a long-time customer, name is Jim. He used to come in and order pitchers of vodka and orange juice with a straw. He couldn't drive home after a few hours and a couple of those, so he'd order two cabs to take him home, one cabbie would drive his car, the other would drive him, then turn around and take the first driver back to his cab."

"He still around?"

"He's a snowbird, comes and goes. Anyway, on this particular night, he ran into his attorney at the bar and the attorney told him there was no need to call the cabs, his limo was waiting outside and he'd have his driver take him home. So while the attorney was paying his tab, Jim wandered outside and climbed into the back of the car with his pitcher in hand. Only it was the wrong car. He was so drunk, he'd gotten into the back of a patrol car parked outside by the road."

Victor tilted his head and laughed. "With a pitcher of booze in hand."

"Yes indeed. The deputy was going to haul him off to County but the attorney straightened it all out. We still see Jim and his attorney from time to time. He's no longer drinking pitchers, though."

"It's a cozy little place," he said.

She leaned forward, elbows on her knees. "Yeah, a good drinking bar. John D. MacDonald used to walk there when he lived down on Point Crisp Road. I'm sure you've heard about some of the artists and writers who live here, Thornton Utz, Julio de Diego, Dik Browne, Ben Stahl, Al Buell, Mack Kantor. Some of them hang out together."

He nodded. "How long've you been here, anyway?" he asked.

"Going on eight years. In this town, that's just about long enough to start calling yourself a native. Where'd you come from?"

"Santa Fe," he said.

"Really. That's quite a change, coming from there to here." She turned to look at him.

"There's an implied question there, I think," he said.

"Um-hmm."

"Oh, you know, the usual," he said, leaning back, crossing his legs in front of him.

She inclined her head. "The usual as in, you're fleeing the snow and ice, or . . ."

He shrugged. "A love affair that didn't last. But it turned out I liked it here so I stayed."

She bit her lip. "How long ago?"

"Been about a year, I guess." He smiled slightly. "You don't have any boyfriends or husbands lurking around that luxury apartment of yours, do you?"

"Would you stop with the apartment? I scour antiques shops, estate sales, get my parents old castaways."

He leaned forward, watching her face. "You haven't answered the question."

She shook her head. "I'm not seeing anyone."

He reached over and took her chin in hand, peered closely at her in the low light. "You're too pretty for that. What happened, is there a guy out there wandering around with a broken heart?"

She pushed his hand away. "I'm not a subject for your next book. What do you write, anyway? Someone said World War Two thrillers."

"Spy novels." He grinned. "Lots of sex and danger. You like that sort of thing, Birdie?"

She looked at him defiantly. "What, the sex, or the danger?"

He laughed. "I meant the books, but you're a bit dangerous yourself, aren't you? Cool and mysterious—"

"That's enough," she said.

They fell silent, sat and watched the dark waves out in the gulf, crests shimmering under the moonlight as they swayed and climbed their way to the beach. A watery dance, one step forward, two steps back.

He rose, stretched out a hand to help her up.

She stood, and they were face to face. The breeze picked up and a heavy wave slapped against the sand. She pushed the bangs out of her eyes and turned away, but he tugged at her wrist.

"I was thinking we could stay a minute longer," he said.

She smiled a half smile. "But the mystery . . ."

He pulled her closer. "Too late for that," he said. "I've already had a sample, remember? Here I am, back for more."

His eyes were dark aqua in the moonlight, mocking and reckless, she objected to his freshness but was drawn to it like a wave drawn to the shore by the moon. She leaned into him and brushed her lips against his. He smiled into the kiss, his forearm resting on top of her shoulder, after a moment it slid down and he gathered her fully to him. They hesitated, the kiss deepened and lengthened and became a hypothesis. *Maybe*, it said, *maybe we could if.*

When clouds began to flitter across the moon he looked down at her, kissed her mouth briefly, took her hand and led her back to the car. There was a song playing, Bonnie Raitt in an old recording, her teasing voice sliding around the bright horn and honky tonk piano. "No baby, no, that ain't the way how . . ." Birdie glanced at him in the dark, he met her eyes, grinned.

He drove along the winding path that led to her apartment and they got out, climbed the stairs. As she put a hand to the door she heard a noise behind them, familiar footfalls scrunching on the pea gravel. She looked over her shoulder, peering beyond the cavernous banyan.

She laid a hand on his arm, said quietly, "Um, something unexpected. Would you wait here?"

She went down to Nicholas, meeting him at the start of the walkway. In a low voice, "Nicholas, this isn't a good time."

He looked in her face. "Baby, why'nt you call? I tried you twice, where've you been?"

She knew, with sinking heart, that he was drunk, she couldn't send him home in his own car. She thought quickly. "Have you talked to Claire? Let me call her for you, maybe she can come and give you a ride, okay?"

He was trying to focus, his eyes were roaming. "You're, uh," he put a hand to his eyes. "I can't do this alone," he whispered, pitching into her.

She looked up at Victor, frowned, said, "Nicky, sit here, alright? I'm gonna go call Claire."

She unlocked the door and Victor followed her inside. "I think I'll stick around, make sure you're alright," he said.

She paused, phone in hand, looked at him. "I'm so sorry about this."

Claire arrived a short while later, sleepy and apologetic. They put Nicholas in her car and she turned to Birdie. "I wish he wouldn't do this, I don't know what gets into him." She offered a sympathetic smile.

Birdie said, "I'll call you tomorrow, Claire. Sorry to roust you like this."

Victor was waiting inside. She shut the door, spread her hands helplessly. "I'm embarrassed," she said. "I hope you won't think this is typical."

He shook his head. "Just to be clear, this is an ex, right?"

She bit her lip, nodded. "Mm-hmm. He's just having a hard time."

He peered at her closely. "You doing alright?"

She lifted a shoulder. "I was the one who left him." She moved further into the apartment. "Why don't you stay awhile? You want an after dinner drink?"

"What've you got?"

She sifted through bottles. "Kahlua, Grand Marnier, umm, scotch—"

"What kind?"

"Single malt, how's that?"

"That'll do."

"Coming right up. Neat, splash of water, over ice?"

"Ice, thank you."

She went to the kitchen for ice, handed him the glass and went around the sofa, tucked her legs beneath her. She sipped from her glass, placed it on the table.

"Bonnie Raitt, huh?"

He nodded. "I listened to a lot of her living out in New Mexico, uh, California—"

"California?" She tilted her head.

He looked at her over the top of his glass, lowered it and cradled it in his hands. "I lived there, too. My family is from New Mexico. I, uhh, met someone and she had a job offer here so I came with her." He shrugged. "I'm an author, it's not like I have to work from a fixed office somewhere."

She nodded. She was accustomed to assessing people's expressions, watching their hands, listening, looking for signs, it was part of her job. She waited for him to go on but he was finished.

She swallowed some of her drink, said, "That ex-husband you saw earlier, he finished the marriage with a lie. It's something I'm good at detecting." She paused. "I think you're lying to me. I don't know why, and at this point I haven't invested enough to care. But if you expect to see me again you'll have to—"

"She died," he said.

She looked at him in silence. Swallowed. "Victor," she said, "I'm sorry."

He nodded, glanced down at the glass in his hand. "There was a congenital problem no one knew about. She had a heart attack at work one day and just like that . . ." he shook his head, took a drink.

"Let's not talk about this," she said gently.

"No, I . . . I didn't say anything because it isn't the kind of thing you bring up in light dinner conversation. The relationship was in trouble and I felt guilty, we'd had a disagreement the day before." He smiled slightly. "I'm sorry I misled you, it was just too heavy to relate, and too soon."

She set her glass aside. "Are you okay now?"

He nodded, leaned forward, "Something tells me it's going to get interesting if we do this again." His eyes scanned her face, she didn't respond.

"Life isn't predictable," she said finally. "No assurances, you know? Sometimes you just have to close your eyes and press the pedal . . ." She shrugged.

"You gonna give me sleepless nights, Birdie?"

She met him halfway, kissed his mouth, long and slow. "One way or another, I expect so," she said.

He laughed softly. " 'One way or another'. I like that. I like you, and I sure like the way you look at me." He rose from the sofa, said, "Thanks for tonight."

She walked him to the door, waved as he drove off, went and collected his glass and placed it in the sink. She didn't go to bed right away. She sat out on the lanai for a while, sipping the remainder of the scotch, looking at the stars, thinking that there were worse things than being liked.

She thought about her friend Kiki who'd gone to cooking school in Paris. She had told Birdie once that there was nothing more exciting than looking up into a night sky over a strange city and knowing that you were young, and free, and could go anywhere and do anything you wanted. Kiki had traveled to London, she'd visited Stonehenge and said that it was mysterious, haunting, and beautiful. She met a man on the trip who had taken her to Morocco. Birdie had never seen or done any of those things.

She got up and slid the door closed, and went to bed.

A few days later, he called her at home. She was on her way to the car and nearly didn't answer, but sprinted back up the stairs and grabbed the phone on the fifth ring.

"Did I call at a bad time?" he asked.

"Not really. I was just on my way out the door," she said, heart pounding, either because of the run up the stairs or the sound of his voice.

"You still off tomorrow? Maybe we could do something."

She hesitated. "Okay. What did you have in mind?"

"I'm still learning the area. Have you been to Selby Gardens?"

"Not in a long time, it's an interesting place."

"Alright, the gardens. Lunch somewhere after that?"

"Sounds nice," she said.

"Pick you up at ten," he said, and hung up.

They walked slowly through the green lushness of the conservatories, taking in the still beauty of the tropical foliage, the light filled rooms, breathed in the close, humid air. The delicate artistry of the orchids was almost an afterthought for Birdie, it was the atmosphere she went for. She was spellbound by the otherworldliness of the spaces, the beauty for her was in the silences.

Going around a corner she bumped into Victor, who was gazing at yellow orchids floating on thin peduncles high overhead. He turned suddenly and took her shoulder, looked down at her.

"What?" she whispered.

He bent, kissed her mouth, grasped her shoulder more tightly and kissed her again, his tongue swept her lower lip before he let her go.

Her cheeks flushed and she paused, pointed upward, said, "It reminds me of a ghost orchid, have you ever heard of them?"

"No, I haven't." He took her arm and began to walk her outside, in the direction of a banyan grove.

"Ghost orchids are rare, very frail looking. I've seen pictures, they're white, with green stems, they don't have any foliage."

"Rare, you say. Where do they grow?"

She smiled. "Here in Southwest Florida. In the swamps down around Naples. They grow on the trunks of trees and hang, like they're suspended, in midair. Very unusual shape, like a small frog in the middle of a leap. Here's the other cool thing, they're pollinated by giant sphinx moths. Isn't that crazy?"

He said thoughtfully, "Sounds like a good premise for a science fiction mystery."

They stopped near the water's edge, looked out over Sarasota Bay. There were boats anchored nearby, catamarans and sloops, a ketch with a buccaneer's emblem on the mizzen, a yawl moving toward the mouth of the bay.

She said, "Do you ever miss your home, being in the desert?"

He stood watching the boats, didn't respond immediately. "Every place has its attractions," he said finally. He turned to her. "Why are you here, Birdie?"

"Me? I moved here with my parents who wanted to be in the sun."

The yawl had disappeared past the curve of the marina. Its spreading wake was making sucking noises against the rip rap at the edge of the lawn.

"That's why your parents are here, but what about you?" He was watching her face.

She shrugged. "It's beautiful, the sun, the heat, the laid-back lifestyle. I love it here and I like what I do." She hesitated, then, "I didn't go to college, I started working almost right away."

"Did you want to?"

She shook her head, leaned against the prop root of a banyan and looked at him. "No, it wasn't my thing. My parents offered it and I told them not to waste their money. They bought me the condo instead."

He smiled. "A girl who knows her own mind."

She laughed. "Most of the time. Once in a while it pisses me off when someone treats me as though I'm stupid just because I chose not to take that route. Some of the smartest and some of the dumbest people I know are college graduates. I see a little bit of everything where I work, I like the ones that are polite, tip well, go with the flow. They don't look at me like I'm a hooker, they know I'm there to make a living like anyone else." She paused. "Sorry, I got carried away."

He smiled. "I get it. You don't care what others think of you, I'm like that, too. But on a bad day, one person with an attitude can get to the best of us."

"Yup. It's like that with your books, isn't it? You want people to like them but not everyone will, and you're at peace with that, you just don't want attitude."

"Mm-hmm. I get the blowhards who think they know everything, critics who live to criticize. Ultimately, writers write to please themselves, but I feel I owe others something too. A good story, well told."

She touched his arm. "I like history, maybe I'd like the way you write about it."

"You'd have to be the judge of that. Are you hungry? I think we've seen what we needed to see here. I was thinking about Tail O' the Pup."

"Sure, I love their Texas Tommies," she said.

Later, when they reached her apartment, he put a hand on the door above her head, cupped her chin with the other hand and kissed her mouth.

"You're not planning any sudden moves or announcements, are you? Because I'm crazy about you," he said.

She leaned into him, breasts brushing his chest, fitted her mouth to his and gave her response. She said, "Call me, I'll be here."

But he didn't call. Not after a day, or two days. She assumed he was traveling.

Three days passed, she figured he'd met someone else and changed his mind about her. She began to throw imaginary darts at his body as he lay dying on the floor.

Four days.

Chapter Two
July - September 1978

Thunder boomed in the distant west. Birdie could see flashes of lightning through the doorway of the bar as they lit the dim gray clouds hovering over the gulf. At this time of day, summer rainy season, a kind of wistful introspection overtook island residents. They huddled indoors looking out, drinking their cocktails — this was a drinking town, no mistaking that — watching and waiting, flirting with strangers, pulling on sweaters against the chill air conditioning. They ventured out again into the balmy dark after the rain had stopped, breathing in the sweeter air, driving streets lighted with flashing trails of yellow and red and green, awash with oil and rain.

The Crescent Club was packed that night, Georgette had called in sick and Birdie was covering her shift. She was busy with requests for comforting drinks, gin and tonic, Jim Beam and coke, beer and wine. Many of the regulars were in, Joe from the marina, Will and Emily, Dave and Denise, Diana from Siesta Market with someone new, a blond with blue eyes.

The shift ended at nine o'clock and she drove home on slippery streets noisy with the splash of tires, listening to Ronstadt's

Prisoner in Disguise, caught up in the melancholy feel of drumming rain and errant love and blackened sky. When she reached home she stood in the shower for a long time, dried her hair, reached for this dress and that before deciding on a faded blue cotton that came to just above her knees. She didn't call beforehand, thought destiny would decide the outcome for her, finally turned the key and pointed her car in the direction of his house.

She tapped on the door and after a while he stood at the opening in jeans and a washed out tee-shirt, if he was surprised he didn't show it. He drew her in and looked down at her, said, "What are you doing here, Birdie?"

"I wondered if you wanted company. Tonight."

He looked at her curiously for a moment. Finally, he took her hand, led her down the hall to his room and sat her on the edge of the bed. "I wasn't expecting anyone. I need a shower, wait here," and he vanished.

She did as she was told, sat and waited, looked around. It was a good room, dimly lit by a standing lamp behind a leather chair in the corner, with pictures on the walls, silent candles perched on a ledge above the bed. She was aware of a taut stillness inside her, a warmth and expectancy wound tightly. She knew what he would be like, had known from the first touch. She kicked her flip flops aside, waited.

He leaned against the doorframe studying her, re-entered the room without speaking. He knelt on the floor in front of her and placed his hands on her knees, began to slide her dress back until it reached the tops of her legs. His movements were sure and unhurried. He paused, looked up. She met his eyes and smiled. Neither of them moved.

She slid from the bed down into his lap, thrust the towel aside, wound her knees around his waist, her arms around his neck, and began the first long, deep kiss.

They didn't make it to the bed.

Afterward, they moved up onto the cool, silky sheets and he pulled the blanket over where they lay, half-asleep, half-awake, talking. He had been absorbed in the writing, sometimes it was like that, the words just came and days got lost. It had happened before, might happen again, had she missed him, yes? She forgave him with a kiss.

Victor went to the kitchen and returned with a bottle of red and a glass, poured, and they talked more. What was she like as a young girl, what did she do on her days off, what had her first time been like. Then it was his turn, holding her hand all the while, turning it over in his as he answered, kissing her palm, drawing idle circles on her breasts with his forefinger, then he was rising above her, she knew what that meant. This time it was slower, he made her wait for it, and it wasn't until the clock near the bed shone midnight that they culminated the act and gave in to sleep, vast, and warm, and satisfying.

"Birdie, you listening to me?"

"Sure, I heard you."

"Really. Well, I just saw you put a bottle of Don Pilar Anejo on the speed rail."

"No I didn't."

Georgette walked to the stainless steel shelf at the front of the sinks behind the bar, pulled up the offending bottle, held it out. "What's gotten into you lately?"

Birdie rolled her eyes, took the bottle. "I'll take care of it," she said, en route to the back room.

Georgette followed her. "The other night you forgot to burn the ice and I had to take care of the sinks the next morning."

Birdie turned. "I was a little off for a day or so but I'm fine now."

Georgette stood in the doorway, studying her. "How long have we known each other, Birdie?"

"Oh, Georgie, about three years, you know that."

"And you know you can come to me if . . ." she put a finger to her mouth, bit on it. "Who did you go out with the other night?" she said suspiciously.

Birdie lifted a case of Schweppes and reached for a ginger ale.

"Can we let this go now? Honestly Georgie, you're like a dog with a bone."

"Haven't you been talking to that good-looking writer guy? The one Kiki brought to your party a couple of months ago?"

Birdie sighed, straightened. "Yeah, so what."

They looked at each other.

"I know your secret," said Georgette. She grinned.

"Look, it's not exactly a secret, okay? It's just . . . you know we shouldn't be seeing customers. And all I'm doing is seeing him, don't go making this into a big romance, Georgette, I don't even know very much about him."

"You will, Birdie. I know you, you have good instincts."

"I dunno Georgie, this one's got secrets of his own."

Georgette cocked her head. "What do you mean, like he's got a record or something? Because he doesn't give off that kind of vibe to me."

Birdie answered slowly. "No, not like that, but everyone has secrets. He's just a little harder to read than most."

They were silent for a moment.

Georgette said, "You okay, though?"

Birdie roused herself, said. "Yup, smooth sailing."

They went back out into the bar.

Sunday breakfast with the parents. She thought about telling them she was seeing someone, decided against it, in the end they knew somehow.

"Your cousin Elizabeth is getting married in February, on Valentine's Day, did we tell you?" asked her mother over vareniki and vodka.

Birdie took a bite of the dumpling, cherries mingled with sour cream, savoring the tartness. "I think you told me. It's going to be outside in the snow."

"How are they so sure there will be snow in February on the 14th?" said her father.

Birdie said idly, "I think there's *The Farmer's Almanac* for things like that."

"And you, daughter of mine, what are your plans for this week?" he asked.

Both faces were turned toward her. She swallowed vodka, wiped powdered sugar from her fingers. "I have a date on Tuesday," she announced.

Her mother patted her hand. "That's nice. How long have you been seeing him?"

Birdie was still. "It's very casual," she said finally.

"What do you mean casual, you only wear jeans on these dates?" said her father.

Birdie laughed. "No! I mean, well, yes, sometimes." She brushed her bangs aside. "I met him through a friend, a couple of months ago. He's nice, kind of quiet."

Her mother said, "What does he do?"

"He's a writer, well, an author. He writes books."

Her father placed his elbow on the table, leaned forward. "What kind of books, good books?"

She laughed. "He writes espionage, you know, daring femme fatales and handsome mysterious spies, trying to save Europe from Hitler and the fascists in World War Two."

Her parents looked at her wordlessly.

"And Stalin?" said her father.

"I haven't read all of them yet," said Birdie, throwing back the rest of the vodka.

"You should bring him to breakfast, let us meet him."

"Mother, I don't think—"

"Or dinner." This, from Fa.

"Yes, dinner would be best."

"Dinner, definitely."

"Find out when he's available for dinner, I'll make something special," said her mother.

Birdie had no words.

Claire worked for a small firm that specialized in family law. She was a paralegal, the right hand to a divorce attorney. She never divulged specifics about current cases but had occasionally, over drinks, been good for a story or two about divorces gone wrong or behaviors that sickened even the seasoned lawyers for whom she worked. Claire was twenty-six and had never been married, Birdie assumed that was why.

They were having dinner at Claire's place that night, Birdie had provided take-out to remedy the dilemma of Claire's cooking which, for as long as she had known her, was close to inedible.

"So here it is, Friday night and you don't have to be at work. I'll bet it feels strange," said Claire, laying a rib on the plate, wiping her mouth and hands.

"Georgette and I switched. I filled in for her one night and this was the trade off," said Birdie. "What's even stranger is that it's Friday night and you're not out with someone." She looked at Claire questioningly.

The other woman shrugged, reached for her beer. "One of these days," she said.

Birdie looked at her. Tall, same thick dark hair as her brother's, hazel eyes, southern Alabama accent left over from their youth. She had a good education, was surrounded by men all day.

"Claire, you need to start dating," she said.

"Now, why would you say that?"

"No particular reason. Got any juicy cases you're working on right now?"

Claire paused. "Just finished deposing a case where the wife was pretty steamed at the husband," she said. "He was screwing around with, of all people, her younger sister. When she confronted him he was pretty cocky, told her she was never going to touch his assets in a divorce because she had signed an ironclad prenup."

"You see a lot of that, guys taking advantage of prenups?"

"Hush now, I'm telling a good story here. So the wife decided to hit him where it hurt. He's one of those wine aficionados, you know, with a big cellar full of hundreds of expensive wines from around the world. She got a couple of girlfriends to help her while he was up in New York on business. They soaked all the labels off those expensive bottles of wine, threw them away, and rearranged every bottle in the cellar. When he got back, all hell broke loose."

Birdie was laughing. "He married a smart one."

Claire wasn't laughing but her eyes were sparkling. "Maybe, maybe not, we're gonna see."

They played Rummy, Claire dealing the cards, Birdie winning the first two rounds. When Claire got up to go to the refrigerator, the doorbell rang.

Birdie glanced at the clock. "It's nine forty-five, you expecting someone?"

Claire didn't respond, she went to the door. A moment later Nicholas was there, looking down at her. "Hey Birdie, I didn't expect to see you here tonight, how you doin'?"

She looked up. "Nicky, you drive over here with that beer in your hand?"

He sat on the sofa, took a swallow. "I'm not drunk, if that's what you're thinkin'."

Claire put a cold bottle in front of Birdie and returned to her place on the opposite side of the coffee table. "You had dinner, Nicholas? There are ribs from Old Hickory in the kitchen, help yourself."

"I'm fine," he said, "Thanks for asking."

Round three. Birdie took the top card from the stock pile, added it to cards in her hand and spread the meld face up on the table in front of her. She added a face card to the discard pile, sat back and took a swallow from the bottle.

"The music's stopped, why don't you go put something on, Nicky, make yourself useful," said Claire. She took a drink of her beer, hesitated, reached across the table, laid a king on Birdie's meld. They looked up as the sounds of Traffic filled the room, Steve Winwood's voice winding its sweet way around the flute on Freedom Rider.

By the time John Barleycorn Must Die was reaching its end a half hour later, Birdie was ready to leave. She said her good nights and walked around the circle to her car, glancing overhead at the black sky and the moon hanging low in the west.

She heard a door slam in the distance and looked around, waited. Nicky's familiar footsteps.

He came up behind her, stood too close. "Hey baby, I may have had one too many, think you could drive me home?"

She turned, looked at him, and got in.

He went around to the other side and got in, too.

Stocking up on juices at Siesta Market the following day, Diana was at the register, couldn't stop smiling. "They must be treating you right," said Birdie as she handed over cash to pay for the goods.

Diana smiled again. "You'll never believe it," she said, "I was on Ocean Boulevard last week in front of Foxy Lady. I tripped, and there was this guy who kept me from falling and making a fool of myself. He said he was visiting from the other coast and did I want to have a drink with him. I thought it was the least I could do." She handed the bagged items to Birdie with her change. "Next thing I knew, we were having dinner and he was asking for my phone number."

Birdie stood listening. "This the one who was at the club with you?"

Diana smiled, her blue eyes sparking. "Yes! He called last night, he's coming over again for a couple of days."

"Diana, that's great, I hope you have a good time," said Birdie. "Keep me posted." She waved, moving out the door. Diana had been married once, briefly, to a firefighter who was killed in the line of duty. She had confided this to Birdie one night at the Crescent Club. Birdie wondered sometimes if the grief was still a problem, if Diana would ever be able to let go of it. Maybe she had.

Victor came to visit her at work, sitting at the point end of the bar. She leaned on the bar and told him it was where most of the regulars sat.

"Am I taking someone's seat?" he asked.

"Not at the moment. They'll start coming in an hour or so, then you'd better skedaddle."

He leaned forward. "I want to kiss you," he said in a low voice. "Badly."

She looked at him longingly. "Better not, I would be seen as unprofessional."

"I have to see you."

"I don't get off until we close at two, then I have to break down the bar."

"I have no other place to be at that hour, come over when you get off. By the way, I called the other night, Friday night, when I got home from Tampa. There was no answer."

She nodded at Joe, who wanted another beer, and moved toward the refrigerator. "I was playing cards with Claire," she said calmly. "You remember her."

"Right, the sister-in-law."

"Ex," she reminded him. "Ex sister-in-law."

He nodded thoughtfully, took a drink and looked down at the bar.

He saw her later, saw all of her after she emerged from the shower, hair wet, body still water-warm and ready for him. He sat next to her on the bed and slowly kissed her mouth, the hollow of her throat, whispered his intentions against her ear, she laughed. Then the play began, a few strokes here, soft caresses there, he liked to take his time, build heat and intensity. It made her feverish to continue but he just laughed, got up from the bed and returned with a tumbler of wine.

"My father is impressed by writers," she said, watching him.

He kissed her knee, looked at her, "Is that a fact?"

"His eyes got big when I mentioned it's what you do for a living."

"Mm-hmm," he said, his mouth warm and inquiring, "I don't think he would be very impressed by what I do to you."

"You mean, at this moment?"

He pushed apart her thighs. "At what I'm about to do," he said.

Breakfast the following morning. "So, to continue last night's conversation," she said.

He looked up from the paper. "I think your demands are getting a little audacious," he said. "I'm doing the best I can but—"

"Oh shut up," she said good naturedly. "I meant my parents. I made the mistake of telling them I was seeing you and now they want to invite you to dinner."

He turned to her. "Seriously?"

"Yeah."

He shrugged. "Sure, I can do that."

"Really?" She eyed him curiously.

"Of course." He grinned. "I wouldn't pass up a chance to learn firsthand how you became who you are. Maybe we'll do a little information exchange."

"You are a cruel, cruel man."

He sat back, looked her over. "If you play your cards right, I might not pursue it."

She shook her head in mock disgust. "A blackmailer too. What have I gotten into."

He took her hand and led her away from the table. "We need to do more research for the book."

She had begun to crave him, loved the knowing smile that was meant for her, loved the way he wove her name into sentences, loved the relaxed way he carried himself. Moreover, she loved the way he spoke to her in bed, loved the heavy heft of him in her hand, loved the small sound he made at the point of no return, loved the breakfasts he made afterward. Did she love him?

She was leaving the World of Books the next afternoon and across the street in front of her, coming out of the restaurant, was Claire, with a man. Something unquantifiable caused Birdie to duck back into the enclosed area of the bookstore, hold the volume in front of her face, peer over the top. There was Claire, leaning against his chest for a couple beats of a minute, smiling up into his face. She said something, walked away down the sidewalk, she didn't look back.

But the man stood with hands in pockets and watched dreamily as she walked away, watched for another minute more. He checked his wrist and pivoted, began moving in the opposite direction.

Birdie exhaled, closed the book, got into her car and drove away.

Museum admission was free for Florida residents every Monday, and Victor said he needed to be inspired by art. Birdie told him about the incident with Claire as they were moving across the manicured grounds toward the entrance.

"I was a little shocked, and I behaved like a juvenile, it was shameful. Peeking behind a book, spying on a friend."

He said, "She was out of character, it provoked a like response from you. Had you ever seen the man before?"

She paused. "I don't think so."

"Never seen him around her office?"

She considered. "No, but I can't say I've never seen him, I just can't place him."

He put a restraining hand on her arm as they stood at the glass doors. "Any chance you misinterpreted?"

"Victor, casual acquaintances don't *look* at one another like that."

The immense canvases of Peter Paul Rubens were behind them, they were poised in front of The Abduction of Deianira.

"Wife of Hercules," said Victor.

"I know about him," she said. "He was a demigod. His father was Zeus but his mother was mortal."

"That's him. It's a very lush painting, don't you think?"

"I think it's beautiful," she said. "I would hope if someone abducted me, you would rush to my aid like Hercules."

"You should probably be clothed, unlike his wife. You'd be easier to carry that way."

She turned to him. "Yes, but it would make a less beautiful painting. What was your major in school, by the way? I'm wondering how you know so much about these things."

He shrugged. "Economics."

She stared. "How did you—"

He took her elbow and steered her to the next painting. "It's a long story. Maybe over a beer sometime."

They entered the next gallery, stood at Still Life With Parrots. "Here's one I know a little something about," she said.

"Okay," he said.

"It's an African grey parrot and a scarlet macaw. Georgette's father has an aviary at the back of his house."

He said, "How is Georgette, by the way?"

"She's alright. She's seeing a doctor later this week."

They finished their tour and skipped lunch, Birdie wanted to go home and get ready for the trip to her parent's house that evening. "Dinner will be a massive affair, Victor. Really. Breakfast, lunch and dinner all at once, they could feed a whole country in one meal."

He laughed, kissed her mouth. "I'm looking forward to it."

Her mother had never quite understood the game of baseball, hadn't appreciated Nicholas' southern mannerisms, couldn't fathom his disinterest in the fine arts. Birdie had been aware of those feelings but never addressed them, and wouldn't, if it came to it, respond any differently to her mother's impressions of Victor.

Birdie was mildly perplexed by how little she herself knew of him. Her father was able - smiling, genial - to access a side of him she herself had not mined. Here was Victor, reciting Anna Akhmatova over the zakuski; Victor and her father commiserating over poor Anna, the poet who was tortured into compliance by that

Bolshevik Lenin; tearing into Trotsky and his Marxist theories while tearing into the rye bread; Victor, over the roast, laughing at her father's stories about plans gone wrong.

"It was a bochka roof, built in the shape of a pyramid. Oh! A real work of art, it was. You know this bochka?"

Victor shook his head, he had never heard of it. Her father used his hands to explain. "Comes from the old 16th, 17th century style. Made of wood, usually, curved at the sides, both sides meeting in a peak at the top. Twenty of them. I came back the next day, six of them collapsed." He laughed, picked up his fork. "I thought I'd never work again."

"My first novel was a little like that," said Victor. "But you make mistakes, you learn, you get better as you go."

"How many books have there been?" asked her mother.

"Eight so far, Kira. I'm working on the ninth. In fact, your daughter is helping me with some of the research."

Birdie put a hand to her mouth, knew what was coming next. But no, no she was wrong.

Her mother looked at her, glowed. "I knew she had it in her," she said. "It just took the right person."

It was her father's heart Victor had set out to win. By the third vodka, they were engaged, he and her father.

The childhood stories started with dessert. Birdie as a little girl - yes, it was true! - until age five or six, did not like clothes, tore them off every chance she got.

"Fa!" she said to him, "Umolknut'." *Shush*.

Victor smiled, touched her chin. "I kind of like the image of you running around free as a bird. Maybe that's how you got your nickname, hmm?"

Her father grew quiet. "Yes, freedom. We know how important that is, do we not?"

From Victor, "That's why the written word is so vital, because truth matters, it has to be recorded and passed down to each generation, or it becomes lost."

Even her mother, when she looked at him, was falling in love.

They slid the doors open wide, let the night air in and went and sat beneath the midnight blue sky, drank her father's wine and talked about this and that.

The evening wound to a close.

"You'd better drive, let him think he's won," Victor said to her as they approached the car. "Your father, he's a sly one. He wanted me too drunk to do anything with his daughter later on, but I was on to him."

She laughed. "Oh? What was your plan?"

He grinned. "I'm a vodka drinker from way back. Didn't you notice those bottles in my living room?"

She was floored. "I thought they were just for the party."

He touched her arm. "Birdie," he said, "I like your father but he's a man, and he thinks like a man. I can never forget that."

Back at his house it was time for more research. He told her that her breasts were his inspiration when he was working on certain scenes in the manuscript. The protagonist's breasts were hers, creamy white and round, with pink tips, he said, covering the real ones with his mouth. He described how they shifted beneath sheer fabrics when she walked across rooms, he wrote about them brushing against the chests of dangerous men who aspired to affect the outcome of the war. In one scene, they spilled over the arm of her lover while he held her from behind on a balcony in Paris. In another, they were shown off provocatively in a dress designed to lure an officer from his post.

"And did it work?" she asked.

"It worked on me," he replied, pulling her over so she was on top. The room was in shadow, the candles on the shelf above his bed flickered in the breeze from the open window. He smiled lazily up at her. The clenching hands, the lowering eyes, the tightening breath, the pleasurable shudder as he slid into her.

The flowers arrived the following day. She read the card and carried them into the bedroom, unwrapped and placed them on the table next to the bed. They were tulips, with light pink blossoms and creamy white tips. She put them in a tall vase, arranged so they were spilling casually over the sides, smiling at the memory of the night before.

Chapter Three
October 1978 - January 1979

The rain was too heavy to leave open windows, she had to close them and switch on the air conditioner. It poured all day, was still pouring heavily when she left for work, she was drenched running to her car and drenched again running into work. She'd brought a change of clothes, her customers weren't so lucky.

They were playing downbeat tunes on the jukebox, the rain seemed to draw that out of people, and they sat listlessly around the bar telling sad stories, staring into their drinks, talking about lost loves, making forlorn jokes about the ones that got away.

One customer sat at the end of the bar and watched people coming and going. He was new, had been in twice that she knew of, ordered the same thing each time, rum and coke, well brand, no lime, sat and nursed it for a while before ordering another. He was waiting, she didn't know what for.

He was short, with neatly brushed hair and a sensuous mouth, a professional look about him, she couldn't say how she knew but years of observing people told her so. The way he held his hands maybe, his posture, he spoke carefully, as though he was used to explaining things. He seemed weary, in need of a vacation. She placed the drink on the coaster, shifted the napkins. "You from around here?" she asked.

He lifted his eyes, looked into hers. "No, visiting."

"Where're you from?"

Georgette was behind her. "Birdie, something's wrong with the tap line again, you think you could give it a look?"

Birdie turned. "Sure, be right there." She slapped the bar twice gently with her hand, looked at the man with the pain in his eyes. "I hope you have a nice visit," she said. "I hope you find what you're looking for."

Tommy was hanging around the side entrance when she went to get a breath of fresh air, he was wet as a dog, smelling of patchouli, looking for a handout. She dug around in her pockets and gave him two fives.

"Tommy," she said, "Clean up your act, you're a nice-looking man. Go over to the veteran's building, see what they can do for you."

He gave her a shy grin. "Thanks, Miz Birdie. You're a kind one."

He disappeared out into the rain, headed toward the Crescent Beach Market, she knew he had rounds to make.

A group of four ran inside at eleven o'clock laughing over their soggy adventure, ordered whiskey sours and white Russians, they livened things up for a while. One of them stood at the jukebox and slid in quarters, and a few upbeat songs played after that, the Beatles' Got to Get You Into My Life, Frampton's Baby I Love Your Way. By closing, Birdie had had enough of damp floors, damp spirits, damp everything, and was ready to go.

At home she slammed the door behind her and tossed keys on the table, went into the bedroom and began to undress. The telephone rang once and was silent. She stopped, listened, and moved into the bathroom, emerged later to a steady and insistent pounding at her front door. Frowning, she went and opened it.

Victor, leaning against the doorjamb, just barely, and drenched. She stared. "Is this the way you shower now? You go outside, let the rain do it for you?"

He closed his eyes, she touched his arm, took him inside.

"So what brought this on, Victor? You got lonely, decided to risk your life and take a drive?" She smoothed his hair, cupped his chin and peered into his face. She had helped him to remove the wet clothes, put him in the shower, given him aspirin. They were sitting on the bed.

He was quietly drunk, with eyes turned inward, not cheerful or combative or talkative. He wouldn't remember anything the next morning.

He said, "I tried calling. It wasn't her, you should know."

She smiled tenderly, he wasn't making sense. "Yes, I know, it rang once, but I was changing and couldn't get to it fast enough."

He grabbed her wrist, looked at her frantically. She tilted her head. "Victor?" she whispered.

"I think of you all the time," he said.

She touched his cheek, he slid down, put his head in her lap and his arms around her waist. She turned off the lamp and sat and rubbed his shoulders for a while.

He was asleep in minutes.

When she awoke, it was almost dawn. He had begun to make love to her, slow, dreamy, rhythmic movements, caresses that built into one long, high pitched arch which spiraled upward for miles, then fluttered downward, soft as a transparent cloud.

She lay still beneath him, heart thudding wildly against his, savoring the feel of him inside her. "Victor," she whispered.

He kissed her neck.

"I'm glad you came to see me."

"Mmm."

She wound her arms around him. "What was it you wanted to tell me last night?"

A pause. "That I missed you."

It had been four days.

She moved, sat up. "I'm going to make tea, do you want some?"

"Yes."

When she returned he was out on the lanai, dawn was just a whisper of pink on the horizon. As she approached, he held out his hand and she took it. "Sit here with me," he said.

She set the tray on the table and perched at the edge of the lounge. "I brought these, too. They're plushki, cinnamon buns."

"Thank you," he said.

"I plan to spoil you on my days off."

"Sorry about last night. Sometimes . . ." he hesitated. "You know how it is."

"Why don't you tell me?"

He looked at her thoughtfully, his eyes slid away. He said, "I wanted to be with you. You don't mind, do you?"

"No, of course not, I love it. Victor, why do you say that?"

"I had a lover once who didn't like surprises." He paused. "She also didn't like to be touched."

She sat very still, then leaned against him, took his arm and hugged it across her chest. "What was wrong?" she asked.

"That was it," he said. "She was just that cold. She didn't mind sex, but afterward, it was as if an invisible line had been drawn around her. No body parts touching in bed, no brushing against her if we passed in the hall, no spontaneous hugs when we were out together, no touching hands, no touching, not anywhere . . ." He fell silent, reached forward and took the tea.

She was horrified. "How long were you together?"

"I don't know, four or five months maybe. At first I thought there'd been some sort of trauma, but since she wasn't averse to sex, I assumed things would get better. She was a lovely person, very gifted, another writer. But it got to me, that lack of touch. I had trouble writing, it felt like something inside of me was dying."

She turned around so she could look at him. "I saw a documentary about that once. The scientists used monkeys to show that babies who are separated from their mother's touch will literally die, it was hard to watch. They performed another experiment where people who wanted to make a call from a phone booth would touch the arm of the person ahead of them in line to see if they could persuade them to change places. Those who were touched were much more likely to say yes."

He nodded, took her hand, kissed it.

She set her mug aside and curled up into him. "I'm sorry about what happened," she said, "but I'm glad you came when you did. I need someone like you, Victor. I need to be touched, and often, and I love it when you do."

She felt his arms go around her, felt the kiss in her hair, closed her eyes and smiled.

Claire had been at the back of Birdie's mind ever since the street incident a month ago. The two had talked and visited and she had watched her closely, no sign of anything other than normal Claire, the one who spent her days preparing contracts and affidavits, conducting client interviews, reviewing real estate holdings. *Where had she seen that man?*

Kiki was off to London, she'd found someone to go with her on her vacation, had called to let Birdie know. "He's insane, just what I need, Birdie. I'll introduce you, throw a party or something when we get back."

"But who is he, Kiki? Do we know him?"

"Oh, I don't think so, darling, name's John, he owns nightclubs, drives a sweet red Ferrari. Anyway, I'll see you in a week."

Birdie had hung up laughing, shaking her head.

At work that night, her first customer ordered Johnny Walker Black and kept it up for three hours. He was a talker, wanted someone to listen. When he paid he left a large tip, put his phone number on the receipt, gave her an odd look as he exited the bar. She crumpled the receipt in her hand and tossed it.

The woman seated next to him smirked. "I'll bet you get a lot of that," she said.

Birdie shrugged. She wasn't going to trash one customer to another. He might return one day and hear about it, it would be bad for business.

She ordered another Finlandia and tonic. As Birdie placed the drink on the coaster the woman said, "I can imagine the things you hear. But I guess there's such a thing as bartender-barfly confidentiality, huh?"

Birdie smiled briefly.

"I used to clerk for a circuit court judge, and honey, I could tell you a thing or two."

Birdie cocked her head. "Is that so?" She leaned on the bar. "How does that work, anyway? There are circuit court, supreme court, superior court, family court judges, I can't keep 'em all straight. Is there some sort of directory or something? They all look alike to me in those robes."

"Sure, hon." The woman lit a cigarette, put down the lighter, and explained it using the napkins.

He was back from a two-day trip to New York, taking care of book business. It was mid-afternoon, he stopped by her place on the way home, Birdie gave him a drink and fed him lunch.

"They like the manuscript?"

Victor smiled. "They like it fine. My agent wants me to spice it up a little so I'm revising it."

She finished putting the dishes away, sat on the countertop looking at him. "What does that mean, exactly?"

He shrugged. "Sex sells. This book was a little more serious than the others and they wanted me to lighten it up. I'm adding a couple of scenes that are a bit . . . salacious, you know, wanton."

She nodded. "Do you mind making changes?"

"If I can fit it into the plot it's not a problem, but sure, I wish they'd leave it alone." He smiled at her happily. "I have the rest of the day, we could find out what's playing at the Teatro, I forgot to look when I drove by."

The Teatro was the 99-cent theater up on the Tamiami Trail near the airport, in the north part of town.

"Maybe stop by the Bahi Hut afterward, get a couple of kamikazes," he added.

"I'm sorry, Victor, I didn't know when you'd be back and I promised to drive down to Nokomis."

His gaze rose quickly, he studied her face before answering. "Couldn't you postpone it?"

She hesitated. "I'd better not," she said.

"When it is going to end?" He went to her, stood against her knees.

She was silent. His eyes had turned dark, and brooding.

"Victor, let's leave it alone, it's complicated," she said finally.

"I understand better than you know, Birdie."

"He's having a rough time right now."

His look was level. "When is it going to end?" His hands on the counter were on both sides of her knees. "Let me ask you something, you ever think about me when you're down there *talking* to him?"

She bit her lip and looked away, she hated confrontation.

He turned her face toward his with his hand. "You led me to believe it was over with him long ago."

She swallowed, said slowly and with force, "Neither of us made any promises, Victor. I don't belong to anyone, so what is this—"

He took her by her arms and kissed her, hard. She could taste the bourbon in his mouth, and the anger.

She reached out to touch his chest with her palm, push him away, but he didn't move.

"What are you doing?" he asked. "Do you know me at all, Birdie? Hmm?"

She slid back from the edge of the counter but he gave a low laugh, twisted the front of her blouse in his hand and pulled her roughly to him.

"You're mine," he said, as he moved to kiss her. She bit his lip. He laughed, kissed her, she moaned and slipped her tongue in his mouth. He took her by the waist and lifted her from the counter, carried her to the bedroom where he flung her on the bed, turned and began to undress.

She rose to meet him, pulled him down urgently.

"Mine," he said forcefully, and then tore aside her clothes and ravaged her. *Salaciously. Wantonly.*

She awoke the next morning to deliciously sore limbs and a note on her pillow. *Make up your mind.*

She crumpled it into a ball and threw it hard across the room.

Victor had not called in a week, and Kiki was no help to her. "Darling, I could ask around but I only know a handful of his acquaintances. Annoyingly secretive. Classic introvert, you know." She studied Birdie over her glass. "Why don't you let me fix you with someone who'll cheer you up, I know a dozen men who would—"

"Kiki, that's not what I'm looking for."

They were at Kiki's Mira Mar apartment downtown. It was dusk, they were having a drink before heading to the Columbia for dinner with a handful of Kiki's friends.

Birdie knew Ralph, one of the waiters at the Columbia. He was in hot pursuit of an Italian girl named Colleen, who came to the Crescent Club every Wednesday night with her girlfriends. Recently, Ralph had been showing up on Wednesdays, too. Colleen talked about it one night sitting at the bar waiting for the other girls. She told Birdie that Ralph would have to stop drinking if he expected a date with her.

Birdie had leaned against the bar, raised her brows.

"I know what you're thinking," said Colleen. "I come here and have drinks with my friends every week. But I never order more than two, do I?"

Birdie shook her head.

Colleen said, "That Ralph. I know those restaurant people, they're all the same. They get together after work and what do they do? They go out drinking and carousing. He seems like a decent guy, good looking, but I want someone who'll make something more of himself, you know? I want someone who'll use his head, the one on his shoulders not his pants, you know what I mean?"

Birdie knew, all too well.

She disengaged from her reverie, said to Kiki, "You ever think about changing your life, Kiki, maybe getting married, settling down?"

"What, me? What makes you even ask?"

"You ever been?"

Kiki finished her drink and rose. "Oh darling, why do you want to know such things? We'd better get a move-on or we'll be late."

"Kiki . . ."

The other woman laughed. "Birdie, if there are two things I know in this silly old life, it's gastronomy, and men. I love men the way other women love their shoes. I just can't help myself, too many choices! But you," she waved her hand, "darling, any fool can see you weren't meant for work, you were born to meet a man at the door in a négligée and make beautiful babies. But that's not my scene."

Birdie shook her head and stood to go. "We should take my car, Kiki. You're too high to drive."

It was a fun group, four others, she hadn't met them before and they made her laugh, and Ralph was working that night, she waved gaily at him across the room.

At the end of the night one of the men lingered and asked for her number. She leaned against the building outside the restaurant, a little tipsy, waiting for Kiki to come out of the ladies room.

"I'm sorry, I don't remember your name," she said looking up at him, he wore glasses and was tall, dark and handsome, just as Kiki had prescribed.

He leaned forward and kissed her lightly on the lips. "Bennett Ian Grant, the third," he said smiling, nonchalantly taking a breast in his hand. "My God, you have nice tits," he exclaimed.

"Your initials are BIG," she said, brushing away his hand.

"Yeah," he said, "and that's not all that's big."

"Well," she said, "Nice to have met you, but I don't like being fondled in front of restaurants by men whose names I can't remember." She turned to go.

"So, that's a 'no' on the phone number?" he said to her back.

She laughed, Kiki breezed out of the restaurant, and the conversation was over.

It was three-ten in the morning, she'd worked the closing shift. Sundays were unpredictable, people might be mindful of Monday morning responsibilities, or they might be having a last hurrah before the new week began; this had been the former. She made herself a martini when she got home, sat on the lanai and propped her feet on the railing looking out over the pass. She'd been doing a lot of that lately, drinking and thinking.

The dark gulf waters lay calmly beneath the misty moon, her mind was not so calm. Week two of the impasse with Victor and Birdie was feeling restless, a storm was brewing, she needed something in her life. *Fine.* In her conversations with Colleen at work she'd learned that the girl needed to find a home for her beagle, a playful male named Beauregard. Birdie cautiously agreed to a trial adoption, but the dog's reproachful eyes when she arrived home late at night were too much for her. She'd returned him after a few days.

She missed Victor's ways, the way he tilted his head and looked straight in her eyes when she talked, the way he placed his hand on his thigh when he drove, his hand drifting up and down her back when he held her, the wry way he made his observations, the sultry way he looked at her in bed, the way he slid his mouth onto hers when they kissed.

Make up your mind. She sat and fumed because she knew what Victor wanted. He wanted her to make up her mind not just about

Nicholas but about her life. *Make up your mind* not only about who you want, but what you want.

She sighed, took her empty glass to the kitchen and placed it in the sink. Nicky wasn't the real issue between them because he wasn't really her lover, he was her excuse. Like Ralph the waiter, she was being told to grow up, or else. *Or else what?*

Georgette's house was on Avenida del Norte, on the canal, a three-minute drive from Birdie's place on Ocean Boulevard. Birdie heard the house before she reached it, the parrots were always up at dawn.

She pulled into the driveway and got out of the car. "You're a sweetheart," said one of the birds. The others laughed and cackled.

At the rear of the house, Georgette's father had built a large aviary for his seven blue and gold macaws, African grey parrots, yellow-naped amazons, and umbrella cockatoos. The creatures ranged in age from thirteen to thirty, the house was alive all day with their noisy chatter. Birdie was enthralled with them, loved the affectionate cockatoos, the bold personalities of the parrots, the vibrant colors of the macaws. Georgette's father was a retired avian veterinarian, she had never known her mother, who died in childbirth.

Georgette appeared at the door. "I guess it's time," she said to Birdie.

"Then let's go."

Birdie was taking Georgette to the hospital for an early morning surgical test. It was being done under general anesthesia and she couldn't drive afterward, Birdie was there to provide transportation and moral support. They didn't talk much in the car, Georgette was worried about the outcome and Birdie, not one for false platitudes or assurances, played music in the car instead. Tom Petty's Damn the Torpedoes seemed appropriate, and they arrived at the hospital as Don't Do Me Like That was winding down.

She sat on a plastic chair and waited while the procedure was performed, paged through a magazine, wandered hallways. She hadn't brought a book to read and mentally chastised herself for not bringing one of Victor's. She found the cafeteria, bought coffee and a pastry, took them back to the waiting area. Shortly afterward, she was notified that *the patient* was recovering nicely and would be ready soon for transport home. More waiting, more important-sounding pages over the intercom, more articles about celebrities she'd never heard of. Finally Georgette, looking pale and shaky in the wheelchair, loaded into her car, off they went toward home.

"You hungry? Should I stop for something to eat?" asked Birdie.

"No, the thought of food makes me queasy. Anyway, I think there's plenty at home. My dad should be back soon." Her father had had an out of town speaking engagement that prevented him being at the hospital.

"Okay. If he isn't, I can stay with you. Were they able to tell you anything?"

"It's some kind of disease, I don't remember. The doctor said it won't kill me, but there's no cure."

Birdie glanced over at her passenger. "Georgette, I'm sorry. But isn't that good news? Does it mean they can give you meds for it, something like that?"

"I'm not sure, but I have a follow-up appointment. I was still kind of out of it so I didn't understand everything." She looked out the side window, finished with answering questions.

Birdie helped her into the house, made chamomile tea, and they sat and talked for a while, Birdie told her about the upcoming visit with Nicholas.

"How's he going to take it, Birdie? I'm a little surprised, you were always kind of hesitant to make that final break, you know?"

"Yeah, but we can't go on like this forever, Georgie. I dunno, I may have hung around longer than I should've because I felt guilty about giving up on the marriage. And lately I've felt guilty for leading him on, it was just a vicious circle."

Georgette peered at her. "How were you leading him on?"

Birdie sipped her tea demurely, looked up at her friend.

Georgette's eyes widened, "Birdie, you weren't!"

"Now Georgette, don't look at me like that, neither of us was attached and it's just been an occasional thing, we always did get along that way. It's just . . . Victor."

Georgette looked at her for a long moment, lowered her cup. "You really like him."

Birdie nodded. "How're you feeling? You sure you're going to be able to work the day after tomorrow?"

"Yup." Georgette looked down. "Funny thing. They ask a lot of questions when they're doing all that pre-surgery prep, and I guess I felt kind of weird about the fact that I didn't even know my own blood type, they told me it's O-negative. I already knew my father's because I ran across his dog tags from when he was in the war, he's A-positive."

She yawned. "I think the anesthesia hasn't worn off yet."

Birdie cocked her head. "That's interesting. I don't know my blood type, either. I guess my parents would know." She stretched and rose. "I think you should probably rest, sleep off the anesthesia. Can I do anything for you before I go?"

"No, but thanks for doing this, Birdie."

Birdie smiled and collected her keys. "Any time."

Birdie and Claire were going to lunch at Raul's. Birdie stopped at the law office to pick her up and was told she was still in court. The receptionist told her where to go.

The tall Mediterranean Revival building at Main Street and Washington housed county administrative offices and courtrooms. Birdie took a seat at the back of the room and sat quietly, surveying the proceedings. In ten minutes, the case was wrapped up and everyone rose, murmured conversations echoed through the room.

Birdie stood and waited for Claire, who smiled brightly when she turned, waved happily, she was in her element. "Birdie. Were you waiting long?"

"No, just got here. I thought we could go in my car if you want."

"Yes, fine." Claire glanced over her shoulder at the judge's bench.

"Did you need to take care of anything, see anyone before you go?" Birdie asked.

"No, no. Wait a second." She turned to her boss, the attorney seated next to her, spoke in a low voice. He nodded.

She said to Birdie, "I'm ready, let's go."

Birdie picked up her handbag, she had seen everything she needed to see.

Raul's on First Street had good Spanish food, they ordered quickly and set the menus aside.

"So, you hear from Nicky lately?"

Claire nodded. "He says he's alright but I'm not so sure, Birdie. I think he's going to have to look at other options if business doesn't pick up soon."

Birdie said, "I really like Victor, Claire."

They looked at each other. Claire took a breath, opened her mouth to speak but didn't.

Birdie said, "Are you alright with this? We can avoid it, you know."

"No, of course not. You should be happy and he sounds like a good guy."

Birdie tilted her head. "You should be happy too."

Claire reached for her drink, shrugged. "We should all be happy."

"But maybe not with someone we shouldn't be with, you know what I mean?"

Claire looked at her and her eyes flickered. "You have something to say, Birdie?"

"You have something to tell me, Claire?"

Lunch was delivered but the food sat untouched.

Birdie said, "Of all my friends, you're the one I look up to the most, did you know that? You and Nicky, you both came from nothing and made something of yourselves, no one helped you. Look at you, you're beautiful and smart, you could have anyone you want, yet you choose someone who could damage everything you've worked for."

The other woman stared at her. "Where are you getting this?"

"I saw him in court today, the judge. Wouldn't that be a conflict of interest or something?"

Claire licked her lips. "I don't . . ."

"I was coming out of the bookstore on Main and I saw you together, it was a while ago. Couldn't this jeopardize your job, and his?"

"You're right, you're right, I know." Claire looked away, put a hand to her head. "It's like looking at myself in slow motion, from a distance, you know? I can see what's happening, but I can't make it stop. I've been so good all my life, Birdie, I had had it so hard. And then I met him, and he's everything I ever wanted." She picked up her fork, put it down again.

Birdie said gently, "Is there a way to make it right? Excuse yourself somehow from those cases?"

Claire shook her head miserably. "I can't do it without revealing why."

She swallowed some of her drink. "An era has ended, and it makes me sad. It's no longer you and me and Nicky. But you've moved on and that's a good thing. You know what I've always admired about you, Birdie?"

"Me? Claire, I'm just—"

"You aren't what you seem. You like to come off as a good ole' girl, kind of laid back and down with the common folk, but you're really brainy, God, I wish I had your brain. Why don't you do something with yourself and use it? You know all those things about history and jewels and antiques, I'll bet half those people on snooty old Palm Avenue don't know what you know. Instead, you work those impossible hours at that bar—"

"Okay, enough, Claire. I'm sorry you're feeling nostalgic and all, but where do you get off?"

She picked up her check and reached into her handbag. "Think I'll wander down to World of Books," she said, "see if I can find something new to read."

She and Claire parted on amicable terms, but the conversation left Birdie with a bad feeling. Would it have been better to have left things unsaid, left her friend to her mistake? Driving home, she thought about calling to apologize, decided she'd done enough damage.

"Mother, how much do you think an 18th century bergère would go for if it was in good shape?" asked Birdie. "I was thinking around twelve hundred or so."

Her mother, who was examining a fringed lamp, said absently, "Louis the Fourteenth, Fifteenth or Sixteenth? She paused. "If the original tapestry is unharmed and the wood is walnut, maybe fourteen hundred. Why, darling, are you thinking of investing?"

"No, I saw something in a friend's apartment, that's all."

"I'd say your friend is coming up in the world." She reached to push the bangs from Birdie's eyes. "Are you ready for lunch yet?"

"No, I'm not hungry. What about the gallery."

Her mother studied her for a moment. "Yes, let's see what's new there. I haven't seen Frank in a while."

"What's Fa doing today?" asked Birdie as they headed down the street.

Her mother smiled. "He's doing his day at the hospital. He loves it so, he comes home with all sorts of amusing stories."

"He's a people person."

"Yes, he's always been that way," observed her mother. "He's one of their most popular volunteers."

After the gallery, the fine jewelry section of an antiques store. "You should be using the pieces I give you," her mother said as they leaned over, examining the lighted case of brooches. "They need to be worn." She turned from the display to look at her daughter.

"I wore the Etruscan revival earrings a couple of weeks ago," Birdie said defensively.

Her mother smiled. "I'm sure they looked beautiful."

"Victor took me to dinner at Cafe L'Europe, I wore them there."

Her mother took her arm and they walked out of the store onto Palm Avenue. "We're looking forward to seeing you two on Sunday. He isn't traveling, is he?"

"No." She hesitated. "I . . . I think he'll be there."

"You seem unsure about that."

"Mother, doesn't it seem strange that he likes it so much? Shouldn't he be just a little uncomfortable around you?"

Her mother laughed. "I think he and your Fa get along just fine, and that's a good thing, Bernadette. You should be glad."

Birdie smiled. "Maybe it takes a little getting used to after Nicholas. Nicky's changed, by the way. I think he's had time to do a little soul searching and regret the things he did."

Her mother was silent.

"Mother . . ."

"That's good news, Birdie, I'm glad. I wish it had happened sooner, but his loss is Victor's gain."

"I don't know about that, mother."

"Hmm."

They stopped to look at a storefront, modern Danish furniture.

"What does that mean?"

"I was just thinking about your Aunt Caroline. She was a great beauty when we were younger, you know. We sang in the choir together only her voice was much better than mine, and we swam in the lake in summer, later we had picnics there with our beaus. There was one in particular named Steven, they were mad for each other. But Steven wasn't the kind to go around with his heart on his sleeve, he never made his intentions known, and Caroline wasn't known for her patience. When the war came, Steven signed up and left for his training, then Jack came along and Caroline went off and married him."

They began to walk again, passing chic boutiques, gift stores, curiosity shops. Birdie said, "I never knew all this."

"Well, those things happen, especially in wartime," her mother said.

"She and Uncle Jack are very happy together, so it all turned out well."

"Oh yes, I guess," said her mother. "But you know, a couple of days after Caroline went to see Jack in San Francisco, Steven came to the house looking for her, and I sat and watched his face when he learned that the love of his life had married another. It was a lesson for me to never let someone slip from our grasp because we're too self absorbed or too shy or too proud to let someone know how we feel. I will never forget the stricken look on that young man's face, it was there before he could hide it. His pain was so pervasive that I could feel it too. He made a terrible mistake, and he paid a very high price."

Birdie looked at her mother. "I don't think I was very good at being a wife, maybe it's not for me."

"No? Well, time will tell. People can be good at being married if they're with the right person."

Birdie sighed. "You never had any doubts when you married Fa?"

Her mother smiled fondly. "No, none. I knew he was exactly the sort of man I needed to be with, and that I would be good for him. It's been my own life's work, creating a life with him, having you. I'm a very contented woman."

"You know," said Birdie. "I don't exactly do anything earth-shattering. Kiki has traveled and seen the world, Claire does legal work that changes lives. I pour drinks, go to lunch now and then," she shrugged.

They stopped in front of The Prague, near the Mira Mar apartments where Kiki lived. Birdie could see the muraled walls inside the restaurant from the street, the owners had told her about their escape to freedom over those walls in Czechoslovakia.

"What brought this on, Birdie?" said her mother.

She shook her head. "I think Victor's books have gotten to me. They're full of heroes who gave their lives for a cause greater than themselves, having all sorts of adventures at the same time, and I'm looking at myself thinking about all the things I haven't done."

"We all make choices, darling, are you regretting yours?"

Birdie shook her head. "No, I wouldn't change mine. But I need to do something worthwhile and haven't figured out yet what it is."

"While you're waiting for your revelation, remember this, Bernadette. You provide kindness and good cheer and a listening ear to countless people who come to your door every day, you're a good and true friend to those who know you, and you're a joy to me and your father. In addition, that man you've been seeing looks at you as if the sun rises and falls at your command. You impact more lives than you know, and that's the whole point of life, Birdie. Some people do it on a world stage, and some do it behind a bar on a little subtropical island. Who's to say which of you has a more lasting impact?"

She kissed her daughter's cheek. "Feel like crepes for lunch?"

"Sure, I think I'm hungry now," said Birdie.

She opened the door and they went inside.

She phoned and invited him to dinner at her place, felt a hint of nervousness when there was a pause before he accepted.

"Birdie, how have you been?" His voice was very quiet, she wondered if he had been napping, or worse, with someone.

"I'm okay, tried getting a dog but that didn't work out, I'm not home enough."

She could hear the smile in his voice. "Birdie with a dog, I can see that. What kind? What did you name him?"

Her turn to smile, he was born with a question on his lips. "I'll tell you about it when I see you on Monday."

When she hung up, her heart was racing and her hands were shaking.

On Sunday after breakfast she made the ten-minute drive from her parents' house to Nicholas' place, down the winding lane past the seagrape hedges and beachfront cottages of Casey Key to the south end, turned left, pulled into the driveway.

He answered at the first knock, welcomed her with a hug. "Hey, baby, how you doin'."

She removed her sunglasses. "Nicholas, how're you doing?"

He sat abruptly on the sofa, looked up at her. "I'm sellin' the business."

She sank down next to him, said slowly, "That's a good thing, isn't it? Do you have a realtor?"

He shook his head. "There's a buyer already. Two brothers, they wanna move, they like it here and they've got the money. They came to me, I didn't want to do it but, well, I was hurtin', you know how it's been," he trailed off.

She nodded understandingly.

He looked away, then back at her. "Birdie, I'm not entirely sure what to do with myself now that things've changed so. What . . ." He looked around.

She spoke softly, as if to a child. "You need to pull yourself together, Nicholas. Baseball was your life, and you haven't come down yet from that mindset. But I don't think owning a business is really your thing, you know? Maybe, if you can afford it, take some time to clean up, quit the booze, it's clouding your judgment. Then you can make some good decisions about what to do next."

He took her hand. "You'll be here for me, won't you, babe?"

She hesitated. "Nicky, whenever you call like this, I come. And sometimes it's too tempting, and we do what we did a few weeks ago. But it's too confusing for me," she said. "And it could hurt anyone who happens to be in our orbit."

"Aww, Birdie—"

"Look, I found someone who cares about me, and I care for him too much to put him in the middle of whatever we've got going here. Do you understand?" She touched his arm. "You need to let me go."

He looked at her with eyes the color of the open sea, deep and dark and blue. They'd been alive once with light, but there'd been too much darkness, now they were still and sad.

"Oh baby, I still love you," he said, touching her hair.

"I know," she said, gently. "The problem is, we never really liked each other. Now you've got to figure out how to deal with it because we can't do this, not any more." She kissed his mouth and rose from the sofa. She looked down at him. She had loved him once, now she wasn't sure what she felt. Compassion maybe.

She went to the door and opened it, hesitated, stepped out. Her eyes were moist but she kept moving forward.

Birdie didn't think of seduction only in sexual terms, though it often was sexual. She practiced it as gentle persuasion, subtly surrounding the intended with pleasing sensual comforts to obtain a favorable outcome. The soft, firm cushions, the smooth rugs underfoot, the enticing smells, clean polished surfaces and Birdie, in her flowing lavender caftan, barefoot, not a stitch of makeup except for eyeliner and lip gloss. A long silver pendant rested just above her breasts, daring to be looked at, begging to be touched.

He arrived with wine as if they were on a first date, she received it offhandedly. "Oh thank you, Victor, would you open it, please? I'm just getting this out of the oven, it needs to sit for a while before we can eat."

She poured the wine, they sat talking. He wasn't writing at the moment, he said, this was his in-between time, he had delivered his final manuscript, now it was time to breathe.

She smiled. "Whatever will you do," her voice suggestive, sweetly sarcastic.

He smiled lazily. "I've managed to stay busy, catching up with friends, I went over to Lauderdale one weekend."

Her hand tightened around her glass, her eyes rose to his.

She got up, headed toward the kitchen. "I think it's probably good to eat now," she said, stomach churning.

He complimented her cooking, she told him about work, and Tommy, and the calls she had made to the VA to try to get him the help he needed.

He sat back, watching her while she talked. "You sound like a woman looking for a cause," he observed.

She played with her hair, it was getting longer, she tucked a strand behind her ear. "No, I don't think so, I just feel for this guy. He fought in 'Nam and I think it did something to him. He had the balls to go and I give him credit for that, I just wish there was someone who could help him to move on."

"Still, it was good of you."

She looked down.

He asked what else was keeping her busy.

She glanced up, searched his face for clues. "A couple of dinners with Kiki, and I found a Paul Frankel chair, I think you'd like it. It's on the lanai."

"I'd like to see the chair. And dinners with Kiki . . ."

She shrugged. "You know Kiki, she loves to laugh."

He picked up his glass. "Um-hmm."

She pushed back her chair. "Let's have drinks in the living room, I don't want to sit at the table all night. Brandy alright?"

He followed her. "Sure."

She sat next to him on the sofa, placed a hand on his arm. "Victor—"

He set his glass on the table, he wasn't looking at her. "Birdie, you know things are different."

She said quietly, "If this is about Nicholas, I took care of . . ."

He sighed.

A frisson of fear gripped her.

She swallowed. "Victor, what's going on?"

He turned to her. "Do you have any idea how hard this is for me?" he asked. His voice was low, and intense, and filled with regret.

"I—"

"I come back to a place that's filled with your scent, everything is just as it should be, Birdie, it's like magic, it's all you, right down to the lighting, right down to the way you've worn your hair."

He reached over and picked up the pendant and she shivered. Their eyes met.

"A few weeks ago you gave me a night, we had a night . . . that I will never forget," he said, releasing the pendant, "but there has to be more than that, and I can't make you want something you're not ready for."

He stood, turned back to her. "Birdie, thank you for dinner. I," he paused. "I don't think I should call you again."

Her eyes widened in disbelief. He walked toward the door, she opened her mouth but nothing came out.

After the door closed she sat for several minutes trying to absorb what had just happened, couldn't take it in, sank back into the sofa and curled into herself and lay numb, unmoving.

An hour later she rose and turned out the lights and stumbled to bed.

Georgette set the cocktail tray on the service bar, Birdie placed four drafts and a gin and tonic on the tray, Georgette went out onto the floor. When she returned, she said, "You know, Birdie, it wouldn't kill you to just give him a call, see if he's willing to talk. I know you miss him."

Birdie looked at her.

Georgette held her hand up. "Fine, okay, I get it."

Birdie glanced to her right, a customer at the end of the bar was signaling and she moved toward her.

She wouldn't cry over him anymore. Sometimes she filled a tumbler with bourbon and sat dry-eyed listening to Ronstadt wailing Try Me Again, or worse, Hasten Down the Wind. Sometimes she fell asleep at dawn and woke at noon with wet eyes. When she wasn't crying in her sleep she felt dazed. All this, over someone who had never even admitted that he loved her.

At Sunday breakfast her father told her he had gone to the library and checked out a couple of the books Victor had written. "Very good books," he said. "When are you going to bring him around again? I like this fellow."

"I don't think he'll be around again, Fa, we broke things off," she said.

"What?" exclaimed her mother. "But he's so nice, you're such a beautiful-looking couple."

"Not as beautiful as you think," said Birdie.

After breakfast, her mother took her into the dressing room and sat her down in front of the safe. As she twirled the dial, she said conversationally, "You know, Birdie, your Fa and I had a breakup after we'd been going out together for about six months, it was over the question of loyalties. I felt divided, should I please my mother and father and live the life they wanted, or did I have the courage to step out and be with Anton. I wanted him to make that choice for me and he wouldn't."

The safe swung open, she turned to Birdie. "What happened?"

She looked down, embarrassed. "Mother, he gave me ultimatums. Everything was fine until he got mad about the fact that I'm still close to Nicholas. He wants me to . . ." she hesitated, "I think he wanted someone who was willing to make changes."

Her mother nodded, was silent for a long moment. She said, "Is he worth it, Birdie?"

"Mother, what do you mean?"

"Birdie, I know I didn't raise a foolish daughter."

She swallowed, said slowly, "We haven't even been seeing each other very long, it took me by surprise. No one's ever talked to me like that before."

Her mother sat next to her and took her hand. "Darling, the boys you dated in the past were boys, maybe they were easy victories for you. But Victor is a man, and men don't waste time on little girls. I'm going to give you some unsolicited advice, so you can take it, or not." She cleared her throat, paused. "I think you've always prided yourself on being independent, Birdie, but being detached is not always a sign that you're free, sometimes it means you haven't dealt with your fears."

Birdie slipped her hand away, began to turn.

Her mother grasped her arm. "I credited you with having courage, Bernadette. Don't disappoint me now."

She said, "What if he wants me to change who I am?"

"I doubt it, that's not what I saw in him. Anyway, life is full of change, we all naturally change over time. He seems a good man, Birdie, he may have flaws but you have them too. See what you can do to understand rather than be understood and you'll be fine."

She rose. "Now, I have this ruby ring, it would look so pretty with your milky complexion, where is it? Oh yes . . ."

There was a For Rent sign posted on the lawn at his house. She stared at it, frozen in horror, heart beating wildly. *What have I done?* It had been a little over a month, now she would never see him again.

She pulled into the driveway and jerked the car into reverse, backed away with unseeing eyes, turned right onto Siesta Drive and somehow ended up at home where she threw herself into housework, laundry, cleaning mirrors, scrubbing floors, beating rugs to within an inch of their lives.

Christmas was not in her heart but she went through the motions. At the Crescent Club they strung more decorations around the bar, she passed through the shops in the village buying presents, baked traditional pryaniki gingerbread cookies and took them down to Nokomis.

Nicholas was at home alone and seemed glad to see her.

"How are things, Nicholas? I see you got a Christmas tree," she said, looking around. The place was different, he had moved furniture, the small tree was on a table near the window.

He kissed her mouth lightly, held her at arm's length. "It's been a rocky ride but I'm on the home stretch, Birdie. Have a seat, you want anything? I can get you tea."

She shook her head, held out the cookies. "I remember you liked these, thought maybe you still did."

He took the package. "Well thanks, that was sweet. They'll be gone in no time, I can promise you that." He looked at her, narrowed his eyes. "Baby, you don't look so good, what's wrong?"

She smiled. "Oh, you know, life."

"If I had a way to change things, do 'em all over again, I would have done them differently."

She said, "I know that, Nicky."

"Some of it was the booze you know. I took your advice and cut that out."

"Really? That's good, I know it must have been hard."

He said sheepishly, "Harder than I thought, I had to go to AA. I have a sponsor now, and I haven't touched a drop in over a month."

She touched his arm, smiled. "Nicky, I'm proud of you. Really. You seem different somehow and I'm glad to know why." She paused. "What else is going on? Has the business sold yet?"

He nodded. "It's gone, they gave me a good price. I'm still trying to figure out what comes next."

"You have any ideas?"

He shook his head. "It'll come to me, I've got a peace about it, though."

She said, "I've never heard you talk like this, Nicholas."

He leaned forward. "I'm worried about you, Birdie, you don't seem like yourself."

She looked down. "I, umm, went through a bit of a rough patch myself."

He sat closer and gathered her in his arms. "Birdie, I wasn't much of a friend when we were together before, maybe I can be that for you now, huh?"

She burst into tears and sank against him while he rocked her. "Oh baby," he said. "Seeing you hurt like this makes me want to punch a wall."

After a little while he got up and came back with some tissues, she blew her nose and wiped her eyes.

"Who is the fool that did this to you," he said, holding her against him again. "I want to tear him apart."

She sniffed. "This from the same man who said he was at peace a few minutes ago."

He laughed softly. "It's different when someone you love is hurtin'. I'll always love you, Birdie." He kissed her hair.

"I love you too, Nicky, you know that," she said. "We're just not meant to be married."

"No, I don't guess we are." He sighed, held her away from him so he could look at her face. "I don't think I've ever seen you cry, you look so beautiful, and lost." He kissed her forehead. "Can you tell me what this is about?"

She frowned and slowly put it into words. This time, she didn't cry.

Birdie felt she was living in stalemate, lunch or dinner with girlfriends, work five days a week, Sunday breakfast with the parents. She tried to imagine an obituary based on those activities and it depressed her. She went to a movie at the Teatro to escape reality, a romantic comedy called Foul Play. It made her laugh and she returned to the apartment in a more upbeat mood, ready to face another day. Work, her father had told her growing up, was the best medicine. She wasn't so sure, she thought maybe it was laughter.

Kiki called, she wanted to get together. "I never see you anymore," she complained. "You've become a recluse."

"I have not," said Birdie, "I just work a lot, I have bills to pay."

"Darling," laughed Kiki, "you need to find yourself a man who will pay the bills for you, didn't your mother teach you that?"

"How're you doing with that?" said Birdie.

"The search continues," said Kiki, whose affair with John had run its course. "Hope lives eternal."

They agreed to get together for dinner Monday night, Kiki said she would phone Claire and invite her to join them, "although she's becoming almost as reclusive as you. What am I going to do with you two." She rang off.

Birdie had two Christmases every year. The first was observed with presents on December 25th, along with the rest of the country. But since her father, who belonged to the Russian Orthodox Church, celebrated on January 7th, her family drove north to St. Petersburg every year on that date for Christmas mass at St. Andrews. After the ceremony they returned home, looking for the first star in the evening sky, symbol of the arrival of the baby Jesus, then they scattered pre-purchased hay beneath the dining table, symbolic of the stable where the infant received his first distinguished visitors, and had their celebratory meal. The roast goose, the pryanyi chai tea, the honey cake.

New Year's Eve was busy at work from opening until closing, it seemed everyone on the island was there at some point or another. She wrapped her wrist, put on a smile, mixed tequila sunrises and brandy alexanders, poured wine and opened beer, and when the clock struck midnight, she and Georgette and the other bartenders lifted champagne glasses and drank to the New Year with the rest of the crowd. In the middle of it all, she wondered where he was, said a mental farewell to the old year, and to him.

The following day, her father gave her his New Year's gift.

"Fa, the box is so big, I can't imagine."

The box proved to be empty but it contained another. On and on it went, like the famous matryoshka, Russian nesting dolls, until she unwrapped the last box, and inside, beneath the neatly folded white tissue paper, was the gift.

She swallowed, looked up at him. "Fa . . ."

"Go on, open it," he said gently.

She picked up the book, opened the cover, flipped past the title page, then the single line on the typed dedication page. *For Birdie, who deserved better.*

She closed her eyes, swallowed hard.

"He wrote that for you, wasn't that nice?" said her mother.

Birdie nodded, looked up at her father, rose to give him a hug.

"I think I might know where to find him," he whispered.

Birdie liked the scents of warm ink on aging paper, dusty leather and moldering glue. Whenever she entered an old book store, heard the tinkle of a bell over the door and the hushed rustle of turning page, she was overcome with a kind of wistfulness that only bookstores with their histories and silences could give.

Today, more people than usual. There was a special sign on the door outside, the interior was redolent with coffee and fresh doughnuts. A table awaited, a stack of books, a neat row of pens.

She thought suddenly, *I can't do this,* and turned to go but someone said to her, "I think we've met before," and she paused.

"Yes, I remember, you were Birthday Girl," he said, and when she turned she saw that he had the clearest blue eyes she had ever seen, a smile that understood everything.

She said, "You must be a friend of Kiki's."

"Everybody knows Kiki," he said.

"Are you here for the book signing?" she asked.

"I kind of have to be," he said. "I arranged it."

She was still for a moment. "Oh, you're the owner! I'm sorry, we did meet once before, didn't we? I like your store."

"Thank you, I've only had it for a couple of years. I'm Gene."

This produced a smile. "Birdie."

"Are you here for the book signing, Birdie?"

"Oh, umm . . ."

He glanced around. "Is Kiki coming? She said she might."

"I don't think so," she said. "There's an event at the restaurant this afternoon. You should give her a call though, she could use some cheering up."

He nodded to someone behind her. "Time to get started. Nice to see you, Birdie."

She looked over her shoulder and directly into Victor's blue-green eyes.

He talked about the plot and the historical background, the mood in Europe before the war, bargaining with the tyrant, the betrayals, the fading hopes, finally the inevitable. She stood behind a tall shelf of books, closed her eyes and listened to his voice as he read, she could not have said afterward what about.

There were twenty minutes of questions from the people who came to see him. She turned and began to watch. What did he think of rapprochement, where did he travel for the research, who was his inspiration for the main character. And the charming double agent? At this, he shrugged, smiled, evaded.

They crowded around the table, he picked up one of the pens and began to sign the title pages of their books. "Is this for you, or is it a gift?" he asked. "You're too kind," he said. He posed for photos, made jokes about travel and airports.

At the end, a woman waited for him to finish, chatting with her friend.

The friend said, "You dedicated the book to someone, someone with an odd name."

The pen stopped, continued. "Mm-hmm," he said.

"Birdie. Who was Birdie? May I ask?"

He didn't look up. "Someone I lost along the way, that happens sometimes," making small talk. He handed her the volume. "Thank you." Capped the pen, stretched, looked around, discovered her.

They didn't speak for a long moment. She said, "You didn't lose me," tried to smile but was afraid she might cry.

He looked at her, eyes roaming her face. He opened his mouth to speak and Gene approached from the other direction to shake his hand, ask if he needed coffee, and let him know there were only fifteen minutes remaining.

She couldn't stay and face his dismissal. She turned and left, the jingle of the bell on the door ringing in her ears as she hurried down the street to her car.

Chapter Four
January – February 1979

She took a shift that night for one of the girls who pleaded illness due to migraine. Business was light, early spring had strayed into false spring with plunging temperatures and strong winds, islanders were staying home, donning socks and burrowing under blankets. It was Southwest Florida, anything under sixty degrees threw lifelong sun worshipers into hibernation. Birdie wiped down tables, cleaned mirrors, swept floors, shivering in her tee-shirt and short denim skirt. She was home by two-thirty.

That morning, the phone rang as she dressed for the weekly breakfast with her parents.

"Don't come today, your mother has flu and you shouldn't be within a mile of the house," said her father.

She was startled, her mother never got sick. "Fa, has she seen a doctor?"

"It's not that bad, but we don't want you to catch what she has. Don't worry, we'll see you next week if not before," he said.

She was reluctant. "Are you sure about this, sure you don't want me to do anything?"

"You're a good daughter. Stay home," he said.

She hung up, at a loss what to do.

She made tea and toast, put on Bonnie Raitt, listened to the heartache and fatalism of the singer's voice on the bluesy Guilty. Settling on the sofa, she picked up the book her father had given her for New Year's but set it down again, her mind was elsewhere.

She'd had a chance to make things right, let Victor know her feelings, but she'd handled it badly. Now he was gone, back to Santa Fe, and she would never see him again or touch him, she'd lost him. She wanted to cry but she couldn't go through that again. She got up from the sofa and went into the kitchen, began to pull out baking pans and utensils, doing did what she always did when trouble came, she got busy.

It was hours before she looked up and saw the fog that had invaded the grounds outside. The banyans were wrapped in a clinquant haze of silent gray, it was not evening yet but it would be soon. She wiped her hands and moved from the kitchen into the living room, peering outside.

She went to the cabinet and poured a glass of wine, took it to the sofa and sat, brooding. It wasn't raining and she had been indoors all day, she needed fresh air. She returned to the kitchen, used a funnel to pour the wine back into the bottle, slipped the bottle into a paper bag and snatched her keys on the way out the door.

The swirls of fog and setting sun had created penumbras around the still sea oats on the beach. Birdie sat among the half shadows and breathed in the heavy air, raised the bottle of Barolo to her mouth and took a last swallow of the Fontanafredda, not the best way to enjoy a good wine but no one else had to know. She stuck the bottle upside down in the sand and stood, a little unsteadily, on her feet, and moved closer to the beach.

At the darkened shoreline she eased her top over her head and dropped it to the sand, looking out over the water. The waves were flat, glistening lightly under a crescent moon. She giggled to herself, crescent moon, Crescent Beach. A blurred movement caught her eye as she glanced down from the heavens, and a sharp voice interrupted her boozy ruminations.

"What the hell do you think you're doing?"

She whirled and caught her foot in her opposite leg, toppling over in the soft wet sand.

A figure loomed out of the mists and roughly grabbed her arm, hauling her upright.

She was face to face with Victor who was breathing hard, eyes angry, features flushed.

She jerked away from his grasp but he caught her again, this time with both hands around her upper arms. His fingers hurt her flesh.

"Oww!" she said. "Let go of me. Where did you come from?"

"I've been looking all over for you. As it turns out, your father said you like the beach at night so here I am. What have you been drinking, Birdie?"

"None of your business, you don't own me," she said bitterly.

His voice was clipped. "So you've said."

They were face to face. For weeks she had yearned for him, now that he was here, unexpectedly, she stood smarting from his tone and words failed her.

"Don't you want to know why I came?"

She looked at him mutely. He was still angry, and in her slightly befuddled state she was having trouble making the pieces fit. *What was he doing here with Fa?*

He reached down and retrieved her top. "Put this on."

She glared at him. After a moment she took and slid it over her head. "I was just going for a little swim—"

"I could see. I gave you credit for being smarter than that."

She cried exasperatedly, "Stop it! I'm sick of people telling me they're disappointed, that I don't belong here or there, or I'm too smart or too good or . . ." she said suddenly, "why don't you just leave me alone?"

He looked at her closely. "Is that what you really want, you want me to leave?"

"It's something you're good at, aren't you? Well, who am I to stop you?"

He hesitated, then released her and turned, began to walk away.

She swallowed, she hardly knew what she was doing. "You hurt me, Victor," she called after him. "I spent two months crying for you."

The retreating figure stopped, faced her.

She couldn't see his eyes through the dim haze but he stood, waiting. A sob involuntarily escaped her throat. "Did you come looking for an apology, is that it? You want me to beg?"

He was still, there was something in his posture, she didn't know what. She sank to her knees. "Alright Victor," she said urgently.

Her mouth twisted. "Don't go. I've never wanted anything more in my life and I'm sorry I drove you away." She began to cry, put her hand to her mouth to hide it from him. "Please don't go, Victor. Please . . ." She was bowed, sobbing in earnest.

After a time she felt his hands on her arms, he was crouched beside her in the sand. "Birdie." He took her in his arms.

"I've been miserable," she cried weakly. "And I'm sorry I was so stubborn, I—"

"I couldn't stand another day away from you," he said.

She stopped, laid her face against his chest and breathed him in, nearly laughing with relief.

She raised her head. "I mean it, Victor," she said sniffling. "I want you to be the only one who touches me, but I want so much more."

"Do you? Birdie, I'm a serious man. I'm looking for a partner, not a child." He was speaking gently.

They looked at each other wordlessly.

"I miss you more than you know," she said, wiping her eyes.

He knelt and slid his mouth over hers, told her things words could never say; then, there was no space between them as they kissed and kissed. The water and the sand fell away and the sky opened, and she knew what a fool she had been, and as he brushed the tears from her cheeks she resolved never to let him slip away again.

He smiled and drew her bangs from her eyes. "Why don't we go home," he said, rising, drawing her up with him. "Maybe you could show me how much you missed me."

She smiled, she was so happy she nearly cried again.

She lay afterward, warm and sleepy, molded against his body, trying to crawl into him, she couldn't get close enough.

He kissed her hair. "I missed you so."

She murmured, "I miss you, too. Nothing feels right without you."

"Are we made up, then?"

She kissed his mouth passionately. "We are. But how are we going to see each other?"

He looked at her oddly. "What do you mean?"

"Well, where are you staying? How often do you visit?"

"Wait, wait, wait, I see now. You think I've moved."

She said patiently, "The For Rent sign on the lawn. I was there."

He grimaced. "Idiot realtor's son staked it at the wrong address when I was out of town. It was probably there for several days before I returned and removed it. No, Birdie, I own that house, I'm not going anywhere."

She called her parents to let them know their ruse had worked. "You and your partner in crime were very convincing, Fa," she said. "But I nearly drove down to check on you anyway."

"We'll expect you and your Victor for breakfast on Sunday," he said, and hung up.

She turned and smiled, he laughed when she told him.

"Like an engraved invitation," he said. "I like that."

"O-negative? Are you sure that's what she said?" Victor was seated across from her at the Mel-O-Dee the following morning, eating waffles. He paused and looked thoughtfully out at the passing traffic.

"Yeah, why?"

He was slow to respond. "They cover genetics in your biology courses?" He turned to her with clear eyes, cool and direct and intelligent.

She put her coffee cup on the table. "It wasn't my best subject. I remember something about chromosomes. And we had to dissect those poor frogs." She wrinkled her nose. "What's so important about O-negative blood? Is she inclined to hemophilia or something?"

"I researched it for one of my books. I'm no expert, but what I learned is that there are four basic blood types, A, B, AB, and O. Each of those blood types represents, for lack of a better term, a blood sugar. Type O immune systems don't have blood sugars and they don't recognize the sugars that are in A and B blood. So if someone with an O-type received a transfusion from one of the other types by mistake, their system would think something's attacking and the blood cells would try to fight it off. The person would likely die because the types are incompatible."

She swallowed, said slowly, "So, if her father is A-positive—"

He said gently, "He probably isn't her father."

They sat in silence for a moment.

"I don't know if she realizes it," she said at last. "She was kind of quiet, but that may have been the anesthesia wearing off."

"How close are you?" he asked.

"It's not something I'd volunteer," she said, "but I'd be honest about it if she asked."

He took her hand. "I'm ready to go. You?"

They were headed to St. Armand's Circle to shop before going to Claire's apartment for lunch.

"I don't mind you coming over late at night," said Victor as his car crossed the bridge. "In fact, I think it's kind of sexy."

She laughed. "You have a one-track mind. But when I finish work I have to shower to get rid of the smoke it takes a little time to settle down. I don't usually get to bed until around three-thirty or so when I have the late shift."

"You could keep a few things at my place," he said. He glanced at her. "Think about it."

They had reached the enormous circle and Victor was driving around looking for a parking spot, he slid the car effortlessly into a space and turned off the ignition, looked at her. "Ready?"

"Yup," she said.

Two hours later Claire was all smiles as she opened the door. It wasn't a large place but it was beautifully appointed and there were new pieces. In addition to the 18th century bergère from a couple of months ago, there were a Hudson River School oil painting, an aptware teapot from Provence. *Oh, Claire, what have you done.*

Over lunch they talked about living on the circle, the pleasures and the problems.

"The restaurant smells used to make me hungry but I've gotten over that. Parking in back can be a hassle, but it's nice being above the shops and only a block from the beach," said Claire.

"Does the noise ever bother you?" asked Victor.

"I've gotten used to it, most of the time I just tune it out. It's been almost three years, I feel very much at home here."

Birdie said, "This is great, Claire. When did you learn to cook like this?"

Her friend smiled. "Steak salad and French bread are kind of hard to mess up."

Claire turned to Victor. "I'm sorry, I haven't read any of your books. Historical fiction, is that it? Birdie tells me they're very good."

He laughed, glanced at Birdie. "It all depends on what you're looking for."

"What are they about?"

"World War Two in Europe. Spies, double agents, provocateurs, that sort of thing."

"Lots of sex and danger," said Birdie. She caught Victor's eye and he smiled.

She added, "Claire deals in sex and danger too, don't you, Claire?"

There was a pause. "Family law," said Claire shortly. "You know, adoptions, annulments, child custody, property settlements, things like that."

"And divorces," said Birdie.

"Those, too," said Claire with a reproving look. *That's enough of that.*

Victor talked about his recent trip to New York, he disliked the weather, and the atmosphere.

"Couldn't they just talk to you on the phone?" Claire asked.

"Most of the time. But the marketing team's different, they want to get a feel for who and what you are. They're selling not just a book but an author, a package, to retailers and the media."

"I'm thinking about going to Paris," said Claire. "Paris has loads of atmosphere, and it's the right kind."

"What made you decide to go there?" asked Birdie.

Clair shrugged. "I have vacation coming up. I've never been and I think it's about time."

"Spring is a good time to go," said Victor. "But it's Paris, so you'll like it no matter when you visit."

"Yes, I'm sure you will," said Birdie. She looked at Claire and their eyes met. Claire looked down, toyed with her napkin.

Birdie put the Genesis Wind and Wuthering album on the turntable, started chopping vegetables. The beauty of Your Own Special Way always evoked an emotional response in her and she thought about the past two weeks as she moved about the kitchen. She felt that she had turned in a new direction, it was a subtle change and she welcomed it, was calm with it. There was no sense of resistance, no fear.

After putting dinner in the oven she showered and changed into a long black dress, light and delicate, with drooping sleeves, her Stevie Nicks dress. Victor was due shortly.

"I haven't seen much of you at work lately," she said later, over the zharkoye.

"I'm outlining the new book but if you make this for me again, I swear I'll visit you at work every day," he said. "What is it called?"

She pronounced it for him. "You say it like jar-koy-ya. Something to keep you warm at night."

"You and your mother, you Russian girls can cook."

She laughed. "My mother's English and Irish. Her parents were horrified that she lowered her standards to marry a Russian from a supposed lower class."

He was amused. "But why? It seems to me your father's done very well for himself."

She shrugged. "That's how snobs are. They don't think anyone can be successful apart from them."

"But isn't Kira a Russian name?"

"That's just tradition, in Russian culture everyone has an affectionate nickname. Her real name is Katherine. Her parents disowned her when she married my father so she took on his culture. She secretly stayed in touch with one of her sisters, but left the rest of the family behind."

He gazed out the dark window. "My father was an engineer. We weren't close, my parents didn't spoil me but they paid for my college."

"What about your sister?"

He shrugged.

The gulf was calm that night and the window was open, candles burning like constellations throughout the apartment. Victor's face was wistful in the soft glow of the flames, she saw that he was about to say something and then didn't. He looked vulnerable, it made her want to reach out to him but she sensed it would be the wrong thing to do. She tried to imagine him as a young boy but couldn't.

She took a swallow of her drink. "Where are they now, New Mexico?"

"No, they live down in Mexico, a little place called Ajijic, a lot of artists and ex-pats living there. It appealed to my father when he retired, that's where he wanted to be."

"He's retired," she repeated, and looked at him. "How old are you, Victor?"

He grinned boyishly. "Thirty-five."

She raised her brows. "Mexico's kind of a laid back place for a straightlaced engineer, isn't it?"

He picked up his glass. "My mother's a painter. My father mellowed as he got older, now they're living the hippie lifestyle."

She got up, started clearing plates. "Your mother's an artist? Is that where your creative side comes from?"

He gathered the rest of the dishes from the table, followed her into the kitchen. "She does nature paintings. The picture in my living room was painted by her long ago."

She turned to face him, the long diaphanous dress silhouetted behind her. "Really? It's very beautiful, you must be proud of her."

He shrugged, she moved past him into the living room. "Do you want something to drink?" she called over her shoulder.

He leaned against the doorframe. "Yes, please."

She opened the cabinet, moved bottles. "I also have weed if you want it. There's a joint in the cache box on the coffee table."

She went and got ice, poured, placed the glasses on the table and settled on the sofa. "Chartreuse alright?"

He sat beside her. "I've never had it."

"Mmm, I think you'll like it."

He produced a lighter from the cache, lit a joint and inhaled, after a moment the strong sweet scent filled the room.

"It's very quiet, we should put on some music," he said.

She rose and went to look through records. "Anything in particular? There's an old Dylan album I haven't played in a while."

"Which one?"

"Blonde on Blonde."

"That's good, it has Leopard Skin Pillbox Hat."

He handed her the joint and she took a hit, looked at him. "I don't think we've done this before," she said.

He leaned against the cushions, facing her. "I've kind of gotten away from it."

"Any particular reason?" She took another hit and handed it back to him.

He reached over and plucked at the shoulder of the dress, it went down easily. "No, when I came here I didn't have a dealer, so I just let it slide." He kissed her bare shoulder, his mouth left a hot mark on her skin.

"Try the Chartreuse," she said.

He sampled from the glass. "Very herbal, I like it. Where does it come from?"

"It's made by French monks, a hundred-ten proof, they intended it to be medicinal." She shifted against the cushions.

He traced her breast through the filmy material, his eyes rose to hers.

"This dress you're wearing, I can see through it and it's turning me on."

She smiled, leaned into him and kissed him slowly, gently sucked his tongue, kissed him again. "Glad you like it," she said in a low voice.

She took the joint, inhaled, handed it back to him. The guitars on Visions of Johanna sounded lush and full, she was feeling a little lush and full herself. She reached for her glass and swallowed some of the liquid, smiled at him.

He smoked slowly, looked at her thoughtfully. She liked the way he was looking at her, liked playing cat-and-mouse, it excited her. Was he going to do this to her? Or that? Should she touch him? Now? Or no, better to make him wait.

"I like this song," he said, "but I think he should slow it down, make it more wistful and romantic."

She reclined her head against the arm of the sofa and stretched out. "Oh, I dunno," she said. "Nothing says romance like, 'It's not that way, I wasn't born to lose you.' "

He looked at her with those washed out blue-green eyes and something unspoken passed between them. She hesitated, almost said the words aloud, set them aside for another time.

She went to the turntable and moved the needle past the next few songs, returned to the sofa. He took her wrist and pulled her onto his lap.

He took a long hit from the joint and placed it between her lips. After she exhaled she set it in the ashtray and unbuttoned his shirt. "I don't want this in the way," she whispered, slid her fingers along his ribs and up his chest.

He smiled and leaned up to kiss her mouth, deep, continuous kisses tinged with herbs and weed and seduction, her head was floating in a dreamy euphoria, body responding to the unrestrained pleasures of touch.

His voice was low against her ear, "I love your pale skin, it does something to me." Hands gliding over her dress, "I like the way it looks against mine when I'm inside you." He slid down, kissed her stomach, she whimpered.

The sensations were very warm and fluid, and while Dylan sang of eyes like smoke and voice like chimes, she could feel Victor's heart beating against her palms, his thighs tightening around hers, could hear her own voice, "Please, please . . ."

He raised the dress above her head and it floated to the floor, shrugged out of his jeans, lifted her hard against him, at last he was where she wanted him. She drew a sharp breath and they began the slow, sweet, singing ascent to ecstasy.

Georgette had received a letter. She placed it on the surface in front of Birdie and said, "What do you make of this?"

Birdie scanned the contents quickly, it was only one page, and looked up. "What's this all about, Georgie, have you ever heard of her before?"

"No!" Her friend was close to tears. "It came in the mail a couple of days ago addressed to me, it's from Miami. I don't know anyone from there."

Birdie glanced at the paper again. "It says she thinks she's your sister. Has your father ever mentioned anything about her?"

A shake of the head. "All I know is, my mother died when I was born."

Birdie hesitated, said gently. "He is your father, right? Not a—"

"Birdie!"

She shrugged. "I don't know, Georgie. You hear about women dying and family members raising the baby, there's nothing wrong with that. What are you going to do, write her back, call her?"

"I'm not sure, maybe it's someone playing a hoax or something."

"Why would anyone do that? There'd have to be a motive, extortion or something, you don't have that kind of money."

"I've been thinking. My doctor said it would be good if he knew my family history because of what happened with me. I could ask if she knows of any illnesses in the family."

Birdie nodded. "Maybe she could tell you things about your mother that your father, well, doesn't talk about for whatever reason."

Georgette eyed her suspiciously. "Like what?"

"Oh, I don't know. This says you also have a brother in Miami. How is that possible? At the least, you should give her time to explain."

"Speaking of time, we'd better unlock the doors," said Georgie, checking her watch. She refolded the letter and put it in her pocket. "I'll think about it, I don't know yet."

Birdie laid a hand on her arm. "This was a shock, but maybe some good could come of it, you know?"

Georgette gave a brief smile. "Yeah, I know. Thanks, Birdie."

A couple of customers filtered in shortly after ten and business was steady after that. A group of snowbirds whose wives had driven to Orlando for the day arrived a little after lunch, they were having a guy's day out. They put two tables together and ordered pitchers of beer, traded stories and insults, took turns at the jukebox.

One of them lit a joint and Birdie had to go to the table to deliver the news. She bent low, said, "Guys, so sorry, but the law is the law, you can't do that in here. You gotta put it out, you understand."

"Aww, darlin', just one toke," one of them said. The rest laughed.

She stood, winked at him. "You understand. Put it out, I can't allow it in *here*."

He finally got it. Stood and scraped back his chair. "Sorry miss, I'll put it out." He walked outside.

Georgette came out of the back room, looked at Birdie. "Someone lighting up again?"

"Yeah, I sent him outside."

Georgette shook her head. "Someone snorting coke in the bathroom the other night, first time I've seen that."

"Doesn't mean it's not happening when we're not around, I just don't want to get known for it, you know? If we see too much of it, we'll have to tell Charlie so he can do what he needs to do. I don't know about you, but I don't want to have to deal with it here."

Georgette nodded. She never did drugs, was straight-laced about them. Birdie didn't care what others did, but she was protective of her workplace. She'd heard about bars where dealers hung out and were well known. It gave the places a reputation, a seediness she didn't want to be associated with.

They went to Crescent Beach on her next day off, he called the night before and suggested it, maybe Anna's afterward for sandwiches, he'd heard it was a good place to go.

She was surprised. "I can't believe you haven't been to Anna's yet."

He was unconcerned. "I'm not here all the time, and when I am I'm usually holed up somewhere trying to be creative."

She got it. "Okay, to the beach, then to Anna's. And you're in for a treat."

The beach was practically deserted. It was before Easter so season hadn't started yet, and a lot of the locals were at work. They took a swim in water that was crystal clear and lukewarm, wandered the shore for a while, sat side by side in the powdery white sand, pleasantly somnolent, enjoying the unobstructed view of the gulf and the horizon beyond it.

"The water is the color of your eyes," she said to him.

"That's a nice thing to say."

"I don't say things like that often, but I think them." She put a hand on his arm and kissed his cheek, leaned against him.

They made love in the living room when they got back to her apartment after lunch, as soon as they stepped inside he pulled her down to the thick wool rug and stripped her out of her bikini, kissed her and kissed her until she was delirious with wanting him.

It was a warm spring afternoon, breezes blew the curtains inward, there was the scent of dried sea on their skin, sandy hair falling across her eyes, mingled breath as tongues met and entwined. He took both of her hands in his and looked down at her as they moved together, the slow swell, the surge like a tide, the spilling overflow, then the still quiet like the one that follows a sea storm.

He held her afterward, on the red and black and gold rug, and she turned her head and kissed him.

"I love you," she said, her mouth against his.

He tightened his arms around her and buried his face in her hair. "I love you, free-as-a-bird," he said, "I love you."

Birdie unlocked the front door with her spare key and walked softly through the house to the bathroom, removed her clothing and showered. The hot water felt good between her shoulders and she stood for an extra minute as it coursed down her back.

When she finished, she took the robe from the hook on the door and went into the kitchen for a snack. Rummaging through the refrigerator she found the remains of last night's stroganoff, pulled it out and unwrapped it. She carried it into the living room and turned on a lamp, flipped over the book she'd started, Victor's fifth novel.

"You feel like sharing?"

She glanced up. "I'm sorry, was I too loud?"

He sat on the sofa next to her and kissed her head. "No, I was waiting up for you."

She held out the fork. "It's not hot but it tastes fine."

"I'll warm it up." He took the plate and went into the kitchen.

She picked up the book and began to read.

He returned after a few minutes. "Anything exciting happen tonight?"

"Diana came by with Roger. They announced they're getting married, everyone's invited."

"She the one with the blond hair, he's blond too?"

She nodded. "He visits from Boca Raton, stockbroker who made it big up north and moved down here. Anyway, I guess he'll want her to move to Boca with him but nothing's been decided. Oh, and one of the new bartenders didn't show up for his shift so he's officially fired."

Victor raised his brows. "Maybe I'll apply. We can spend more time together. Sex in the stockroom."

She laughed. "We see each other three or four times a week, don't you get tired of me?"

He didn't smile. "It's actually two, maybe three times a week."

She met his look. He rose and went back to the kitchen, returned after a few minutes with the plate.

They began to eat, passing the fork between them. "I like the book so far," she said.

"You should live here with me," he said.

She looked up. "Did you use someone as a real-life model for the Hungarian countess? I was wondering about those exceptionally big bosoms."

He set the plate on the coffee table. "I love you and I want to be with you more," he said.

"Victor, it went very badly the last time I tried living with someone."

"It was with someone different," he pointed out.

"But I was involved. What if it turns out I'm the one who's bad at it, and not him? I don't want you, of all people, to be hurt."

He reached forward, touched her face. "I'm a big boy, and besides, I don't think that's going to happen this time around."

"Tell me something," she said, watching him.

"Mmm?" He smiled.

"Is there a reason you haven't married?"

"Who said I haven't married?"

She raised her brows. "Are you joking?"

He shrugged. "I was married briefly, in college. I had very romantic ideas about how it would be. Turns out I married for love, she married for security." He paused. "I divorced her the week before graduation."

She was amazed. "Why didn't you mention it before?"

He said patiently, "Birdie, it was years ago. I was young, it wasn't exactly my finest hour." He sat back, looked at her. "Surely you didn't think—"

"That you were a virgin before me? No, of course not, Victor, but you have a way of surprising me sometimes." She hesitated, settled back against him with a laugh. "You may be quiet, but you're never boring."

He wrapped his arms around her. "So you'll live here with me?"

"You have any other surprises I should know about?"

He kissed her hair. "There's the wife and four kids and dog up in Utah. I guess I should have mentioned them earlier but I forgot."

She laughed. "I'll think about it," she said.

Chapter Five

March – May 1979

She began moving things into his house a week later. First, her clothes; then, sorting through furnishings, a few pieces here, a few there, Asian and Russian pieces that mixed well with the things in his house. By late Tuesday, she was in residence.

"You have a safe somewhere in the house?" she asked over dinner that night.

He set the wine glass down and looked at her. "A safe? To keep valuables in?"

She nodded.

He shook his head. "I keep the few papers I need in a box at the bank."

"I forgot to mention it, I need a safe. I can't leave certain things behind at the other place."

He smiled. "Am I allowed to know? Are you one of the lost Romanovs?"

She laughed. "No, nothing like that, it's just, I have a collection of good jewelry, it needs to stay with me."

"Okay, so what kind of safe?"

She spooned more potatoes onto her plate. "Can we put it on an inside wall?"

He smiled, he was amused. "Sure, we can do that."

On Sunday, breakfast. He held her hand as they walked up to the house.

They greeted him like a member of the family, her mother kissed his cheek, her father made familiar jokes while she and her mother set the table. They ate outside on the terrace, the weather was typical Southwest Florida in spring, light clouds pushed across the sky like lambs frolicking across fields, soft lemon sun shining through. The air was warmish but not quite, Birdie wore a long dress.

"Where does this new novel take place, Victor? Birdie tells us you've started working on it already." Her mother had begun to take a maternal interest in the books.

Victor nodded. "It begins in Italy, with the fascists. I may have to go there briefly to get a feel for the locations, but a lot of the research has been done already."

Show me what's under that dress, popetto mia.

Oh yes, do it like that, bella tesoro.

"You don't take a break between books, make time to relax?" This, from Anton.

Victor turned to him. "Normally, yes, but I wanted to get this completed so I could take a longer break next year. I'll finish this and set it aside, probably get it published around the usual timeframe next fall, it depends on my publisher."

Birdie took a deep breath. "Mother, Fa, I'm going to be living with Victor from now on," she said. "I'll leave his telephone number and address with you so you'll be able to reach me, I mean, us. That will be my new number from now on."

A look passed between Victor and her father.

"You're serious about this?" said Fa.

"I am," said Victor.

"You're adults," said her mother, matter-of-factly. "Be good to one another, be happy."

Victor turned to Birdie, took her hand and kissed it.

The phone rang, her father went inside to answer it.

"Where do you live, exactly," said Kira to Victor. "Birdie said you have a place somewhere near hers, on the key?"

"Yes, I own a house only a mile from Birdie's condo. You'll come, of course, and see us there."

She smiled. "We had contemplated a house there ourselves, but one weekend we happened to take a drive and there was this property for sale, with the view, and the seclusion, and Anton fell in love. He knew just the sort of house he would build for us here. That's his gift, you see. He knows, just one look, how things are, how they should be. Very discerning, my Anton."

"A visionary," said Victor.

She nodded solemnly and they looked at each other.

"I should show you the hidden room sometime," said Birdie. "Fa built it, just for kicks. You'd never find it on your own."

Victor raised his brows. "A hidden room? I'd like to see that."

Kira smiled. "It's his study. There's a glass ceiling which is lovely at night for star gazing."

Birdie said, "I would like more tea, anyone else?"

Anton returned to the table but didn't return to his seat. "Birdie," he said. "That was Nicholas on the telephone." His voice was very quiet and his gaze was direct.

She tilted her head, her brows furrowed. "Nicholas? Why's he calling here?"

"He said he has been trying to call you at home but couldn't reach you. It seems," he hesitated, looked at Victor.

She became still, a slow chill crept up her spine.

"It seems his sister has been found dead."

She gasped. Victor grasped her wrist, put an arm around her waist. "When did this happen," he said in a low voice.

"Last night, apparently."

"And how is . . . Nicholas?" asked Victor.

"He's distraught, naturally. He wanted to talk to Birdie."

Her mother said, "Call him back, let him know he can talk to her later."

Birdie heard the calm voices around her through the roaring in her ears, felt the pressure of Victor's arm, but deep inside, her heart and mind were racing. Her breathing came in short bursts, she put a shaking hand to her mouth, felt cold beads of sweat on her forehead as she began to shiver. From far away, her mother's voice, "She's in shock, get her into the sitting room."

She heard herself say faintly, "No, I should—" but she was being carried swiftly down the hallway and placed on the sofa, a pill placed gently between her lips, water spilling down her neck. Victor was beside her and she was limp against his body, someone was putting a blanket over them, gradually her eyes became heavy and the trembling ceased and was replaced by a quiet darkness as the sedative, and Victor's arms, took effect.

Nicholas was calm, calmer than she'd expected him to be, but he had cried, and she knew it was for the best, it wouldn't do for him to keep his grief bottled up inside. He stood alone at the gravesite after the funeral, the rest of their friends had gone to their cars, the relatives who had driven down from Alabama had left already.

Victor waited for her while she went to say goodbye.

She put a hand on his arm. "Nicky, how're you doing? Do you want me to stay with you a while longer?"

"No, no, I'll be going now, too," he said. He smiled wearily and turned to her, glancing toward Victor's car. "He taking good care of you, Birdie?"

She smiled briefly. "He is, Nicholas. Are you taking good care of yourself?"

"I'm clean, if that's what you're askin'. You met Peter, he's been . . ." His voice trailed off, eyes meeting hers. "She was seein' someone, you know, I don't know who, but he wasn't worth dyin' over. If I find—"

She clutched his arm. "Don't go there, let it rest with her, you hear?"

His eyes suddenly filled. "She told you, didn't she? Baby, if you know anything, please—"

"Nicky, let it be. You've been doing so well, just stay focused, she wouldn't want you—"

"Nicholas, if you need anything, if we can do anything . . ."

They hadn't heard Victor's approach, he stood at Birdie's elbow, hand extended.

"Thank you, thank you so much." Nicholas took the hand, shook it. He gave Birdie a last look, walked away to the waiting limousine. Two men stood waiting for him, Birdie had met them earlier, was glad he had friends who were there for him.

She didn't speak to Victor in the car, he turned on the radio instead. They went into the house and she sat on the sofa, he went to the kitchen, made tea, returned to sit with her.

"She needed someone to talk to and all I did was give her a hard time," she said. "That's all I can think about, what a terrible friend I was." She felt weary, beat-up from sorrow.

He leaned close, brushed the bangs from her eyes. "Birdie, sometimes no matter what we say, no matter what we do, people commit themselves to a certain path, and we can't go there with them. Do you know what I mean?"

She looked at him, there was pain in his eyes. She kissed his cheek and leaned against him.

He went on. "We're not invited on that journey, they don't want us along, and we can't go where we're not invited. My sense of Claire is that she was a lovely young woman with all the promise that that entails, but she was in over her head. She saw something she wanted, didn't realize she wasn't equipped to handle the consequences, but it never occurred to her to say no. She wasn't listening to you, she wanted what she wanted. Some people are . . . they're wired that way, Birdie. Maybe he could have stopped it, or maybe he tried to end it and that's what made her do it, but we'll never know. What goes on between two people in love is one of the great mysteries."

She swallowed. "How did you get so wise, Victor?"

He wound his arms around her, kissed her head. "Lots of mistakes, Birdie. I should be the smartest man alive by now but I'm not."

She put her arms around him. "I love you so," she said.

"I'm sorry our first week living together was such a drag," he said.

"Well, it will get better."

"Do you want to stay in tonight or go out?"

"I think I'd like to cook, can we stay in? Tonight, all I want is to be alone with you."

He kissed her mouth. "I like the sound of that."

Kiki was introspective when they talked a week later.

"Kiki, if you can't come, just say so, you don't have to give a reason. We'll do dinner another time," said Birdie.

There was a long silence at the other end of the line. "It's just that I'm not sure about his schedule," she said, finally.

"Okay, well, you've got the new number."

There was another pause.

"It feels strange without Claire around, doesn't it?" said Kiki.

Birdie drew a deep breath. "Yeah, I miss her too."

"Do you ever ask yourself why?"

"She didn't leave a note."

"Yes, but you knew her better than anyone, Birdie, she must have told you something. I keep thinking we missed something. Maybe . . . maybe she tried to tell me but I wasn't listening."

"No, don't do that to yourself. Sometimes people are just messed up inside and they're so good at hiding it that even their closest friends don't know. Anyway, let us know about dinner, okay?"

Kiki promised and rang off.

Later, Birdie puzzled over Mystery Man with Victor, but he had no ideas.

"Some master of intrigue you are," she said accusingly.

He smiled, propped a foot on the desk and looked at her. "If I were writing her story, I'd say it was a suave, stealthy stranger who slipped into the restaurant late one night, intending to neutralize the dangerous spy who had infiltrated the organization as a sommelier. She heard noises and went to the wine vault, caught him plunging the dagger, recognized that she was right in suspecting the evil sommelier, and when their eyes met over the body—"

She put up her hand, laughing. "Okay, I got it."

"You know, half the time I'm walking around with different scenarios filtering through my head, it's something writers do, indulge in hypothetical conversations that we play out so by the time we get to the typewriter, it feels like we're writing what we know, not just something imagined. Does that make sense?"

She nodded.

"It's why I need so much time alone, I have to work things through, no noise, no beautiful distractions."

She smiled, moved to his lap, put her arms around his neck.

"You live in a fictional world, is that what you're trying to say?"

He kissed her mouth, smiled. "Sometimes. Sometimes I have to move deliberately between the real world and the . . . the world I've created. You're like a bridge between the two, Birdie. When I have a hard time finding my way back, you're the one who helps me across."

"I think that's the nicest thing anyone's ever said to me," she said.

His eyes were serious, their color warm in the lamp light. "I love you," he said in a low voice. "I love the way your eyes change color when you're listening to a story. I love the way you move around the kitchen when you cook, like you're bossing it around. And I love that scent you wear, like some kind of spice, I smell it everywhere in the house."

She smiled, he kissed her and went on. "I love that lean you do on the bar at work, it's the sexiest thing I've ever seen. I love that you're smart and can put me in my place when I need it, you look like a nineteen-year old little girl but when you open your mouth, Lord have mercy on the man that tries to pull one over on you."

"Hey, enough now," she said.

"And this remarkable, lithe little body." He carried her from his lap to the sofa and leaned over her, ran his hand up her thigh, began to stroke her flank. "I love what it does to mine."

She laughed softly and reached for him.

A few days later, her safe was installed. After he'd finished paying the man and the truck pulled away, Victor turned to her. "It's all yours."

They went into the bedroom where she hauled the suitcase onto the bed, began to pull out boxes and bags.

"Wait," he said, opening one of the boxes. "What is this?"

Sitting cross-legged on the floor beside him, "Oh, that's an imperial topaz brooch."

"Looks expensive."

"Well, that's why we need to put it in a safe."

He studied her, looked back at the brooch, "Tell me about it."

She took the piece from him, removed it from the box, rustled around and pulled a small jeweler's loupe from another bag. "It's an antique. Outside, here, you see it's stamped with a 56 zolotnik mark, which in Russian is 14 carat gold." She leaned close and pointed. "There's the maker's mark. A maker's mark is a jeweler's mark, like a personal trademark, in this case, you see here? It's in Cyrillic, it says AB, only the B in Cyrillic means V." She looked at him.

He nodded, picked up another box, opened it. "What about these?"

"Turquoise diamond drop earrings, half a carat. I like this style, it's Art Deco, which means made between 1910 and 1930."

"What's a full carat?"

"Full carat is a fifth of a gram, 200 milligrams. I've never worn these, no place to wear them so I keep them as an investment."

"What about this?"

She glanced inside. "An a jour piece." She fingered the brooch. "I like these unusual pieces, see the back? There's a stained glass window effect."

He handed her a velvet bag. "What's in here?"

"Victor . . ."

"I'm seeing a whole other side of you. Birdie Noonan, businesswoman."

She looked at him through lowered lids. "These are not business for me." She rose and went into the closet, began to place items in the safe.

"How did you come by them?"

"My mother gave a lot of them to me. I bought the rest, here and there, my parents taught me to save my pennies, the advice came in handy."

He lounged on the floor, watching her. "How did your mother come by them, if you don't mind me asking. You said she isn't Russian, and some of them are Russian."

Her gaze met his. "You'd have to ask my father."

She closed the safe, picked up the empty suitcase, stowed it in the closet and shut the door.

He said, "You seem to know a lot about this kind of thing, have you ever considered taking it further?"

She sat on the floor across from him. "Not really, I kind of picked it up as I went along. Hanging out with my mother, going to auctions, listening to others, you know how it is, Victor, something interests you so you read things, do the research. You do the same in your line of work."

He shifted, leaned against the bed, looked at her. "Is that how you acquired the antiques at the condo?"

"I grew up around antiques. My parents always furnished with them so that's just how it was. They talked about them, I learned gradually, when they got tired of something they'd give it to me so I already knew the provenance, then I started shopping for my own pieces."

"Birdie, I think you have something, call it a hobby or a kind of specialized knowledge, that has potential value to others. You could do more with it, if you wanted to."

"Victor, I already made my choice. Isn't it a little late to change horses in midstream?"

He was silent, studied her face. "Why don't we go out for dinner tonight?" he said, finally. "I heard about a place up on Longboat."

He took her to the tiny restaurant, on the bay side of Longboat Key, called Euphemia Haye. Pressed tablecloths, French farmhouse decor, quiet music, cuisine elegant but not stuffy, the scent of garlic heavy in the air. She loved it.

"I heard the owner named the place after his grandmother," he said.

"What a lovely thing to do," she said. "This is beautiful, Victor, thank you."

He took her hand. "Antique furnishings."

"Um-hmm, well kind of."

"Someone with your knowledge could be a resource for people like this who need to find furniture." He looked at her.

"Victor, I have a vocation."

He nodded. "Yup, you do, and you're good at it. But Birdie, just because you're good at something doesn't mean you have to stay at it for the rest of your life. You know what I did before I wrote books for a living?"

She finished the last of the creme brûlée and sat back, looked at him. He continued. "I worked for a brokerage firm, I was a stockbroker. My degree was in economics. My uncle got me a job at Dean Witter, I went through their school, turned out I was pretty good at it. Maybe I would have done well but I hated it."

She swallowed some wine, he signaled for the check. "Why economics?"

"My father saw that I had a head for math, and philosophy, I guess he realized I took after him that way. I was under a lot of pressure, Vietnam was gaining momentum then and I needed a deferment, my uncle had a seat on the New York Stock Exchange and knew people. Between the two of them I didn't have a chance."

The check was delivered, he continued talking. "I did it for two years. After the first year, out of sheer unhappiness and a way to escape, I began to read a lot more, and write. Turned out my college roommate had gone to work for a publisher, he was coming through town one weekend, one thing led to another and now I'm doing what I want rather than what I feel I have to do." He leaned forward. "Decisions can be reversed."

She stared at him. "Victor, I'm not unhappy like you were."

He began to take out his wallet.

"You don't have to be unhappy to make a change, Birdie. Just remember that."

Spring had arrived in full, the air warm but not yet humid, the gulf waters warm but not bathwater warm like they would be in midsummer. At the bar, business was steady, the regulars were there every Friday and Saturday night, the four o'clock crowd took up their seats on weekdays.

A new bartender named Vicki was hired and fully integrated by the time Georgette was ready to leave on vacation. On her last shift, Georgette reported the conversation she'd had with her father regarding her trip.

"He said he didn't think I had any business nosing around my mother's past," she said.

"That's how he phrased it, your mother's past?" said Birdie.

"Yeah. I've been thinking of it as finding out about my own past but when he said it like that, it put a different spin on it, you know? Made me wonder. I don't know, Birdie, maybe this trip is a good idea and maybe it isn't, but I'm glad Lee's going with me. Moral support and all that."

Birdie nodded as she pulled the last of the napkins from the bag and finished restocking the bar. "Victor wants me to go with him on one of his trips," she said.

"Really? Where does he go?" asked Georgette.

"It depends. Sometimes he makes research trips to the places he writes about, usually Europe for a few days to a few weeks. Other times he goes to book signings and publicity events. Those could be anywhere in the country."

"Sounds nice, but you never seemed interested in traveling."

"I am, but I never had the chance. All I ever did was work," said Birdie.

Georgette looked hard at her. "Birdie, seriously, you should go with him if you can, the further the better. Didn't you ever have a dream of doing something big or adventurous?"

Birdie looked at her and smiled. "What do you want to be when you grow up, Georgie?"

Georgette laughed, "Funny you should ask that now. I always wanted to be like my dad, do something with animals. You know how I'm always rescuing little creatures, I can't seem to leave 'em alone, or they come find me somehow."

Birdie smiled, nodded at a new customer. "I hope your dream comes true, Georgie, I really do."

"What about you, Birdie, what's your big dream?"

Birdie shrugged. "I like what I do," she said as she turned to go.

Georgette put a hand on her arm. "Don't take this the wrong way, but I think you were meant for other things, Birdie."

She looked at Georgette, disengaged her arm and moved down the bar.

This time the parents were coming to them. Victor had suggested it, he wanted them to know where their daughter and her lover were living in sin, he said, so they could see that it was a responsible arrangement.

Birdie laughed. "They don't think of it that way, don't be silly. What matters to them is that you care for me."

He kissed her hair and drew his arm around her neck. "You believe that, Solnyshka, but parents who love their children need to be reassured. You're still their little girl even if you're in your twenties, and I'm the man doing those unmentionable things to you."

Solnyshka, *little sun*. He had started calling her that, had taken the trouble to learn the Russian, and she loved him for it.

She lifted the spoon, lobster bisque in the bowl. "Taste," she said.

He took her wrist, looked into her eyes, sipped. "A little more sherry," he said, and kissed her mouth.

She lit candles, he put on Django Reinhardt, they served Sauvignon blanc with the stuffed shrimp. The four of them talked about the traffic between the keys during tourist season, the age and construction of the houses around Hansen Bayou where Victor's house was situated, the escaped monkey from the house next door.

Victor described the distraught owner's attempts to coax the animal down from the backyard tree with orange pieces.

"That didn't work and he got frustrated, he started to act like Junior, jumping up and down flapping his arms, there they were, man and beast, yelling at each other like an old married couple."

Kira laughed. Birdie said, "I came home in time to see Junior swing down from the tree, walk nonchalantly to Victor, and climb up his back. Poor Ted, I think he was ready to donate Junior to a zoo after that."

"Are monkeys legal pets in Florida?" wondered her father.

"Anything from giraffes to sloths is legal, but you have to have a permit," said Birdie. "One of my customers tames lions for the circus and we've talked about that."

Her mother inquired about work, Birdie said she'd had to refuse service the day before, due to a forged driver's license. "It's one of the things I hate about the job," she said, "asking for I.D."

"How did you know it was forged?" asked Kira.

"She looked young, acted overconfident, wore too much makeup for a Florida beach girl. She gave me a license with a Miami address but when I asked her which part of Miami, she couldn't tell me."

Her mother said, "What did you do, call the police?"

"No, I confiscated the ID and sent her away."

"You won't have to deal with it for a whole week while you're on vacation," said Victor.

Her parents looked. "Vacation?" said Anton, sampling the word as if he'd never spoken it before. "You take vacations now?"

"Well, I've just never done it," said Birdie.

"Have you made plans, where do you think you might go?" said Kira.

"We're thinking about going out west for a few days," Birdie said.

"I need to go to New Mexico for some book signing events, we thought we'd make a trip out of it. I'd like Birdie to see where I came from," explained Victor.

"New Mexico, that's a lot of desert, isn't it?" said her father.

"I've never really traveled outside of Florida and Michigan, Fa. I want to see what the desert is like." She looked at Victor, smiled.

Victor uncorked another bottle. As he was pouring, he said, "I met a man once in my travels, we were in England, he had come from the Soviet Union, told me he had lived through the revolution, this was an older man, of course. He was sitting in front of an Orthodox church, I asked if he was going inside and he said no, he just liked looking at a beautiful place that reminded him of home. He said he was . . .Tengrist? Is that how you say it?"

Anton nodded, once. "Pagan. Yes, they have shamans, a very old practice in the south, this was not something you would see in the cities, he would be from the country. They worship different gods, a sky god I think."

"You've traveled some. At least, from Russia to here," Victor said to Anton.

"Oh yes," her father said thoughtfully, "traveled even more than that during the war."

Victor looked at him with interest. Birdie was clearing the table, her mother was assisting. They made coffee, Birdie finished the crepes suzette, the four of them ate while her father, prompted by Victor, reminisced about his youth.

"I was only twenty when the war began for us, I was sent to Poland, several of my friends died there. I don't know how I survived, I wasn't skilled enough then to know what to do, I think it was destiny that carried me through it. Later, at the end of the war, I was in Berlin." He chuckled, looked at Victor.

Victor tipped his wine glass. "The Soviet army took Berlin," he said.

"We took Berlin almost without a fight. They had lost much of their signal equipment by then, and we took advantage. The Germans were using the public telephone system to learn our positions, calling civilians to ask if they'd seen any Russian soldiers. We caught on, started answering their phones for them when we heard them ringing, laughing over that, I tell you. Laughed a long time afterward, too." He shook his head, lost in the reverie, swallowed coffee. *Over 20 million Russians died in the war,* more than any other nation.

"When did you come to the U.S.?"

"Oh, not long afterward. An American officer I met in Berlin was from Detroit, very nice fellow, he owned a construction business and offered to sponsor me if I wanted to come over. We had spent a lot of time talking about building and construction, I knew enough English."

Victor turned to Kira, she smiled. "We met at a New Year's Eve dance in Detroit. I was there visiting a friend for the holidays, I found his accent charming."

"I was a construction foreman by then, very worldly and successful," said Anton.

Kira laughed. "Not exactly, but you had dreams, and that was intoxicating. What girl can resist a handsome man with a vision?"

Victor said, "Birdie and I met on her birthday, at her party."

She said, "We talked about Paris, you left early."

Their eyes met across the table. "Well, I kind of had to," he admitted.

She laughed, turned to her parents. "One of my friends had eyes for him."

He took her hand, "I had eyes for you."

After the parents had gone, the kitchen was cleared and the candles were dying out, he sat upright against the headboard of the bed, she was going to the safe to remove her jewelry.

He said, "No, don't," and held out his hand. Sad Eyed Lady of the Lowlands was playing on the turntable, it was one of their favorite ballads.

She went to him, he used the hand to bring her to his side, reached for the necklace and looked at it in the candlelight. It was a long pendant, a large, teardrop-shaped black onyx which rested just above her cleavage. "I loved this on you tonight, you should wear it more often."

"Alright, Victor, I will," she said. Her eyes met his.

She leaned forward, kissed his mouth, a long, promissory kiss. "I've been waiting for this all night," she said.

He watched, smiling, as she stood and unbuttoned the back of the dress and let it fall, stepped out of it quickly wearing a silk chemise. She went to him and straddled his lap, he ran his hands over the garment and caressed her breasts, tilted his head and placed a warm mouth against the fabric.

He looked at her. "I was wondering."

"Hmm?"

"What would that pendant look like . . . from a different angle."

She smiled, kissed him again, parting his lips with her tongue. He groaned. Moving lower, kissing his chest with an open mouth, sliding down to unfasten the pants. She unzipped them and reached inside, took him in her hand and looked up.

"Yes," he said, and smiled. *Yes, that.*

Georgette was back, full of news and angst. She had a sister, and a brother, and a story of her mother, whom she had never met, that was as intriguing as it was troubling. Her mother, she said, was pretty.

"And also pretty free with her favors, if you know what I mean."

Birdie, speaking carefully, said, "Mothers aren't perfect, Georgie."

"I figured that out, Birdie. Anyway, she was married to my half-sister's father, and ran off on him. Then she got pregnant with my brother, or half-brother, and didn't marry his father."

"What about your father?"

Georgette said, "As it turns out, my uncle. But he was the one who raised me, and I think of him as my father, so we squared that away when I got home. It's been a weird week, Birdie, I'll tell you. Things here at the bar seem normal compared with what I've been through."

She added, "There's another thing, Lee and I have called it quits."

"What?"

Georgette looked down, swallowed. "We were just kinda coasting along, you know? I wanted something more, and he was happy with the way things were. So," she frowned, shrugging.

"Oh Georgie, I'm sorry. I know you cared for him."

"What about you?" Georgette looked around. "Everything okay here?"

Birdie laughed. "It's been an interesting week here, too. The night you left, I had a customer who was getting a little loaded but I was busy and didn't realize just how much until one of the regulars, you know Jimmy, took me aside and told me the guy at table four had just pissed in his beer. So I go to investigate and sure enough, there's the pitcher sitting in front of him on the table and he's grinning at me like he's proud of himself. I was just thankful he used the pitcher and not the floor, you know?"

Georgie was laughing. "Been a while since we've had one of those."

"Yeah, well, he wanted to order more, told me he was feeling a little down and liked coming to our place, could he please have another, and my response was too bad so sad, there's the door, don't come back."

"You have a hard heart, Birdie," said Georgette.

Birdie grinned. "Day before last, a guy came in who took one look at the two of us, it was me and Vicki, and said he refused to be served by a woman. So I told him this must be our lucky day. I don't know what he expected exactly, but he stood there a minute and looked at us, we weren't leaving, so he did."

Georgie laughed, shook her head. "You must have seen worse when you were at the Chicken Coop," she said.

Birdie nodded. "The guys who worked there could be brutal. One of them, Scotty, was good looking, girls were always leaving their phone numbers, waiting around for him to get off, you know the type, but he wouldn't take crap from anyone. There was this guy that used to come in, he'd throw money around buying drinks, had a girlfriend who came in too, one of those tall glamorous brunettes. One night he had a lot more to drink than he should have, and got more obnoxious than usual. Before he left, he took Scotty aside and told him he should do something useful with his life, work in construction, fight fires or something. Scotty says, I got something useful for you, buddy. When you take that girlfriend of yours home tonight, pull her arm behind her back and bend her over and do it real slow, she loves it when I do that."

"Oh wow, that's cold."

"The thing is, Scotty got around and everyone knew it, so it wasn't just talk. We lost the guy as a customer but, you know, I guess Scotty got some satisfaction out of it."

Georgette was quiet for a moment. "I guess I'm back on the market now. But maybe not right away." She sighed, looked at Birdie. "You finished?"

Birdie poured the last of the ice into the well and stood. "Yup. I guess we need to open the doors. You ready?"

"Sure." She looked at Birdie. "What about you, you doing okay?"

Birdie smiled. "We're going to New Mexico next week."

"That's cool! What's in New Mexico?"

"Victor's from there, he has a couple of book signings to do but the rest of the time we're just going to chill."

"How long?"

"Charlie's giving me a week."

"You'll like it, it'll be something new and different. I'm glad, Birdie. Sometimes it's nice to get away for a while, you know?"

"I guess so, I'm about to find out."

Chapter Six
June – August 1979

The sunset was an extraordinary color, vivid pinks streaking across a clear sky of light and dark aquamarines.

"Tell me again what you call your house?" she said.

"Cielo Azul, Blue Sky," said Victor, resting his forearm across her chest.

Birdie reached for the glass, swallowed the last of the tequila sunrise, settled back again in his arms. "I like the sunsets here, but maybe you should rethink the house name. Shouldn't it be pink sky?"

He kissed her hair. "Not manly enough. You ready for another drink?"

"Okay."

He said, "If you want that drink, you'll need to move."

She acquiesced. "I'm learning more about you," she said lazily. "You mix a good drink, you speak Spanish, you have a house that looks at mountains."

He smiled. "You like it here?"

"I do, it seems very . . . you. How could I not like it?"

He got up, walked to the other side of the patio and began to pour, a little of this, a little of that. He returned, handed her the glass, sat at the foot of the chaise.

"What would you like to do tonight?" he asked.

"How about more of what we did earlier?" She sipped the drink, smiled at him over the rim.

He grinned, touched her knee. "We'll get around to that later. What about dinner, there's a place downtown that has scratch-made tamales. They use corn husks, green chiles, the works."

"That sounds wonderful. Victor, do all the houses around here have these private courtyards?"

"A lot of them do. The open spaces help the airflow, keep things cooler."

"And they're pretty."

He drank from his glass. "Different than what you're used to. No languid ocean breezes or warm gulf currents."

She said, "No powdery white sand."

"I have to differ with you there," he said.

"Hmm?"

"White Sands National Park has pure white sand dunes."

"Really, where's that."

"About three hours south of here, you want to take a drive?"

"No, we only have three days left, I think I'd rather stay around here, get to—"

Inside the house, a deep bong sounded, they looked over their shoulders. Victor set his drink on the table and rose to investigate, Birdie stayed on the chaise watching the mountain ranges fade from violet to deep purple. She sipped her drink, heard footsteps.

"Birdie," his voice sounded different, formal. She turned. Before her was a woman she recognized, the woman she had seen once before when she'd served her at the Crescent Club. Swimmer's shoulders, haughty, burgundy by the glass. This time, her hand was extended.

"Amanda Babel, nice to meet you," she said, smiling professionally.

Birdie shook hands, looked into blue eyes, did not like what she saw there.

"I was driving by, noticed the lights," Amanda explained. "Victor just told me he's in town for some book signings." *What are you doing here?*

Birdie nodded, smiled, said nothing.

"Is this your first visit?"

"Yes, it is."

Amanda turned to Victor. "Surely you've taken her around? The opera house, Palace of the Governors, the galleries, St. Francis—"

"We've been doing some exploring," he said mildly. "Right now we're just relaxing. Do you have time for a drink?"

She hesitated, looked at Birdie who smiled benignly.

"Yes, I'd like that. Do you still keep white wine around? I could use a spritzer."

"Coming right up."

Amanda remained standing, leaned against the low wall and withdrew a cigarette from her handbag. Victor returned, she lit the cigarette and inhaled deeply.

"Stressful day at work," she said, accepting the glass. "When I saw the lights I got curious. Actually, I'm glad you were home."

Victor turned to Birdie. "Amanda teaches mathematics at St. John's College."

The woman smiled briefly, blew a long stream of smoke, swallowed some of the wine. "Found one of my best students was giving answers to another student and we had to deal with that today. Jeremy is out of town until Sunday night and I don't have him to talk to so it's lucky you were here. There's an assistant dean opening and I want to be considered for it."

Victor said, "Where's Jeremy this time?"

"What? Oh, San Francisco. The project is going on and on, the client is insatiable, a new demand every time he turns around." She looked at Birdie, said, "Jeremy's my fiancé."

"Congratulations. You must miss him when he's away."

Amanda took another drag, looked upward toward the blackening sky. "I'm used to it." She looked at Birdie. "Some women need a man with them all the time, I'm not one of them."

Birdie smiled, took another drink.

Victor said, "What about the promotion?"

She stubbed the cigarette in the ashtray and reached for her handbag. "That's what I wanted to talk to Jeremy about. Wedding's in September but the new position takes off in August. I can do both but it might mean putting off the honeymoon." She produced and lit another cigarette. "That's presuming I get the job." She smiled briefly through the smoke.

Birdie said, "It's too bad he can't be reached by phone."

Amanda shot her a look. "I'm not inclined to bother him when he's on business, it can wait for two days."

"Philip over in Languages got his eye on the job, too?" asked Victor, crossing his legs, leaning against Birdie.

Amanda nodded. "Yes, and one of the newer guys in Philosophy." She shrugged. "You know how it is, competition among college faculty is always political, I'll have to take the gloves off."

"You're well qualified."

She nodded, blew another stream of smoke, looked speculatively at Birdie. "Are you from Florida?"

"For about the last ten years, yes."

More smoke. "What about before?"

"My family was in Michigan, the Detroit area."

Amanda looked at Victor. "Oh, I know people from there. They were in, let me see, I think a place called—"

"We lived in Dearborn, my father owned a business there."

Victor swallowed the last of his drink, rose. "Can I get you another, Amanda?"

She put out her cigarette. "No, I need to go, I have to get ready for tomorrow. Thanks, though." She flashed a smile at Birdie, gathered her handbag, paused. "Have you been to see Father Ryan, Victor?"

He was still, looked at her expressionlessly.

She said, "He asks for you."

"Drive carefully, Amanda. Wouldn't want any accidents before the wedding."

Later, over candlelight and margaritas, stuffed jalapeños and more margaritas, they circled around to the visit.

"Are you coming back for her wedding?" she asked.

"I was thinking about it," he said.

"She seemed tense," she said carefully. "But considering what's ahead of her, maybe she has a lot to be nervous about. She's very unlike you, Victor."

"Um-hmm."

She raised her eyes to his.

"Who's Father Ryan?" she asked.

"One of the priests here in town." He looked around. "You seen the waiter? I think I'd like another margarita." He looked at her glass. "What about you?"

She studied his face, swallowed more of the drink. "I'm fine, thanks."

He said, "Amanda's an acquired taste, comes on a little strong at first but try not to take it personally."

"Victor, I was educated at private Catholic schools, my parents are not poor trash, but she looks at me like I'm one of those women on the cover of Hustler."

He shrugged. "She's like that with everyone."

She sat back against her chair. "How well do you know the fiancé?"

He twirled the stem of the glass in his fingers. "Not too well, he's in advertising. They became engaged a few months ago."

"Does he travel all the time? On weekends?"

He raised his eyes. "I'm not sure," he said after a moment. "I travel, too. Are you making a point, Birdie?"

Their eyes held. "Sorry," she said. "I shouldn't have brought it up. Where can we go tomorrow? I want to see as much around here as possible."

He smiled. "Too bad we're not here in the fall, there's an unusual little ritual you might like called the Burning of Zozobra."

She smiled, drank more margarita and leaned forward. "What is it?"

"It's a burning in effigy of the gloom and doom of the year. A local artist started it about fifty years ago, he created a marionette for a symbolic campfire with his friends, now it's an annual event. The crowds are a little rowdy sometimes, there's a lot of good natured drinking associated with it, and the effigy looks a bit macabre flopping and burning in the breeze . . ."

He trailed off, took a swallow of his drink.

She took his hand, said, "I think it's kind of a nice tradition, burning all your sorrows and troubles away, don't you think? I like the idea."

He grinned, "I thought you might."

They passed a church that looked out of place on the busy street. "What's that?" she asked.

"Oh. A local cathedral."

"It's not like the other adobe buildings, it looks unusual."

"It's called St. Francis Cathedral."

She looked at him curiously. "Do you ever go?"

"What?"

"You're Catholic. Do you ever go?"

He shrugged, shifted in his seat. "Not since I was in high school."

She turned from him, looked out her window. They were driving through the city toward the national forest, he had proposed a hike through the canyon and was driving the old Jeep he kept at the house.

"Canyons, hatch chiles, adobe, calabacitas, this is like a whole other country," she said.

He glanced at her. "In a good way."

She laid a hand on his arm. "In a very good way. Do you think your parents ever miss it?"

"Oh, I dunno. I think they're pretty happy where they are."

"When did they go to Mexico, was it right after you left for college?"

He was silent. *Oh Victor, why are you making me guess?*

"And what about you, Victor, do you miss it?"

They were at the periphery of the city, smaller neighborhoods, fewer businesses, less traffic. He said finally, "I was raised here, I miss it sometimes but I like to travel, then I found a place I like just as much." He turned his head, smiled at her.

He veered off the main road, drove beneath a bridge, went up a hill. The terrain was very bright and dry under the June sunlight, they passed red cactus blossoms, green sage, juniper trees, a hawk circled above them. They bounced and swayed for the next ten minutes as the vehicle progressed along the sand and sediment road. She saw a flash in front of the Jeep and looked off to the right.

"Did you see him?" he asked.

"It looked like a wild dog," she said.

"Coyote. We may see more of them, they're not that unusual."

"Would he hurt us?"

"No, he'll keep his distance."

They had reached the parking area, he pulled the keys from the ignition and they got out. He slung the backpack over his shoulder and they made their way across the lot.

It was an easy walk on the volcanic plateau, the shifting light from the wind and the clouds caused a mélange of mirages to play out on the surrounding rocks. As they made their way through a narrow pass between two cliffs, he explained that the cliffs were basalt, slow moving lava. They walked past the scattered boulders and along the stream, sat for a while and drank water and enjoyed the sun and the sounds of the rushing wind.

He stretched his legs, his polished boots glistened in the sun and he looked comfortable, at ease, and happy to be home. She liked seeing this side of him, Victor the outdoorsman. She was wearing boots as well, he had taken her to a store, insisted, said it would be unsafe wandering the canyon without boots to protect her. She didn't ask what from.

He said, "We could go somewhere else next time, I don't know where, we could play it by ear.

She looked at him and he held out his hand.

When she went to him he removed her sunglasses, kissed her mouth.

She leaned her head against his shoulder. "I love you, I love being here with you," she said.

He took her chin in his hand, brushed back her bangs. "I want to show you all the places you've never seen," he said. "Take you to Paris and London, New York." His eyes scanned her face. "Do you want to do those things, Birdie?"

She blinked, slowly nodded.

He smiled, said gently, "My solnyshka. Wherever you want to go, we'll go."

She laid her head on his chest, put her arms around his back and said, "In that case, I think I'd like to go back to the house. I'm starved."

He laughed.

Another sunset, violent pink over swimming pool blue above a sliver of school-bus yellow. The skies were busy that night, stars came out to play twinkling merrily, later shooting across the universe, dragging tails through the dusty heavens.

He drove to a restaurant fifteen minutes outside of town called El Nido, they were given a table by a fireplace, ordered a bottle of wine. She had worn her copper dress with the low portrait neckline, added drop earrings.

She appraised him while he was looking at the menu.

He glanced up.

"I don't think I've seen you in jacket and tie before," she said. "You look extremely handsome."

"Thank you. If that man in the mirror doesn't stop ogling your breasts, I'll have to have a talk with him."

She smiled. "Maybe he's a jeweler, maybe he's admiring my earrings."

He laughed.

It was a late one, their last night in Santa Fe. When they reached the house he opened the bedroom doors to the courtyard and she uncorked another bottle of wine. They sat on the chaise longues outside looking at the Milky Way high above the canyon. She thought about the last few months, how glad she was that he had been with her, and she told him so.

He reached across to her chair and took her hand. "I'm glad too," he said.

She put his palm to her mouth and kissed it. "Ti moiyo vsyo," she said.

"What does that mean?"

She swallowed. "It means . . . it means, 'you are everything to me'."

He was quiet for a time. "Come over here," he said.

She settled next to him and he wrapped his arms around her, kissed her hair. "Did I ever tell you how my parents met?" he said.

She shook her head, kissed his neck. The skin was warm and she could feel his heartbeat beneath her mouth.

"They met at the birthday party of a friend," he said.

She drew back. "You're kidding me."

"I'm not kidding you."

She smiled up at him. "I like that, very much."

His knee between her legs as she kissed his mouth was warm and encouraging. She sat up, removed her arms from the dress and let it fall to her waist. The starlight illuminated her torso.

"How beautiful," he said, cupping her breasts with his hands.

She smiled, stood, slid the dress the rest of the way off. She paused, turning slowly, performing for him, *you like what you see?* He smiled and beckoned, and she returned to the chair. A million stars in the sky, a head full of sixty dollar wine, she lay naked in his arms while they kissed, reveling in the feel of his clothing moving over her skin, the ancient desert dark and silent around them.

His fingers drifted up and down her spine, brushed the softly rounded rump, the cleft between the curves, her breathing came more rapidly.

He picked her up and carried her inside.

There were words, but none that had a formal lexicon. A press of his hand said *don't stop*, long kisses meant *I love*, hard firm strokes *you are mine*, his tongue in her mouth signaled *what I'm going to do*, staccato sighs *almost there*.

They spoke aloud afterward, warm sentiments strung together in half sentences.

". . . love when we do this," she said.

He kissed her mouth. "I'm very glad . . ."

". . . a whole night isn't enough."

He laughed softly. "That's what days are for, Solnyshka."

They woke a couple of hours later to a hushed rainfall that sounded to Birdie like cats running across tiled floors, tiny padded feet pounding lightly, then the downpour came, releasing the lovely smell of the open desert.

Victor kissed her neck, wrapped an arm around her chest and pressed her tightly to him.

She moaned softly, arched her back against him as he entered.

Round two.

By breakfast the rain was gone. Instead, a silent raven, looking at her from the top of the totem pole. "I think it's a raven," said Birdie, finishing the last of the huevos rancheros.

Victor peered upward toward the sky. "You're right," he said. "Ravens are bigger than crows and have that diamond shaped tail."

"I don't think I've ever seen one this close."

"Ravens aren't unusual around here," he said. "In fact, they're very symbolic."

She looked at him. "What do you mean?"

"The Pueblos north of here have interpretations for omens and spirits, that sort of thing. According to them, ravens are messengers."

"Really."

He nodded. "If this one had approached making a lot of noise, it would have meant there was something he wanted you to know. In this case, he was watching you. It means pieces are falling into place for you like they should."

"You never fail to surprise me, Victor."

"It's just part of the culture around here."

"Pieces falling into place, huh?"

He smiled. "For me, anyway."

They returned to rain on Siesta Key, a warm, lush, tropical rain that blew perpendicular as they ran into the house. Birdie made tea and sat at the kitchen table, wrote a list of items they would need at the market while Victor dealt with their luggage.

They drove together into the village, ran into Georgette at Siesta Market. She was drenched, in a hurry, had run in to buy cold medicine for her father.

"Good to see you two!" she sang as she backed out of the store.

There was a new girl at the checkout counter. "Is Diana still around?" Birdie asked her.

"Until the end of the month," the girl told them. "She's getting married and moving to the other coast."

The telephone was ringing when they returned to the house. It was Kiki, wondering why Birdie was breathless.

"No, don't tell me," she said. "I don't want to hear about your sex life."

"Kiki, we just got home, I ran to get your call."

"Darling, good news, if you're free for dinner next week, we can both be there, me and the boyfriend."

"I wonder if the surprise is a celebrity," said Birdie as they were dressing for the dinner a week later. "That would make sense, it would explain why she's being so hush-hush."

"I doubt it. Kiki wouldn't be able to keep something like that to herself," he said.

"Exactly how well did you know her?"

His eyes rested on hers in the mirror. "Not as well as you think. She was seeing an acquaintance of mine at the newspaper, he introduced us. She's a nice girl, you know how it is, we hit it off but I only saw her a few times."

"She's very pretty."

He grinned widely. "You're fishing."

She laughed. "I guess I am. I'm curious because she's . . . there's something about her that attracts people."

He was watching her, she had begun to apply eyeliner. "She has charisma. But the chemistry that draws us to someone, makes us fantasize about them, it wasn't there with her," he said.

She finished with her eyes, took a brush to her hair. "Sexual chemistry," she said.

"Um-hmm, that too. Certain undefinable things about others, you can't put your finger on it, you just know."

She got up and crossed to where he was lounging on the bed, knelt and ran her fingers through his hair. "Like the way they brush their hair aside with their hand, and when you like the scent of their skin, or the way they say certain words, the way they taste when you kiss them, the way their name sounds when you say it, you mean those things." She leaned closer, brushed her mouth against his.

He smiled, "The way I wanted you the first moment I saw you at the Mira Mar, and waiting for you was torture."

The doorbell rang, his gaze rested on hers and he pulled her in for the kiss.

Another ring. They got up together and went to greet Kiki and Mystery Man.

Kiki wasn't her usual extravagant self. She sat quietly next to Gene on the sofa after dinner, tucked her legs beneath her dress and turned sideways, rested her cheek against his shoulder.

Birdie handed around the Grand Marnier, settled into a chair near Victor.

"You ever been in broadcasting, Gene? You have such perfect diction," she said.

He smiled uneasily. "Singing lessons when I was young, my parents were active in local theater and my brother and I couldn't escape it."

"Did you ever do anything with the music yourself?" Birdie asked.

"No. I was a radio announcer in college, that's as far as I wanted to go. Books were always more interesting to me," he said.

Victor played absently with his glass. "That was me, didn't care much for cartoons on Saturday morning, I wanted to read comic books, R.L. Stevenson, cereal boxes, anything I could get my hands on." He paused. "I remember a book by James Thurber, something to do with a bad pirate who terrorized an island by taking a vowel from all the words . . ."

The two women exchanged a smile.

Gene laughed. "The letter O, or no . . . *The Wonderful O*. I read that book, too. Classic Thurber, a good story that was funny and clever."

Birdie said, "There was an illustrator named Hilary Knight, I liked those funny books he did about a little girl named Eloise who lived at the Plaza in New York City and was always off to somewhere. Eloise goes to France or some such."

Gene looked at her curiously. "By the actress, you mean? Kay Thompson?"

"I don't remember, but I think my mother still has them."

"They may be worth something, you know. First editions of children's books that are in good condition are very popular."

She lifted her glass. "That's good to know, I can ask her." She sipped some of the liquid, looked at Kiki. "Isn't that trip to Ibiza coming up soon? What kinds of plans are you making?"

Kiki said, "I've decided to put it off, maybe go around the first of the year instead. Holidays at the restaurant are busy, you know how it is . . ."

From Gene, a slight smile.

Victor swallowed some of his drink, glanced at Birdie, said, "Never know, the first of the year can be a good time for change."

"He thinks I should open a shop," she said to the others.

Kiki lifted her head. "What?"

Birdie bit her lip. "I don't know . . . I've been tending bar for almost ten years and all that time I've been collecting things, antique and vintage jewelry, furniture . . ."

"She knows a lot about them," said Victor.

"You do, Birdie, I've told you a hundred times, darling, haven't I?" Kiki sat up. "Those stunning earrings you wear must be worth a fortune, you have a real eye for it." She turned to Gene. "Don't you have a friend, the guy who buys the Walt Whitman from you, who does appraisals?"

Gene looked at Birdie.

"The pieces are already appraised," she said. "But I've never run a business of my own. It's a big investment, and I would lose some of the free time I have now."

Victor said, "Your father would be happy to advise you, Birdie, all you have to do is ask."

Gene nodded, said, "It may be worth it to you if it's your passion and it's what you're doing anyway, but until a business gets off the ground there isn't much time for other things. You spend a lot of time figuring out marketing strategies, doing paperwork, taking care of nuts and bolts."

Kiki reached for her drink. "I remember my first taste of the restaurant business. I was bussing tables at a new eatery in New York City and there were problems getting people to see the big picture, you know, how all the little nuts and bolts come together to make a really stellar place. Some kids weren't getting it, they were still leaving napkins on the floor. Finally the maître d' had a meeting, said he was going to be watching us. Sure enough, he started rolling five-dollar bills inside straws and leaving them on the floor, seeing how long it would take us to pick them up. If you did, you could keep it and you made the cut."

She drank from the glass. "I liked him, he taught me to look at a place from the ground up, see the big picture, and not just my little piece of it."

Gene said, "Were you one of the ones who found a five-dollar straw?"

Kiki grinned. "Of course, darling, I've always been a neat freak." She looked at Birdie. "You have to be too, I know. Nothing like sliding on a lemon peel behind the bar when you're carrying glasses to the dishwasher."

Birdie laughed. "You're right, I've seen it all, opening the dishwasher and getting a face full of burning steam, bloody fingers from broken glass in the ice well, speed pours that fall out of bottles and cause a mess. You can't afford sloppiness when time is money."

Kiki yawned. "Speaking of time, darling, I have to be in early tomorrow. Special event at noon to prepare for."

They said their goodnights outside the front door, Gene leading her by the hand to the car, Kiki turning to blow a kiss before she climbed inside.

"That's about as subdued as I've ever seen her," said Birdie, closing the door behind her.

"She seems happy," said Victor.

"Happy? This is no ordinary dalliance, our girl Kiki is in love," said Birdie.

Nicholas may not have been in love, but he seemed happy. He stopped by the Crescent Club later in the week and ordered a coke, said he wanted to see how she was doing.

"I should be asking that of you," she said, settling the glass on a coaster and leaning on the bar.

"You still got that lean goin' on," he said, smiling. "Always loved that sexy li'l lean."

"You drive all the way up here to come on to me, Nicky, or you genuinely wanted to see how I've been?"

"Baby, you may not be mine anymore but I got some fond memories," he said.

Birdie looked at him silently. Finally, "We've been through a lot, Nicky, I'll grant you that. And I have a lot of admiration for the way you pulled yourself together. And you've been a good friend to me when I needed it, I won't forget that. Now don't go doing anything to undo those good feelings, you hear?"

His eyes scanned her face. "I hear," he said. He took a long pull of the coke, said, "I really did wanna know how you're doin', Birdie."

She smiled. "Fine, thank you. Just got back from a week in New Mexico, now it's back to work and the place seems so small after those wide open spaces, know what I mean?"

He nodded. "I remember being out west, and I swear the skies out there really were bigger. I'm southern born and bred, but I can see the attraction."

"I remember you told me once you saw shooting stars when you were out there one night in the middle of nowhere."

He smiled. "I sure did, one of the prettiest sights I've ever seen."

"I put flowers on her grave before I left, Nicky."

He looked down. "I saw them. There were others, too. I think he's been leaving them for her."

She stared at him. "What?"

He raised his head, looked at her. "Do you know who he is?"

"Nicholas, I—"

"She killed herself over him, Birdie, let's just say it. I don't know who he is but he feels sorry, he brings her flowers a couple times a week. Pink roses."

"Oh no." She put her hand to her mouth.

A lone woman walked into the bar, stopped as her eyes adjusted to the dusky interior. She climbed onto a seat at the opposite end of the bar and Birdie went to her.

A few minutes later she was back. "Nicholas, I'm sorry, I know it makes it harder for you."

"I swear if he ever comes when I'm there, I'll confront him, you know I will."

"I wish you wouldn't, he obviously loved her and is mourning too, Nicky."

They were both silent for a moment. The other customer went to the jukebox, inserted some coins, went back to her seat.

"So what about you, what are you doing with your time?"

His glance strayed toward the jukebox where the Eagles' Hotel California was playing, it seemed too loud in the almost empty room at 10:30 in the morning.

"I took the real estate exam and passed, I was thinking I might work with some friends who're doing land development out east of town," he said.

She straightened, looked at him closely. "It would be something brand new for you," she observed.

"Yeah, it would. My friend Mike works with his father who's been doing it for a long time, they have a geologist, a couple of landscape architects who seem to know what they're doin', there's another realtor who's taken a liking to me." He grinned. "It's a good group, they're looking for another realtor."

She smiled. "Sounds like you'd be learning from the ground up."

He nodded. "It feels good, feels right."

Vicki walked into the bar, waved, and Birdie lifted her hand. She looked back at Nicholas.

"I gotta ask, baby, he still treating you alright?"

She swallowed. "I'm in love with him, Nicholas, I moved into his house."

He took her arm. "But does he—"

She leaned so close she could smell the rosewood and laurel soapiness of the Paco Rabanne. "He acts like there are six billion women in the world and I'm the only one he sees."

He looked at her sadly. "Baby, I wish to God I'd done the same."

"But you didn't, and now here we are, Nicky."

Victor looked up at her when she got in. "Bad day?"

She smiled. "Long day." She bent over the bed, kissed his mouth. "Now it's a good day."

He set aside the book, opened his arms to her and she settled against him. "How was yours?"

He kissed the top of her head, hugged her tightly. "You want me to make you something?"

"No, I don't even want a snack."

"I'm having a Dubonnet, I could pour another."

"Well . . ."

He released her, left the bed and returned a few minutes later, handed her the glass, lemon twist floating among the ice cubes. She sipped gratefully.

He watched her as she drank. "I have something to tell you," he said.

"Hmm?" She lowered the glass, looked at him.

"Your father called a little while ago. He said your mother fell yesterday, he had to take her to the emergency room, she'll be alright but she got a little bruised and her ankle is broken."

She stared at him. "Where are they now?"

"At home. He wanted to let you know she's sleeping, they gave her pain medicine, and you should call in the morning. He's tired, he's gone to bed, too."

"How did it happen?"

"That damn Moroccan tile, your father swore he's going to rip it up and replace it with sticky tacking, I can see it now." He smiled, drank from his glass, reached for her and she leaned back into him. "You know how the tiles get a little slick sometimes in the morning and evening from the humidity coming off the gulf, your mother missed her sweater, went outside to get it and slipped."

"Poor mother. I wish I could talk to her right now."

"Solnyshka. We'll drive down together in the morning, first thing."

She nestled against him. "I love you, Victor."

"I love you, Birdie. You know, don't you, that if something ever happened, I would take care of you?" It wasn't a question, but a promise.

She tilted her head, kissed his mouth. "And I, you." Not a statement, a commitment.

Birdie peered at the clock, it was five minutes after six but she couldn't sleep, she got up quietly and dressed, made bacon, waffles, coffee, squeezed oranges. The paper hadn't arrived yet, so for something to do she took apples from the bowl on the table and made a sharlotka, slid it into the oven to bake.

She held the warm apple cake in her lap on the drive down to Casey Key. Victor glanced sideways at her. "Birdie, she's alright, she's good, your father assured me."

"Oh, I know, I just need to see for myself."

When he pulled onto the shell drive beyond the hedge she almost leapt from the car. They walked together to the door and Fa was there to greet her with open arms and a kiss. "She's in the bedroom, Bernadette, go see her."

Poor mother, her forehead was bruised and her arm was bandaged. She was sitting up in bed, hair brushed, pale and smiling.

"I've never felt so silly in my life, Bernadette, really, there I was on my stomach like a wild bird, calling for help."

Fa entered the room with Victor. "Kira, you look none the worse for wear. Feeling a little better?"

"Thank you, Victor, thank you for the flowers. The doctor said I must not walk, however, so here I am, at the mercy of nurse Ella, who is around here somewhere . . ."

"Mother, I can help, too," said Birdie.

Her mother smiled. "That's what the nurse is for, darling, but you've lifted my spirits just by being here."

"I baked a sharlotka this morning. It's in the kitchen, you should have some."

"Thank you, I'll have some later with my tea." She yawned, "Forgive me, the medicine makes me sleepy. I can hardly read a book, my eyes betray me after a few pages." She looked up at Anton who took her hand.

"She had a fracture and had to have surgery," he said, "but nothing to worry about, it just takes a little longer to heal."

The nurse came into the room after a little while and waved them all out, like misbehaved schoolchildren late for class. "Off you go," she chided. "Madame needs rest so she can heal."

They sat under the umbrella outside on the offending Moroccan tiles, Birdie, Victor, and her father, and talked about opening a business. Birdie asked for his thoughts and he was quiet for a long moment, said that it was a good idea if three things were concurrent, a demand for the product, a reliable supply, and a person willing to commit to making the first two come together and grow.

"I'm just not sure, Fa," said Birdie, exchanging glances with Victor. "I have a product that I know, and I know where to get more of it, but I don't know if I have what it takes to work at it steadily for a long time."

"Well," he said, "You have to learn to walk before you can run. But if you don't have a fire in you to chase after it, then don't; we aren't all meant to be in business for ourselves. Just be sure you know what you were born to do, and that you're doing it."

She leaned in, kissed his cheek. "I love you, Fa."

The thick envelope lay on the desk by his calendar. Birdie looked at it and sighed.

The shower stopped, after several minutes Victor entered the study dressed in his work clothes, jeans, shirt with rolled up sleeves, his gold Sperrys. She held out the coffee, "This is for you. By the way, I just noticed the wedding invitation. Do we need to call and make arrangements?"

He took the coffee from her hand, kissed her cheek. "Thank you, I haven't decided yet."

"Victor . . ."

He pulled out the chair. "Leave it alone, Birdie."

She felt her face flush, stood for a moment, turned and left him to his mood.

He worked steadily all morning, she made him a sandwich for lunch, took hers to the beach and ate looking out over the narrow swath of water at the foot of Shell Road. She left for work just before four o'clock.

There were three of them overlapping the afternoon and late shifts, Vicki was scheduled until ten o'clock. "Full moon tonight," she said as she breezed out of the bar. "You know what that means, girls. Good luck!"

After her departure, the pace picked up a little and Birdie and Georgette were progressively busy. A table for six in the middle of the floor was commandeered by sunburned tourists, squeezing as much fun and laughter as they could manage into their last night of island freedom. They took pictures, fed a continuous stream of quarters into the jukebox, and kept Birdie running behind the bar making rum runners, mai tais, pina coladas.

Diana and Roger were back in town, stopped by the bar en route to a table to greet Birdie, Diana's huge ring sparkling even in the dim red lights. Diana wanted Birdie to see it.

Birdie released her hand, looked up and smiled. "Beautiful," she said, and it was. A two-carat diamond solitaire, princess shape, on a simple and elegant gold band. "I can tell how happy you are, Diana, the long wait was worth it."

A young man plopped down at the inside end of the bar around eleven o'clock, said to Birdie, "The usual," and waited politely for her to produce a drink.

She stood, observing him. "I have no idea what that is," she said finally.

"Uh, a Miller please."

"Sure, coming right up. While I get that, you can get your driver's license out. I'll have to see it before I can serve you," she said.

"Oh, uh, you won't believe this . . ."

She smiled. "Maybe I will. Try me."

"Well, on the way here, I think I lost it at the beach. I was there with a girl and, well." He smiled nervously and spread his hands.

"Oh, that's too bad. But this is your lucky night, there's a sheriff's deputy at that table right over there. He's off duty but I know he'd be glad to take your report, the sooner the better since you shouldn't be driving without. You want me to get him for you?" She pointed at the table.

He glanced over his shoulder at Roger and Diana. "Uh, no that's okay, maybe I'll go look for it again." He turned and left.

The Band's The Night They Drove Old Dixie Down was playing and everyone was singing along, the good vibe lasted until the crowd began to dwindle around one-thirty, last call. Only one couple remained at closing, arguing quietly over their beer, they looked up as Georgette approached.

"Leave. We're having a private conversation here," said the man.

"I heard. We'll give them five minutes," Birdie said to her in a low voice. She took another look at the man, it was the first time she had seen him with someone.

At five after two Birdie left the bar and approached the deuce. The woman looked up at her but not the man. She crouched down, put her hand on the table, said. "The bar's closed, sir, it's time to go. We've closed out your tab, now we need to close out the till."

The man stared at her. "I'm not going anywhere until we finish," he said.

Birdie rose. "Time for you to leave," she said. "Pay the tab now or I'll have to make a call."

The woman said, "Martin, you heard the lady, I wanna go home."

"I'm not ready to go yet, you can't leave me."

She rose from the table. "You just told me for the last time what I can't do. I can, and I will." She picked up a purse from the floor and walked out the side door to the parking lot.

The jukebox had been turned off, Bernadette was behind them, silently wiping down the surface of the bar. Birdie was still standing at the table.

The man stood suddenly and looked at her. "You did this," he said. He reached into his pocket, withdrew a knife.

Birdie was absolutely still. Behind the bar, Bernadette froze, then walked quickly toward the back room.

The blade was only about four inches, but Birdie was terrified of knives. She stepped back, said quietly, "Sir, the only thing we need to do here is remain calm. You have the tab, let's take care of that and you can be on your way."

He grabbed her arm, pulled her close to his body, she could feel the length of the blade against the side of her throat. He was trembling and smelled like sweat. "That's not going to happen, you insulted me in front of her. I just found her and now she's leaving." He said into her ear, "You'll pay for this."

She could feel his hot breath on her cheek, his sweaty hand on her forearm, but she didn't turn her eyes, didn't want to see the knife.

He said, "Don't move or I'll cut your f***g throat."

Her mouth was dry and her stomach was churning. She swallowed, fought to control her breathing, long breaths, so he wouldn't know her fear.

"It cost me to get her back and now it's going to cost you for losing her. Everything's got a cost."

He began to drag her slowly toward the door. "We're gonna take a little trip," he said, and her fear began to choke her, she had a hard time swallowing, felt tears begin to form.

Suddenly he jerked her to a halt.

"Better yet, down on your knees. Do it!" He screamed the last two words. He loosened his grip on her arm and she pulled away and fled, ran toward the stockroom where she was sure Georgette had gone. She screamed Georgie's name. The stockroom had a lock on the door, was close to the back entrance of the building.

As she ran she heard the sirens.

Even after the shot of whiskey at work to calm her nerves, after a long hot shower after arriving home, she didn't feel ready to talk.

Victor's only knowledge of the event was a call from a deputy informing him of her delay due to *an incident*. He'd greeted her at the door with a long embrace, a kiss on the forehead. He was waiting patiently for her.

She went to him, sat next to him on the sofa.

"What can I get for you?" he asked, his eyes searched her face.

She shook her head. "How was your day, did you do your ten pages?" He worked, every day, to write at least ten pages longhand, good or bad.

He laid his hand on hers. "Birdie . . ."

She removed her hand. "I just want to be normal, Victor, can you understand? I've had too much reality today."

He paused, said carefully, "Not dealing with trauma isn't normal, Birdie."

She looked at him for a long moment, everything inside of her was taut, extraordinarily still. "Really? Interesting that you of all people should say that."

He flinched. She looked away, bit her lip. "I'm sorry, I shouldn't have said that."

He was silent. She rose, went to the bedroom and dressed, she was exhausted but couldn't sleep, felt cranky and overwhelmed.

She returned to the living room, lifted her keys from the table. "I'm going for a drive."

"No."

She turned. "What?"

"Please, I'll come with you, you've been through an ordeal and shouldn't be out there alone."

She started for the door.

"Birdie—"

"I'll be back," she said stubbornly.

Strong arms behind her, gently removing the keys from her hands. "No, Birdie."

She reacted suddenly, violently, with a fear and a force she didn't know she had. "No!" she shouted. "I'm going, let me go!" She tried to push him away, kicked at him, told him she hated him, but his arms weren't letting go.

To her horror she began crying, then sobbing, struggling to turn away but he continued to hold her as she twisted and writhed and clawed at him, for how long she didn't know. She was terrified of his arms, panicked, couldn't bear to be touched, fought wildly, panting for breath until she had no more strength, until he was holding her up while she cried, as he murmured incoherent words.

She didn't know how they arrived at the sofa, she was in his lap and he was holding her while she sat helplessly and cried and cried against his chest. From somewhere he produced a wad of tissues and she leaned her head against his shoulder and blew her nose with shaking hands. Her eyes stung and her nose felt swollen.

Outside, the sky had become pearlescent, nothing stirred, foliage hung limply from their trees. A small watercraft moved through the bayou a block away, the sound of its engine drifting faintly over the water.

He stroked her hair. "You didn't cry at the funeral," he said, "and you've been worried about your mother. Now this."

She said miserably, "I said terrible things to you, Victor. I wish I could take them back."

He was silent. Finally he said, "It's enough to know that you love me. We'll leave it at that."

She kissed his cheek, saw that his eyes were moist, and a shot of pain went through her. She kissed his mouth. "I love you more than I've ever loved anyone, please forgive me."

He said quietly, "You were distraught."

She paused, said, "That man tonight, I recognized him but not her. He's been coming in alone for the last six months or so, I think he was looking for her. I don't know how they ended up there tonight, we were busy and I didn't notice. Maybe she finally showed, or maybe it was her idea, she wanted to be in a public place. I think they were married, she had a ring."

She rubbed her eyes, continued. "They seemed so serious, he was trying to convince her, she wasn't being convinced. I think it took a long time to reach the point they were at. Before she left, she said he had told her for the last time that she couldn't do something. Control issues maybe. Anyway, he took it out on me."

He hesitated. "This happened toward the end of the night, were other people around?"

She shook her head. "No. It was just Georgette and me, we did last call and they were the only ones left, he refused to go and I approached them. I think he forgot Georgette was there." She had difficulty describing the assault, her hands shook and her focus drifted.

He stopped her. "Birdie, you've already been over it with the deputies, they'll deal with trying to find him. Do you think you could sleep now, maybe a walk on the beach?"

"No, I wouldn't want anyone to see me like this."

"What about something to eat?"

She shook her head.

"You're supposed to work tonight, what arrangements were made?"

"He said not to come in tonight, I'm supposed to take a few days off." She looked at him, tears began to form. "I can't even think about it," she put a hand to her mouth.

He kissed her hair. "Let's go to bed. You need to rest even if you can't sleep."

She rested fitfully, scenes from work played out in her dreams and she woke with a cry when the phone rang later in the day.

Victor sat on the bed and took her hand. "That was the sheriff's office." He hesitated. "Birdie, that was his wife you saw in the bar." He looked in her eyes. "She shot and killed him at home early this morning, she said he tried to stab her. When the deputy took her statement, she was able to corroborate your statement and Georgette's from last night. He wanted you to know."

She lay in the pillows, greeted the news in stunned silence. He smoothed the bangs from her eyes. "My brave girl, it's all over now."

She nodded, felt again the sharp metal against her neck, the sickening smell of sweat when he pulled her against him, his stale breath in her face. She wrenched suddenly from Victor's grasp and vomited onto the floor next to the bed.

Chapter Seven
September – November 1979

He went to his sister's wedding alone, taking the redeye to Santa Fe with a return ticket for the following night. Birdie had closing shift the first night, slept until noon the next day.

She went with Georgette to Diana and Roger's wedding on the grounds of the historic Ringling mansion. The ceremony was elaborate, violins playing andante, Diana lovely in her cream silk dress standing beside her groom in the early twilight. After the sun had set, the calypso music began. Champagne was poured, and Roger's friends, who had come over from Boca Raton in their expensive cars and private planes, mingled with the Sarasotans to feast on succulent lobster, rich caviar, plump oysters.

Georgette was flirting with a man in his 50s with a sparkle in his eye when Birdie tapped her on the shoulder.

"Georgie, I think I'm ready to go."

Georgette turned to her companion. "No problem," he said. "I can get you home."

Birdie let herself into the house and opened the windows. It seemed sad and empty without Victor there.

He arrived after eleven looking morose and bedraggled, smiled briefly when she met him at the door, kissed her and headed to the shower.

She handed him his glass of bourbon when he re-entered the living room. He put a hand around her waist, twirled her and kissed her mouth. She laughed. "That's the kind of greeting I like."

"I can't tell you how good it is to see you here when I come home."

"I missed you. And it was lonely last night," she said.

"It was, was it?"

"How was the wedding, was it—"

"Boring," he said. "It was held at the boring country club, and afterward I had to talk to boring academics about topics which held no interest for me. All the while, all I could think about was getting home to you."

"Victor, what a romantic thing to say."

He took her hand and led her to the bedroom. "I brought you a present."

"Oh?" She dimpled. "I like presents."

He drew her to the bed. "Sit here. I'll be right back."

He went to his suitcase, returned with a bag.

She took and opened it, withdrew a small box. "Victor, what is this?"

He knelt on the floor in front of her. "I don't want to go anywhere again without you."

She swallowed, looked at him.

He smiled. "Remember the day we went to Crescent Beach and had lunch at Anna's afterward? Then we went back to your place."

"I remember. We said . . . we said we loved each other."

"Yes. But for me, it happened the first time I saw you, looking flushed when everyone sang Happy Birthday, the way you pushed back your bangs, those flowers on your dress that matched your hair, then we talked, and just like that, my life was changed. There was something about you that spoke to me, and it hit me hard, Bernadette."

He paused, smiled. "I want it to go on forever. Do you want that, too, Birdie?"

He swept the bangs from her eyes, kissed her mouth, said, "Open the box."

She studied his face, looked down. Inside, emerald-cut antique topaz mounted on a platinum band.

She swallowed. "Is this . . ."

"Forever, as in married, husband, wife, the whole thing. Solnyshka, will you do that with me?"

She looked down at him, set aside the box, took his face in her hands and kissed his mouth. Her heart was beating fast and loud.

"Yes," she said, through the kiss and the smile. "Victor, I will stay with you forever and be your wife."

"No more living in sin," he said to her as they drove to the house on Casey Key the following Sunday.

"We could stay engaged indefinitely," she said. "Are you worried the sex won't be as good once we become legal?"

He grinned. "With you? Birdie, I will always want you, morning, noon and night. I want you right now. I want to pull the car over and raise that skirt—"

She laughed.

It was a hot early September morning, but the shade of the umbrella, the gentle gulf breezes and swaying casuarinas brought the temperature down, made sitting outside pleasant. The broken ankle ordeal behind her, Birdie's mother had decided to forgive the tiles and be more careful using the terrace after dark. The beautiful Moroccan tiles were staying.

Birdie's father was jovial. His wife was on the mend and his peace was restored. "I did not like that nurse. She ordered me around like I was an imbecile, you must do this, you cannot do that. In my own home! I was glad to see her go."

Her mother was amused. "Anton, she made the most delicious breakfasts, you said so yourself."

Victor said, "You seem to be doing pretty well with that cane, Kira. Are you pain free as well?"

"Oh, now and then I need to take something, usually when I haven't paced myself."

"Mother I would be glad to help if you need it, you know that," said Birdie.

"As a matter of fact, we just hired someone to come in twice a week to help with the cleaning and other things. A nice Italian girl with experience."

"You mean through a service, something like that?"

Her mother said, "Yes, through a service." She frowned. "That's a beautiful . . . what is that ring, Birdie? It's new."

"This? Oh, it's something Victor gave me this week, a gift. Do you like it?" She held out her hand.

"Stunning. Victor, really, you made a beautiful choice."

Birdie looked at Victor, smiled.

He said, "Yes, I think so, too."

There was a brief silence. Birdie picked up her tea.

Her father grinned, said slowly, "Kira, I don't think you're . . ."

"I asked her to marry me . . ."

"What . . . ?"

Her mother's hand went to her mouth.

After the initial congratulations and tears of joy, there were questions about wedding plans but Birdie was nonchalant. "Maybe in a month or so," she said. "Nothing elaborate, we both want something simple."

"Where will you live, are you going to stay here, go back to your home out west?" asked her mother.

"Probably stay where we are, we're not sure yet," said Victor.

Birdie's father rose, went inside, she knew what he was going to do. He returned with the bottle of Stoli and four glasses. Birdie smiled, she had prepared Victor.

He talked while he poured. "Kira and I met thirty-one years ago." He picked up his glass, looked at his wife and smiled. "It has been a good life, and despite what you think you see, I am not a perfect man so it has been love that has kept us together. Love makes us stubborn so that we stay instead of go, it makes us humble, so we admit our mistakes, it makes us forgiving when we don't feel like forgiving, it makes us wise beyond our years." He lifted his glass. "Za lyubov." *To love.*

The four of them drank to love. They also drank to *Our parents.* Later they drank to *Our lovely ladies.* Then there were discourses on family, children, and the virtues; honesty, patience, selflessness.

"You still have family back in New Mexico, Victor?" asked Kira.

"My parents live in Mexico now, I don't see them much," said Victor. "They're very close to each other, like you, very happy together."

"Ahh, this is good," said Anton. "A good role model, you see what it's like, how it should be." He looked at Birdie. "My daughter here, you'll have to be careful. She has a mind of her own."

"Fa!"

Victor laughed. "It's a very good mind, Anton, keeps me humble."

Anton said thoughtfully, "That, and the ability to forgive, those two things show what we're made of, Victor."

They left shortly afterward, driving home in the late afternoon brightness, Victor pensive, Birdie pleasantly sleepy, looking forward to a Sunday afternoon nap.

But it was not to be. As soon as she lay on the bed and closed her eyes he was there, raising the skirt. "What's this?" he said, kissing her shoulder, busy hands rearranging clothing, lowering panties.

She didn't mind. She turned onto her back, slipped him out of his pants and into her as quickly and deftly as a backstage dresser at the opera. She loved his trim hips and flat stomach, welcomed his swollen warmth inside her, raised her knees and drew her arms around his waist and kissed his mouth, pressing further into him.

The nap came later, on tousled sheets amid mussed clothing and tangled limbs. She didn't care about the clothes, she had him, he was what mattered.

Georgette and Kiki wanted to make plans, hold showers, but Birdie held them off. She and Victor didn't have a date yet, and she wasn't a bridal shower kind of girl.

"You know me," she told Kiki, sitting outside in front of The Broken Egg as they finished a leisurely breakfast. "Have you ever known me to be involved in something like that? I just wouldn't enjoy it."

Kiki sipped coffee and looked at her. "Well okay, but we need to do *something*. It's a happy occasion and I want to celebrate with you."

Birdie looked at her. "What do you mean, 'I', isn't Gene still in the picture?"

Kiki smiled. "I'm seeing him tonight." She leaned forward. "Birdie, I've never known anyone like him. My whole world is rocked. I'm reading Proust, for goodness sake, and Thomas Mann, and James Joyce, and liking it!" She laughed.

Birdie smiled. "You seem good together, Kiki, I'm glad."

"Five months, I think that's some sort of record."

Georgette was pleased and proud when she heard the news. "I think I was the one who set you up, Birdie. You can thank me for that beautiful ring."

"Say that again?"

"Well you know, when he came in to the bar that day and I pointed him out. I must have known even then—"

"Georgie, get out of here!"

"Okay, Birdie, I can see you're just trying to weasel out of naming your first daughter after me."

Birdie laughed, added the fresh lemon peels to the caddie. "Good one, Georgette."

"Seriously though, Birdie, have you made plans yet, or are you playing it by ear?"

She shrugged, "We're talking things over, you know how it goes. This isn't my first wedding, we want a ceremony that's nice but relaxed. As far as children, sure, of course." She smiled dreamily.

"Birdie, don't tell me—"

"Oh, no! No, but it's something to look forward to. With my strawberry hair and his auburn, I'm guessing a child with any other hair color would be a little remote, but who knows."

"You'll find out, it'll all come together," said Georgette sagely.

"Yup, it will."

Nicholas wasn't home when she knocked, his car appeared as she started backing hers out of the driveway. He was carrying a sack of groceries and she followed him into the house, stood at the kitchen doorway watching as he transferred items into the refrigerator, folded the paper bag and stowed it in the cupboard beneath the sink.

They sat on the sofa in the living room while she told him and he was silent for a moment, the iced tea glass suspended halfway to his mouth. He placed it carefully on the table in front of them as he looked at her. His expression was wistful.

"I guess I knew it would come to this, Birdie, but a piece of me was hopin'."

"Oh, Nicky . . ."

"Birdie, I have to ask you something, and it's important."

"What is it, Nicholas?"

"Can you find it in you to forgive the way I treated you? It's been weighing on me and I . . . I just can't feel good about letting you walk out of here without knowing how truly sorry I am. Baby, I hurt you so. I don't know why I did those things, but you didn't deserve them."

"Nicholas," she said, "I'm not sorry we were married, though I'm sorry we had to go through what we did. But we made it through, and we're both in a better place now. We've even learned to be friends, haven't we?" She smiled softly and cupped his chin. "And I've forgiven you, Nicky. You're a good man, I want nothing but good things for you."

"Thank you, baby."

"Are you still going to follow through on the land development work?" she asked.

"Yeah, it's lookin' that way." He hesitated. "Something else came up, Birdie. I saw the man Claire was with."

She straightened. "What do you mean?"

"It was almost inevitable. He was leaving one day as I got there, and I stopped and asked what he was to her, just like that, told him I'd seen the flowers."

Her eyes widened. "What did he say?"

"He was one tragic man, Birdie. Said he knew who I was, I think he wanted to talk to someone about her anyway."

"Oh no."

He nodded. "They were together for almost two years, he has a wife and two sons, said he tried to leave but his wife threatened public humiliation. He's a judge, Birdie, some of Claire's cases were being heard by him and they could've both faced legal consequences. Claire," he hesitated, his face a study in pain, "Claire wanted him to leave, move somewhere else and start over with her."

She was one step ahead. "He couldn't do it. He had ties here."

He was looking out the window at the sky. It was a bright, cloudless day outside, hot and muggy, September in all its glory. His gaze went back to her face. "He couldn't do it. He said he told her he wanted them to stay together, he'd recommend her for work somewhere else, but she didn't want to be kept any longer, she wanted him all to herself."

Birdie thought about the art pieces she had seen in the apartment. "Poor Claire," she said.

He nodded, was silent for a minute, said, "I was feeling a little down a couple weeks ago so I went to that church on Main Street. The man who got up to talk said some of the most amazin' things, Birdie. About forgiveness, and how God forgives us for the bad things we do even though we can't repay him, and how we should do the same. He said the other person might not even care, but it takes away the bitterness that hurts us and everyone around us."

He shook his head. "You know, I've been blaming that man for . . . for cuttin' her wrists like she did. But Birdie, I swear I just don't think I can hate anyone that much for the rest of my life. The man's eating himself alive over her, and I have to ask myself how hating him is gonna make things right again. He had a hand in my sister's death, but I gotta forgive him." He looked at her and his eyes watered.

She took his arm and drew him to her in an embrace, kissed his neck, and they sat like that for a long moment.

"You're going to be all right, Nicky," she said. "You're headed in the right direction and I couldn't be more proud of you."

He drew back and looked at her. "Baby, we're both gonna do alright. We both are."

Victor was on a phone call with his agent. When he hung up, he swiveled in his chair, looked at her in the doorway and said, "It seems there's growing interest in the World War Two genre. The last three books made the best seller list, so the publisher's willing to go with a more substantial printing for this one, and a better deal for me. Where do you want to go to celebrate?"

She smiled widely, moved toward him. "I'm so happy for you!"

He grasped her hands, drew her into his lap. "Happy for us, Birdie. This is all about us from now on."

"But you did the work, Victor. I didn't write those books."

He smiled, "True enough, but you're my muse." He kissed her. "And now we're both reaping the benefits. Come October 29th, we'll own everything together."

"Then make a reservation for Tuesday at the Greenhouse," she said. "I've been wanting to try it."

"What's your shift today?" he asked.

"Four till closing, why?"

"Good. We have time to go to the beach."

"The beach?"

"Yeah, good place to talk. Come on."

It was late morning and the sun was high overhead, he took her hand and they made the short trek to the upland, the soft deep stretch of beach behind the vegetation. They didn't need towels or accessories, they sat directly on the sand looking out over the distinctive turquoise colors of the Gulf of Mexico.

"I do love this place," she said.

"I know, I can see why." He turned to her. "We need to talk about how and where we're going to live."

"You see how I like to live, Victor, I'm a simple girl. What do you have in mind?"

"I've been mulling things over, I think I should sell the place in Santa Fe."

"Oh . . . I really like the idea of having a place out west. It's so beautiful there."

"On the other hand, we don't need two places here."

"I know." She hesitated. "The condo is right on the water and it's sentimental, my parents bought it for me, but your house is so pretty, and a little larger."

"Can you get time off to visit New Mexico again?"

"Doubtful. Not twice in one year."

"Birdie. You know you don't need to work, I'm considered a very well-to-do man."

She looked at him. "I love working," she said slowly, "I know it limits the amount of time I have to spend with you but I've never not worked."

He leaned in, kissed her mouth. "Think about it, no pressure."

She rested against him, head on his arm. "I confirmed the date with the Selby people."

"Good. A nice place for a wedding, pretty and low-key."

"I won't wear white, I think it would be silly, no one would be fooled."

"Wear whatever you want, Birdie. You're a beautiful woman, no matter what you put—"

She faced him. "Really. Suppose I decide on a tuxedo with suspenders?"

He grinned. "Especially if you wore suspenders."

"Well, what if I wore my mother's navy wedding suit from the 1940s?"

He frowned. "That might be carrying it a bit too far, don't you think?"

She kissed his neck. "Okay, what about a bikini? It's Florida, I could put on a gold Lamé bikini . . ." brushed his lips with hers, kissed his mouth slowly, deliberately. Two men passed by on the way to beach, one of them glanced back, gawking.

Victor pushed her hair back, smiled. "It would be a very short ceremony. I would have to hurry you off to that banyan grove and plunder you right there."

Mock consternation. "Plunder me? And how would you do that?"

It took six minutes to drive home, where a thorough explanation was provided in the bedroom at the rear of the house. Torn clothing strewn across the floor, writhing flesh, impassioned screams silenced by kisses deep and luscious.

"Yes? Now?"

"Yes! Oh God, oh God."

Plundering.

Birdie gave notice at the Crescent Club, in two weeks she would be unemployed. But as Victor pointed out, she had other options.

"You realize now we can go wherever we want, whenever we want, Solnyshka. We can stay here, go there, I can write anywhere."

"What do you want to do?"

"I'm not sure yet, we could go back and forth, we'd still be close to your parents."

"And what about yours, Victor? Will they come to the wedding?"

"No, but maybe we'll go to Mexico to see them."

She was quiet. "Do they know we're getting married?"

He said patiently, "They didn't go to New Mexico for Amanda's, they won't come to Florida for ours. They're in their own world down there."

"Why is that, Victor? Did something happen?"

"No particular reason, they just have each other." He turned, resumed his writing.

She saw his evasive eyes, unavailable arms, head canted away. She saw, but said nothing.

They took the old fashioned vows on the lawn at Selby Gardens and were pronounced husband and wife by the judge who officiated. Afterward, the wedding party, a Monday afternoon cocktails, hors d'œuvres, and cake reception, Birdie in her silver cocktail-length dress and Victor in his tailored gray suit; that night, their own private celebration at home. The following day, an early morning flight to Paris.

They stayed five days and five nights at their hotel in the 1st Arrondissement. By day they explored the ancient city, photographed the Eiffel Tower, the Champs-Élysées. They walked the steep steps of the Sacré-Cœur, went across the chilly Seine, wandered the crooked streets of the Latin Quarter. At night they dined in dimly-lit restaurants and busy cafes, sampled bottles of wine and VSOPs, then explored each other on the silken sheets of their bed at the Paris Ritz.

"Time for the real honeymoon," he'd say, somehow the straps of her gown would disappear down her arms, and long nights of bliss would begin.

"My husband," she would say, over the telephone in the morning. "My husband would like coffee and croissants." She liked the words, they sounded good to her ears.

"I will take that dress for my wife," he would say in halting French to the shop girls in the city. She liked that, too.

They returned to their house on Anglin on a dull, overcast day in November. It had rained, the trees were dripping and the streets were running rainwater.

"Is this a sign of something, the fact that it's been raining each time we return?" she said to him over a nightcap that evening.

He smiled. "Maybe things are sad around here when we're gone, and everything cheers up because we've come back."

"I can live with that," she said. "What should we do tomorrow?"

"Let's take care of the legal stuff, make the wills, do the life insurance and bank signatures, and see a realtor. I'd like to do it all before we leave for New Mexico."

"That'll all take a couple of days, won't it?"

"That's fine, we need to check in with your parents, anyway."

Four days later they were back in Santa Fe. As their rental car sped east through town to the house at the edge of the canyon, Birdie recognized street signs and businesses from her previous trip, it made her feel like she was shedding her tourist persona, putting on a resident mindset.

But something was wrong, she saw it in his face when he walked the house flipping on lights.

"What is it, Victor? Is everything alright?"

"Hang on." He put a hand to her arm. "Stay here." He moved down the hallway, came to her after a couple of minutes, scowling.

"Birdie, I need to make a call. It'll be a minute, would you get us a drink?" He kissed her head, went in to the study, closed the door.

She slipped out of her coat, it was chilly but she had worn a sweater and long slacks. In the living room she found the glasses, poured bourbon, saw the open magazine flung over the sofa arm, paused. *Time.*

She thought about the irony in that, swallowed some of her drink and waited.

Victor came down the hallway, saw her and smiled tiredly. She held out his glass.

He took the drink. "Thank you. Are you hungry?"

"Yes, but it can wait," she said, and took another swallow from her glass.

He removed his coat, threw it over the arm of the nearest chair.

They looked at each other silently.

"Then why don't we have our drinks first and decide where to go? Do you want music?"

"Victor, who has been here?"

They edged around the furniture and sat on the sofa facing one another. He took the magazine, tossed it on the coffee table.

He swallowed, looked at her, said lightly, "Amanda, but she won't be coming back, not to worry."

"Why not, Victor? Not to worry about her coming back, or not to worry about her?"

He swallowed again and gave a short laugh. "Honestly, I'm not sure."

Someone was pounding on the door, they both looked up. Victor glanced at Birdie as he rose from the sofa. "I'm sorry," he said. "She can be a handful."

As he opened the door, Amanda shot through the opening, face contorted. "Are you kidding me? After all we've been through, now this?" She swore at him as he reached out to touch her, turned and saw Birdie on the sofa, watching them.

She whirled toward Victor. "What is this Victor? You bring your little whore back here to screw you anytime you feel like it but you tell me, your own sister, I'm not welcome—"

"Hey, hey." He glanced toward Birdie. "Amanda, stop. She's my wife, we're married, so stop the histrionics."

She laughed, swore again, started moving into the living room but he caught her arm and said, "You here to pick up your things? Fine, I'll help you." He steered her down the hallway toward the guest room, closed the door.

Birdie, left alone, gulped the last of her bourbon. Her hand was still steady but her insides were twisting like a tornado. She went to the cabinet, poured another.

They returned after about ten minutes, Amanda carrying a small bag at her side. She turned at the door, acknowledging Birdie, said, "Congratulations. I hope you'll be happy here."

Birdie smiled. "Thank you."

"I'll let my famous brother fill you in on the history of our happy little family, but just in—"

"That's enough, Amanda," he said, grabbing her arm.

After she was gone Victor leaned against the door, looked across the room at Birdie.

"You might as well come over here," she called to him. "Whatever you think I might say, it probably wouldn't hold a candle to whatever she did."

"You think?" he said.

She gestured with her hand. "Come."

He went to the sofa. She held out his drink, he took it and sat down. She tilted her glass against his. "Za lyubov, you remember what that means?"

He swallowed, drew a hand through his hair, hesitated. "I've got a lot of new phrases swimming around in my head. To love? Is that it?"

She nodded, spoke in a low voice, "The last time we were here, I told you that you were everything to me. In Russian, that has a deeper meaning than just telling someone you love them. When I say things like that, Victor, I mean them, I'm not a whimsical kind of girl."

She looked in his eyes, they were flooded with tears.

She took his glass and set it down, moved closer and drew him to her.

They didn't speak for a while. She kissed his forehead, his cheek, then his mouth.

He said, "Please, I don't want to talk or explain or discuss just now, I will, but not tonight."

She began to make love to him, opening her mouth to his, brushing the tips of her breasts against him, stroking him through the denim. "I love you, Victor," she said.

Off came the sweaters, the pants, the rest of the clothes, then the intimate scent of skin, the quick intake of breath. She liked being on top, could feel him better that way. His eyes were open, watching her. "You are everything to me," he whispered, sitting up, taking her waist in his hands.

She smiled, closed her eyes. *If only you would talk to me.*

They went looking for a realtor the next day. The woman was too talkative, Birdie felt she would go mad if she had to listen to her for very long. They tried another office, a smooth talker with an English accent. An English accent? It was too weird somehow, in the northern New Mexico desert. The third try was a small, five-man office, a couple of secretaries, it felt right.

"I know that neighborhood, I have to tell you, homes sell pretty quickly there. What are your plans?"

He was a listener, not a talker, they liked that. They shook hands before leaving, went to dinner at a new place called Cafe Pasquals, a pink adobe structure on a downtown street corner. While they ate, they talked. Nothing fancy, they agreed, maybe a house in another neighborhood, maybe somewhere else.

"You said, Victor, that you'd lived in California for a while. Where was that?"

He took a swig of the beer, settled it on the table. "Down around Palm Springs, Palm Desert, Rancho Mirage."

"What was the attraction?"

"Oh, I dunno, I was bumming around after graduation, last hurrah before going to work for my uncle, checking out the country. I liked the climate, and the landscape. It's similar to what we have here, desert, mountain ranges, hot days, cool nights."

She nodded. "I've heard Palm Springs is very pretty."

"Yeah, it is."

She looked at him. "I've never been to California, it would be nice to see it sometime."

He put a hand to his mouth, looked at her. "It's not that far, you know."

She finished what was on her plate, leaned back, smiled at him.

"I feel like a world traveler. Sarasota one day, Paris the next, off to Santa Fe, now an adventure in California," she said as they drove toward the street address in her hand.

He laughed. "You've got a good start. Now that we have your passport, we can go just about anywhere."

"I'll make a list," she said.

"I have to limit my travels somewhat," he said. "If I'm not disciplined about my work schedule, I won't produce."

"Turn here," she said, pointing.

He did, and they began to look for the house. Birdie saw it first, the graceful phoenix sculpture rising from among the palms in front. Victor turned the rental car into the driveway and the house was before them, an L-shaped ranch, 3,000 square feet of flat roof, gleaming white stone and glass, all according to the paper the realtor had given them. They had wanted to arrive ahead of her so they could form their own impressions.

They got out of the car and walked around the property, saw the rectangular lap pool at the side of the house surrounded by a cut stone wall, wandered further and saw the clerestory windows at the back of the house.

They looked at each other and grinned.

The engine sound of another car pulling into the driveway, a door slammed. "That will be Sheryl," he said.

She came around to where they stood, hand extended. "Good to see you again," she said, shaking their hands, each in turn. She had dark auburn hair, it looked like they were at a convention for redheads. "So, you like midcentury design. Well, you're in the right place for it."

Victor nodded. "We'd like to see inside."

At the hotel that night, optimism. "You think they'll take the offer?" she asked.

He shrugged. "All we can do is wait, but it was our good luck that he likes espionage novels."

She laughed, she was excited. "I've never bought a house before."

He was businesslike. "You just have to know how to negotiate."

"She said it would be a couple of days."

He nodded. "We'll hang out while they decide, get to know the area. How does that sound?"

They didn't need that long, the offer was not accepted and he talked with Sheryl the following morning to discuss their next move.

"This is part of our strategy," Victor said to Birdie over lunch.

"Really? It looks like they turned down the offer."

"They were supposed to. We gave them a low offer just to gauge their interest. Now we're proposing a figure closer to what we're willing to pay and giving them twenty-four hours."

"This is like being in a Moroccan souq," she said.

He laughed. "A little bit."

They explored the city, drove down Palm Canyon Drive, admired the skirted fan palms lining the streets, browsed a few shops, went to the art museum. Everywhere they went the purple San Jacinto Mountains loomed in the near distance.

The following afternoon their offer was accepted. They celebrated with a bottle of wine and a night of passionate sex.

The Santa Fe house and Birdie's condo sold in the same week later that month. After a tiring three-day sprint to sign closing documents and make necessary arrangements, they decided to wait until spring to return to the new house. By then, they would be ready to tackle decorating and refurbishments.

In the meanwhile, the holidays were approaching.

Chapter Eight
December 1979 – February 1980

Birdie was happy to be home, she'd missed the warm nights, relaxed lifestyle and quiet quirkiness of the key. She commented on this to Georgette as the two sat visiting at the Crescent Club one morning.

"I can see where you're coming from," said Georgette. "I would miss being away from here, too. And the desert wouldn't be my thing."

"I dunno, the desert has a different kind of beauty, Georgie, not lush but kind of clean and pared down. Everything's different, the air is drier, there are different animals. We have those cute little anoles here, they have funny little roadrunners there. We have the gulf, they have the pretty San Jacinto Mountains, and it's nice looking out the windows and seeing them. Anyway, it's a getaway house, most of our time will be spent here."

"What about his family, did you meet them while you were there?"

Birdie hesitated. "His parents live in Mexico," she said, "so I haven't met them yet."

"They must not be very close. I mean, Mexico's right across the border, isn't it?"

Birdie shrugged, "I don't know, Georgie, families have issues. He has a sister, though, she lives in Santa Fe."

"So, what's she like?"

Their eyes met. "She's a little high-strung."

"Well, it's not like you live next door to each other so . . . everything's cool, right?"

Birdie smiled briefly. "Right."

Georgette said, "You heard about Tommy?"

"Tommy . . ."

Georgette cocked her head. "You know, the guy who came around looking for handouts."

"Georgie, he has some problems, he was in 'Nam—"

"He got killed by a drunk driver."

Birdie stared at her. "What?"

"Yup. Some woman driving down Midnight Pass up by the Greenhouse, broad daylight, so drunk she didn't even realize she'd hit someone crossing the road."

"Oh nooo."

"I'm sorry, Birdie, I know you liked him."

Birdie nodded, frowned, reached for her drink.

They listened to the jukebox for a few moments, Lynard Skynard's Sweet Home Alabama.

When the song ended, Georgette said, "Diana and Roger stopped in to say goodbye."

"Oh, I'm sorry I missed them.

"Yeah, she was disappointed too, she said to tell you goodbye temporarily. They went to the Greek Islands for their honeymoon, he rented a sailboat and they cruised around for a couple of weeks, she said it was like heaven. I believe it, the pictures were like something from a movie. She looked like a million bucks, said they'll come back to visit from time to time, maybe you'll catch her then."

"And what about you, Georgie, have you been seeing anyone?"

"No, but I will, Birdie. The thing is, working here, I don't have much time. You know how that goes."

Birdie said absently, "Kiki knows everyone, you should ask."

Georgette smiled briefly, moved down the bar to greet a new customer.

Her parents greeted them on Sunday like long lost lovers, lots of hugs, pats on the hand, little kisses.

"So, how is married life treating you, how do you like the new house?" asked her father as they lingered after breakfast. An early chill was in the air, too damp for sitting out of doors.

Victor responded. "We're planning mostly cosmetic changes, but they won't start until we go back in March."

"I wish you would come out and see us there," added Birdie. "I think you'd like it."

Her parents looked at each other. "Maybe," said her mother. "I'm a little bored just sitting around, but I would like to divest myself of this cane first."

Birdie frowned. "Why are you still using the cane, I thought you were getting better?"

Her parents shared a look.

"It's not healing like we thought," said her father. "It was a compound fracture, sometimes they take longer."

"You sure about that, Fa? Nothing else?"

Her mother touched her arm. "Birdie, I may have to face the possibility that I will need the cane for the rest of my life."

Birdie bit her lip. "Mother, I'm sorry. Is it painful?"

"Only a little bit."

"March or April is about the time I'll start putting the next novel to paper. I'll be busy with the book tour prior to that—"

"What is this tour?" asked Anton.

"Just a series of interviews and book signings to promote the latest novel," said Victor.

"Are you going with him, Birdie?"

Birdie looked at Victor. "I'd like to but we hadn't really discussed it," she said.

"Those tours aren't my idea of fun," said Victor. "My publisher and agent set them up, they're all business, two cities crammed into one day, fast paced with no time for sightseeing. They're exhausting, it's better I go alone."

"Do you have to do them?" Kira asked.

"The publisher wants it, my agent wants it, I like meeting the people who read the books but I could probably do without the interviews."

"What about the next book, do you have a setting in mind?" asked Kira.

"Yes, I think it's going to be Romania," said Victor.

"Romania, huh?" This from Fa.

Victor looked at him with a certain smile. "The Carpathians."

"The Soviet and German armies fought there."

Victor nodded. "A storyline involving the changes in Romania, culminating with her switch to the side of the Allies in '44, I'm already starting to study up on it."

Tchaikovsky's Piano Trio in A Minor was on the turntable, the four sat in silence for a few minutes listening to the cello and violin, then the piano started again.

"Have you given any more thought to a business of your own?" asked her father.

Birdie laughed. "We've been so busy, I haven't had time to think about it."

"It may be a lost point now," said Victor, looking at her. "We'll live here most of the time, but we want the freedom to go to Palm Springs when we feel like it. It's hard to maintain a business if you're not around to keep it open."

She nodded, they were in sync.

Birdie had planted a garden. She'd started with a few tropical plumeria, bottle palms and red ti plants to complement the existing vegetation. It turned out she had a green thumb so now she was on her hands and knees gently patting soil around the ground orchids, heliconias, and fringed crinum lilies she had added to bring an island of color to the middle of the back yard.

She sat on her haunches and used her wrist to brush the bangs from her eyes, surveyed the area opposite the house. Tomorrow, some fruit plants and vegetable seeds, a small garden with herbs for cooking and baking.

The sound of wood rattling against wood, an opening door. She glanced over her shoulder.

"My wife, the home economist," said Victor, smiling, moving toward her in the grass.

She grinned, held up her dirt-stained hands. "I'm a happy girl," she said.

"Then I'm a happy man," he said, glancing at the new flowering bushes. "Very nice, it's looking like a real garden."

"Thank you!"

"Your father called, he wanted to know if we would like to go with them to the opera on Saturday."

"What did you say?"

He smiled. "I said yes, of course."

She laughed. "Have you ever seen an opera?"

"No, there's a thriving opera in Santa Fe but I've never been, have you?"

"Yes, once, La Boheme, it was quite the production, very extravagant. My parents love it so I'm glad you accepted. Which are we going to see?"

"The Magic Flute, Mozart."

"Oh, fun. It has some humor in it."

"I suppose we'll have to dress. And they want supper beforehand, we're supposed to choose the place."

"I think it'll be a nice evening."

He reached down and pulled her to her feet. "Ready for lunch?"

She grinned. "Are you offering?"

He kissed her nose. "I was going to make an omelet, I'll share if you want."

"I want, thank you. I have to water these and then I'll be in. Ten minutes."

He released her and walked toward the house. She stood and watched him go, hips relaxed, shoulders back, she loved that walk.

An early supper Saturday at Pattigeorges on Longboat Key, it was popular, her parents had never been and wanted to try it. It was a good choice, they liked the menu suggestions by Kiki, liked the waterfront location and the accommodating service, important since they had to be at the theater early.

"They're used to it," Birdie told her father seated next to her at the table. "This is a social town and people are always dashing off somewhere."

"A circus town," her father said. "Built with circus money."

"Yes," said Birdie, "that, too."

Victor smiled. "Every town's got a story."

"What is it like where you came from, Victor?" asked Kira, sipping wine.

"Santa Fe was settled by the Spanish," he said. "Pueblos lived in the area originally but had left 200 years before the Conquistadors arrived, then there was the war with Mexico before statehood. So, there are heavy Pueblo, Spanish and Mexican influences."

"When you drive into the city the first time," said Birdie, "you notice the Spanish-Pueblo architecture. All the buildings downtown have to maintain that historical flavor. It makes it very different from Sarasota, or Palm Springs or Detroit, or anywhere else."

"Mud, water and straw," said Victor, looking at her father. "Formed into bricks, left in the sun for ten days to dry. The adobe roofs are flat, hidden behind parapets, round roof beams are embedded in the walls, windows are square and set into the walls."

"Interesting," said Fa. "This is how you lived when you were in New Mexico?"

Victor caught the eye of the waitress and nodded.

"No," he said to her father. "Spanish Colonial Revival, like a lot of the houses here."

"It was a beautiful house," said Birdie, fondly. "It had a lovely courtyard." She leaned against the table, looked at Victor and smiled. Behind him, a familiar face walking through, she turned and a look of recognition passed between them. Birdie drew a breath and froze. The woman hesitated, continued walking.

Victor started to turn, the waitress handed him the check.

The Magic Flute was a tale of would-be lovers going through tests of fire and water, and visually dazzling. Birdie liked rich explosions of color, lively drama, beautiful music, but the surprise at the restaurant had sent her mind elsewhere and she found it hard to concentrate.

At the Queen of the Night's solo, the coloratura singing of her desire for revenge, Victor reached into Birdie's lap and squeezed her hand. She leaned against him, her dress, made of emerald silk, was long, strapless, with a low sweetheart neckline. His eyes lingered there, rose to hers, returned to the stage.

Later, a brief glance to her right, Victor's dark profile was intent, Tamino and Pamina had his attention as they greeted the sunrise together at the end of the second act.

They stood outside at the car, her parents anxious that Victor had enjoyed it. "You really liked it, Victor? It's understandable if you didn't, opera isn't for everyone," said her mother.

"Really, I did. Thank you for the introduction."

At home, he tossed his shirt and pants into the dry cleaning hamper, turned from the closet.

She presented her back. "Undo me, please?"

He kissed her neck, taking his time, pressing against her. "Beautiful dress, the kind that makes promises." He slid his hands beneath the silk, began to raise it past her hips. "Time to make good on those promises."

She said, "I think all the cleavage and perfume tonight went to your head."

He stopped, turned her around. "Birdie, what is it, what's wrong?"

Her mouth changed, her eyes were downcast. "The wife, the woman from the bar." She shook her head and leaned into him.

He put his arms around her. "You saw her, you spoke with her?"

"I saw her at the restaurant. I know she was never charged, but still it shocked me. I guess I just didn't expect to see her again. All I could think of when she walked past was what he did, that feeling of being trapped . . ." She began to tremble.

He kissed her hair and stroked her shoulders. "What can I do?"

"I don't know, Victor." There was torment in her voice. "I thought I had forgotten but then I saw her and it all came back. Oh how I wish I could forget that night."

"I suspect this is one of those things that will heal with time. Would you like to talk with someone, a professional?"

She hesitated. "No, I think you're right, I just need time. I'm sorry it's taking so long."

"You've done nothing wrong, Birdie, everyone reacts differently to something like that."

"I feel so selfish," she said. "I know it must be so much worse for her."

"Be patient with yourself." He touched her face, watching her eyes. "I'm going to bring something to drink. What would you like?"

"Whatever you're having, Victor."

"I'll be back. And then, my sun," he lifted her chin with his hand, kissed her mouth, paused, kissed again more deeply. "And then I'll do what I can to help you forget."

They had dinner at the Columbia the next evening with his agent, who had flown down to meet with Victor about the upcoming book tour. Scott liked Sarasota, was thinking about renting a place seasonally, sticking the proverbial toe in. They talked about the area during dinner, switched over to business after the plates had been cleared and the coffee and digestifs were served.

He lit a cigarette and hunched over the table. "Okay, so what they have in mind is a week-long tour that takes in fifteen cities," he said. "You know the drill, the morning television shows, radio interviews, bookstore signings, we'll make sure the local media are informed."

"Give me the specifics," said Victor.

"Last week in February. You'll do the usual whirlwind, Dallas, Atlanta, Nashville, Chicago, Detroit, Denver. I'll get you the list, I left it at the hotel."

Birdie drank her coffee, listening, not listening. The restaurant was below the apartment where Claire had lived and she realized, guiltily, she hadn't thought of her in at least a week. She'd been busy with her new identity, the houses, traveling, weaving two lives into one.

She tuned in again when she heard Scott say, ". . . and Amanda. Kind of nice having her around on that last tour."

Victor glanced at her, she met his look with a stare, blinked, looked away. He said to Scott, "Yeah, well, not this time."

Scott tapped his cigarette on the ashtray. "Oh, too bad."

At the end of the evening Scott picked up the check and they drove home silently.

Inside the house Victor dropped his keys on the table. "Do you want a nightcap? I'm having one."

"Thanks, no," she said, and went to bed.

She was awakened, open kisses on her neck.

She turned. "No, Victor."

He pressed closer, she moved away.

He touched her shoulder. "What is this, Birdie?"

She lay looking at the dark night sky, she had forgotten to close the curtains. "You know what this is, why are you even asking?"

Silence.

She turned her back and closed her eyes.

"Birdie?"

She didn't respond. She got up and went into the bathroom, drank half a glass of water.

She went to bed but not the one she had been sleeping in. She folded back the covers and got into the guest bed.

"Birdie." She was being awakened again.

She opened her eyes. "What."

"You're avoiding me."

"You seem to know a lot about that, Victor. I'm just trying to get some sleep."

He slid into the bed with her, this time she allowed him to take her in his arms. "Can we talk?" he said.

She yawned. "If you do the talking, I'll do the listening."

He kissed her head, tightened his arms, "Solnyshka, will you listen to a story? It's not . . . it isn't pleasant."

She nodded.

He sighed. "Amanda was always precocious," he began. "As she got older she grew wild, my parents did their best to rein her in but I think she was just born that way, wired that way. Around freshman year in school she starting running around, staying out, they were worried sick and I . . . " He paused.

She asked hesitantly, "What do you mean running around?"

"You know . . . she had a reputation."

"With who? Kids you knew, friends?"

Another pause. "Yeah. A few fights ensued, that's just what you do when you have a younger sister. My parents went to one of our priests, they, uh, enlisted his help, they didn't know what else to do. They asked him to work with her, you know, counsel her."

She was fully awake now.

He didn't speak for a long moment. "It seemed to help after a while. He was a good guy, younger than the others, he used to joke around with me when I was hanging out after school. She cleaned up her act, her grades improved," he gave a short laugh. "No more fights, I had him to thank for that."

He was talking against her hair as she lay and watched the glow of the moon through the curtains.

"My parents were grateful, life went on, maybe a year later I started noticing the changes. Her devotion to the church, she never missed a mass or confession, she was there to help out. She went from playing around with all the guys at school to having nothing to do with them."

Birdie swallowed. "How much older are you?"

"Two years. It was my senior year, she was a sophomore. Our family was going to mass, my father, in gratitude, had donated to the parish, everything going fine but I was noticing little things. The way she was dressing, her behavior, nothing you could define but she wasn't like a girl anymore, more like a woman. I started following her, it wasn't hard to do."

Here he paused, said, "I need something to drink, you okay?"

"Um-hmm." She waited for him, heart contracting, *What have I done?*

He returned, tumbler of water in hand. This time she held him, drew her arms across him and felt his voice beneath her arms as he spoke.

"There are a lot of hiking trails in the mountains around Santa Fe. He was taking her there, I should say they were meeting there, no coercion was involved."

"Just to be clear, this was a . . . a priest?"

He nodded, resumed the narrative. "I kept it to myself for a while, I wasn't sure what to do. Then I went to her, she was hysterical, 'How could you, I love him', about what you would expect from a sixteen-year old girl. So I did the next logical thing and went to my parents. They didn't believe me, she'd become such a model of virtuous behavior they couldn't see past it."

"Oh no."

He stopped to drink from the tumbler. "So I went to the priest. Father Ryan."

"Oh Victor."

"I'm not sure what I expected, probably something along the lines of, 'So sorry, it won't happen again', but that's not what I got. No admission of guilt. Instead, he said it wouldn't do anyone any good to stir up strife, I don't remember what else, I got out of there as quickly as I could. I remember . . . I remember telling him it had to stop or I would go to my parents."

He stopped speaking for a long moment. She said gently, "And is that what happened?"

"No. Amanda came to see me in my room, said that they loved each other and it would never change. How is an eighteen-year old boy supposed to take that? In the meanwhile, my parents were treating me like I was the one who had done something wrong, casting doubt on their sainted Father Ryan."

She was silent, he went on.

"He sent for me one day after school. I thought maybe he'd reconsidered. But no, he wanted to ask my forgiveness. He said he was weak and couldn't stop, he loved her. I couldn't handle it, I beat him up."

"You what?"

"I did the only thing I knew to do at that age, I was filled with rage and my own unfulfilled desires. I beat him up, he was like all those boys she'd been with before, only worse because he knew better. And he hadn't behaved like a priest, he'd behaved like any ordinary man, even I knew that. He . . . I broke his nose, ribs, he didn't resist. They transferred him to another parish in the city."

She was silent for a moment. "What happened with Amanda?"

"Word got out, I've no idea how. After the dust settled and Amanda graduated, my parents moved down to Mexico, they were so mortified by the whole incident. Amanda stayed, went to college there, went about her life. Turned out, they never stopped seeing each other, she threw it in my face every chance she had. Right up until a few months ago when she . . ." He sighed.

She was appalled. "Her husband knew?"

"I don't know, he found out, figured it out, the marriage was annulled. She claimed he had an affair with one of his clients, so she moved out. She used her key to the house, didn't bother consulting me. I took exception to that and had the locks changed."

He took another drink and was silent for so long she wondered if he had gone to sleep.

She said, "How are you doing, Victor?"

"How am I doing? I resent them. I resent her and every taunting word she's ever spoken to me. I resent him and his betrayal of our friendship, his betrayal of what he was supposed to be. I resent the fact that my mother and my father, who were supposed to believe in me, believed instead a lie, and liars, and didn't come to my aid. They were so immersed in each other, so vested in their reputation, that I somehow got left out of the picture."

She said, hesitantly, "I think that there'll come a time when you'll have to let go of the bitterness. The others may not know or care, but for your own sake." She kissed his hair. "I think you see it, too."

Out of the darkness, a sigh. "Yes."

"We'll have a child of our own one day, Victor."

He reached up to her, kissed her mouth. "I hope so. Let's make that happen soon."

She went to see Kiki the following day, arriving unannounced, hoping to catch her before she left for her second shift. Kiki worked five or six days a week, was normally at work early in the morning, went home around midday, returned to the restaurant for the evening shift.

No luck. Birdie stuck a note in the door and left.

At home, Victor was gone, too. He'd left a note, she read it and made a cup of tea, went outside and checked the newly planted garden for signs of growth.

When Victor arrived after an hour, she greeted him with relief. "Thank goodness you're here, I was going out of my mind."

He took her arms. "What do you mean, is everything all right?"

She laughed, "No, I mean, yes, I'm sorry. But I think I'm bored, Victor. When you're here, I have something to do, you're good company and we do things together. But when you're not here, it's different."

They sat in the living room. "Maybe I've done you a disservice, Solnyshka, you're not used to being a woman of leisure."

She said hesitantly, "Well, I've always worked. Ten hour shifts is normal in the industry. I never had time to develop hobbies, days off were devoted to laundry, marketing, lunch now and then with a girlfriend."

"Or a late-night date with a lover," he leaned toward her and kissed her mouth.

She smiled, returned the kiss. "You have your writing and research, the guys to pal around with occasionally. I thought a small business might be worth pursuing, but not with a limited commitment."

He leaned back, looked at her closely. "You know, your mother was saying basically the same thing, did you notice?"

"What do you mean?"

"Your father helps out with handyman projects at the parish, volunteers as an orderly at the hospital, but your mother's been feeling a little bored. Birdie, what's her expertise?"

She stared at him, brows contorted.

He answered for her. "She knows jewelry and antiques. You said she taught you everything you know." He sat looking at her, smiling.

It took her a moment. "You think she would do it?" she finally asked.

He shrugged. "You know her better than I, but let's say she took care of business while we were in Palm Springs on your - you could make them buying trips - and you handled the shop when we were back in town. I might be willing to come up with half the startup capital if your father was willing to invest the other half."

She smiled. "My husband, the genius."

"Not if they don't like the idea. Can we talk about something more immediate?" he said.

She left her chair, went to sit on his lap. "What's that?"

"What are we doing for Christmas?"

She laughed. "I've always liked the idea of opening presents on Christmas Eve."

"Is that what you normally do?

"No." She explained her family tradition.

He was thoughtful. "This is a new beginning for us so we'll make our own traditions. Let's open gifts on Christmas Eve. Um, what are your feelings about a service? You already know mine."

"I hate to do Christmas without a service, Victor."

"Let me give it some thought, we'll come back to it. What about Christmas Day?"

"A nice dinner, no doubt about it. But as I said, mother and Fa don't celebrate until January 7th, so we'll have to go it alone unless we invite others to join us."

"Not a bad idea, would you like to do that?"

"Maybe it could be the start of another tradition."

"We'll see, Christmas is only three weeks away, others may have already laid plans."

"Okay."

She shifted in his lap, wound her arms around his neck. "I've been a very good girl this year, just in case Santa is wondering."

He raised his brows. "You have, have you?"

She smiled. "It depends on how you define good."

His eyes met hers. The hand resting on her thigh was warm and sensitive, it slid beneath the fabric of her dress, teased toward the top of her leg.

He said, "I think you've been very good, I'll relay the message. Why don't you kiss me, Solnyshka?"

In a little while they went down the hallway to the bedroom, Santa was delivering early this year.

The holidays behind them, their attention was focused on preparing for Victor's book tour.

"I'm dreading it," she said. "We've hardly been apart since we met and I'm going to miss you. Are you sure I couldn't come?"

"I think it would be better if you were here, Birdie. Spend time with your parents, catch up with your girlfriends, you'll be less miserable."

"How do usually get ready for these trips, Victor?"

"I use the beach a lot, get as much sun and exercise as I can because I'm cooped up indoors most of the week."

"It's the dead of winter, some of those places will be freezing. I really hate being cold, Victor, maybe it's good that I'm not going. Do you mind having to do it?"

"Mixed feelings. I have to push myself, it's one of those necessary things authors do to earn money. But there's another side, it's a chance to meet and talk to people who buy my books."

"You're an introvert, isn't being around all those people hard for you?"

He shrugged. "Too much solitude can encourage self-centeredness. Sometimes it's good to interact with others, learn from them. It can be pleasurable."

"And how did Amanda—"

"She wasn't actually on the tour, Birdie. We used to talk from time to time, I mentioned I was going to be in Albuquerque, and she likes skiing the Sandia Mountains so she met us there. She and Scott hit it off and I think they stayed in touch for a while, I never asked."

She said, "Oh."

She finally connected with Kiki, tried to make plans but her friend was slammed with work. "Super busy, I wish I could but I'll have to get back to you. I've even had to postpone our trip to Ibiza. Too disappointing."

"Everything alright with you, aside from your schedule?" asked Birdie.

"Oh yes, dreamy. Gene is fabulous, well, you know, he has his store to run and can't be available twenty-four seven, but he managed to surprise me on Valentine's. Really, he's such a lovely man."

They hung up promising to get in touch soon.

She turned to Victor. "What do you think about getting a dog?"

He glanced up from his book, looked her over. "What brought this on?"

"Well, you know, I tried it once for a few days, it was nice having something warm and cuddly to take care of. The problem was, I was hardly ever home, but now I am."

He smiled and stretched, closed the book. "Feel like lunch? I need to get out, I've been sitting all morning."

"I would love a couple of meat pies from the French Hearth."

A chilly day with skies the color of shadow, pale clouds pushed west by careless winds. They drove across Siesta Bridge to the mainland and turned right onto Osprey Avenue, then right again, and parked in front of the small blue-canopied building.

Birdie recognized the back of Nicholas' dark head as soon as they entered the bakery. She tapped Victor's arm. "Be right back," she said.

She surprised him with her touch, he whirled around, smiled broadly when he saw her. She kissed his cheek, asked how he was doing.

"Beautiful," he said. "Everything's real fine. And you, how're you, Birdie?"

"We had the wedding, I'm married again."

He regarded her with serious eyes. "So you're not Birdie Noonan anymore."

"No, it's Bernadette Babel now," emphasizing the second syllable. "So, what're you doing today?"

He smiled shyly. "Waiting for someone. We just finished lunch," he glanced at his watch, "and have to get back to the office."

"Well I won't keep you, Nicky. Nice to see you."

He kissed her cheek, glanced over her shoulder, nodded solemnly. "You look beautiful, baby."

Victor had already ordered and found a table, she joined him. "I hope you didn't mind."

"He's doing better, I hope."

She picked up a pie, began to eat. "If you saw your ex-wife, would you talk to each other?" she asked after a moment.

He didn't answer right away. "We might say hello, but there wouldn't be anything to talk about after that," he said.

"Was it a friendly divorce?"

His mouth twisted. "I wouldn't say friendly, I think 'cold' would be a better description."

She stopped eating, looked past him. Nicholas was leaving the bakery with a young woman whose hand was on his arm, looking back over her shoulder at him. Her face was plain but pretty, extraordinary blue eyes framed by long dark wavy hair like Claire's, a classic straight nose and small, pale mouth.

Her heart squeezed momentarily, she looked at Victor. He said, "When you see your ex, how do you get along?"

She looked into his eyes. "We didn't learn to be friends until afterward. I think of him fondly and wish good things for him, but we're both in a better place." She leaned forward and kissed his mouth, smiled.

He wiped his hands with the napkin and said, "I don't think we're home enough to be able to have a dog, Birdie. And traveling with one could be complicated. I'd rather put it off for a while."

She nodded and looked away.

"Did you really want this? Is there a reason?"

She shook her head. "It's the silliest thing, it was a dog that someone at the bar couldn't keep and I volunteered to give it a home, on a trial basis. I don't know what made me do it, loneliness, I guess. But I liked it." She looked at him.

He smiled, leaned in and kissed her mouth. "We'll find something for you to do."

She was shocked by how much she missed him. The everyday closeness comprised of rising together each morning, seeing him bent over the desk in his small study, lovemaking at odd intervals, sharing dinner every evening, touching at every opportunity, all ceased abruptly when he left for Chicago, and her body went through withdrawal.

She stayed busy. She deep cleaned the kitchen, baked vatrushka buns, kulich, and pastila cake with tart McIntosh apples. She washed curtains, bed linens, rugs.

Late on the fourth night, the phone rang, it was Victor.

"You need to come home, now," she said. "I'm exhausting myself from cleaning and I think I'm four pounds heavier from eating vatrushka buns. There's no telling what I'll look like by the end of the week. Please save me."

He laughed, his voice was low and intimate. "I miss you too, Solnyshka. What are you doing at the moment?"

She paused. "I was just about to turn in for the night."

"And what are you wearing? This is so I can picture you in my bed. Alone, presumably."

She smiled. "I'm wearing your light blue shirt, I've been wearing it around the house all day."

He groaned. "I love you in that shirt. Do me a favor, don't put it in the laundry when you've finished with it."

"How are things going so far?"

"Pretty smooth except for a plane delay in D.C., there was a snowstorm. Sales are going well, meeting some nice people along the way. We fly to Birmingham in the morning."

"We?"

"Scott stopped in last night, he's going to Birmingham with me, he'll leave again after Houston."

"Don't be fooled by those pretty journalists Scott likes to hang out with, they just want to be in your next book so they can tell their friends. Remember what's waiting for you at home."

A low laugh. "I remember. You know my favorite memory? Our first night, you were the one who came to me, how could I ever forget that night?"

She smiled. "You'll still be back Wednesday afternoon?"

"Be waiting for me," he said.

She had dinner with her parents on Tuesday, they talked about the house in Palm Springs.

"We both liked it as soon as we saw it," she said. "You saw the pictures, you know what I mean, it's very simple, classic."

"The Sarasota School," said her father.

"What, you mean the architecture?"

He shrugged. "Carl Abbott and other men are doing those things here. They've been doing it for years. If you had wanted a house like it all you needed to do . . ."

Her mother laid a hand on his arm. "We will miss seeing you every Sunday," she said. "We have been spoiled having you around this long, but life brings changes."

Birdie toyed with her spoon. "How would you feel about working together, mother?"

"Bernadette, what do you mean?"

She looked up at them. "Victor and I thought maybe I could have my shop after all. It could be a joint venture. I'll be in Palm Springs a few months a year, while I'm there I could be buying merchandise. In the meanwhile, you would be here, running the shop until I return." She paused. "What do you think about that?"

Her parents exchanged a long look.

Her mother cleared her throat. "Well, I don't know, I think—"

Her father grinned. "I think, what are you waiting for?" he said.

Birdie laughed. "It was Victor's idea. It never occurred to me, but he said he would consider putting up half the startup money, Fa, if you would contribute the other half."

Her mother laughed. "A businessman! All this time, I've been thinking what a romantic man you married," she said.

Wednesday afternoon, Birdie had just begun dinner preparations when she heard the sounds at the front of the house, went to investigate. She opened the door and Victor was there, flowers in one hand, suitcase in the other.

She took the bouquet, kissed his mouth. "How sweet," she said. "I just started heating up the borscht—"

"Dinner can come later, I want you now," he said. Down went the suitcase, up went Birdie in his arms, off they went to the bedroom.

Two hours later, they were eating on the bed, buckwheat blini with red salmon caviar and sour cream, homemade borscht with short ribs, topped with sour cream.

"I think we oughta buy stock in sour cream," he said as he spooned up the last of the borscht and set the dish aside.

She laughed. "Maybe you should, it has vitamins. Might as well make money on it, too."

They made love again after the food was gone. The week of separation was over, they were giddy about being together, the celebration would last all night.

The next morning they rose early and walked to the end of the street to look at the gulf waters, he wanted to see them, said he'd missed the distinctive blue-green color. She hugged his arm, "All you have to do is look in the mirror," she said, "the gulf is in the color of your eyes."

He turned and kissed her mouth. "I think maybe you have a little bit of writer in you. How'd the proposal to your parents go?"

"They like the idea. It's up to you and Fa to go into details, but maybe when we return from Palm Springs we could start looking at storefronts."

"Are you excited?"

She nodded, looking in his eyes. "Having a partner makes a big difference. How did you know, Victor?"

He shrugged, ran his hands down her arms. "You're sociable, Birdie. The thought of spending days and nights sitting alone in a store left you cold but having someone you can bounce ideas around with and develop plans and ideas with, well, that's a different story."

"She won't be there all the time."

"True, but enough of the time. Anyway, I have a feeling she'll be there as much as you want her to be."

She smiled, she was shivering. "Let's go home, I need to get warm."

Birdie coughed repeatedly into the tissue and slumped back against the pillows. Victor entered the room carrying a paper bag, withdrew a prescription bottle.

"This is what the doctor ordered," he said.

She didn't ask what it was, her voice was gone anyway.

He sat gently on the edge of the bed. "It's bacterial pneumonia. He said if we had waited another day you'd be in the hospital."

She closed her eyes and listened, her breathing labored.

"You need to be a good girl and stay where you are," he continued, "while I feed you soups and juices, and these antibiotics."

Her hand shook as she reached for the pill, his hand guided the water glass to her mouth, then he drew the covers up and kissed her hair.

"Poor little girl," he murmured.

She made a faint noise, it was all she had the strength to do, then turned her head and closed her eyes.

When he slipped back into the room ten minutes later, her eyes fluttered open. "Vic," she croaked.

He sat next to her on the bed, smiled softly.

She coughed repeatedly into her sleeve. "While you . . . Casey called."

His eyes changed, he leaned forward. "Birdie? Man, or a woman?"

She breathed laboriously. "Girl." Closed her eyes, was silent.

He smoothed the hair away from her face and kissed her forehead, said lightly, "It's alright, nothing to worry about."

She was ensconced in a hammock in the back garden several days later, the sun shining warmly on her face, she had survived the worst of it and was no longer coughing up awful green globs from her lungs.

Georgette was sunning herself in a nearby lawn chair, reached for a tall iced tea, drank, and swished the ice around in her glass.

"What on earth happened?" Georgette asked. "I thought pneumonia was something our grandparents got, not us. I never even heard of what you've got."

"I was the same as you, thought I had a bad cold that wasn't going away," said Birdie. "Victor's the one who said something didn't seem right. If we had waited a few more days, he'd be collecting on my life insurance." She turned away and coughed roughly.

"You still don't sound good. You going to go ahead with the trip to California?" asked Georgette.

"We're postponing it a week, then we'll leave. Maybe it'll give me time to meet that new guy you mentioned."

"Oh now, Birdie, I knew you'd do that. Bring some poor guy up once or twice in conversation and suddenly he's the father of my children."

"Wow, Georgette, you let him get that far already?"

Georgette rolled her eyes. "See what I mean?" She hesitated. "It's weird, I feel this strange attraction to older guys lately. They've gotta be around forty or fifty to get my attention. I think since my birthday, I've started to tune in to the need for stability or something." She looked over at Birdie laying in the hammock, eyes closed, knees bent.

Birdie said quietly, "You think it has to do with that thing with your mother last year?"

"I dunno, Birdie, what can I do about it, anyway?"

"There are plenty of men in their forties and fifties who might be trying to recapture their youth with a pretty twenty-five year-old like you, Georgie, just be aware of that. We see them every day at the beaches and the bars, it can be tricky trying to sort the good ones from the bad."

Georgette said, "I think maybe it was that incident in the bar last year, it scared the crap out of me and I want to feel protected. Or maybe I'm tired of waiting and I just want to be rescued. I heard somewhere that eighty percent of women feel that way, only most of them don't know it."

Birdie bent forward and coughed. "All those women hanging out at the bar, Georgie, they're not all there because they like the taste of beer. 'Course, the same could be said about a lot of the men. Everybody's looking for something."

"You're one of the lucky ones, Birdie."

She coughed, cleared her throat. "I know that, Georgie."

It was their last breakfast with her parents before leaving for Palm Springs. Birdie had missed the past two weeks due to her pneumonia so there was plenty to catch up on. Family announcements always came first, Uncle Jack and Aunt Caroline's wedding anniversary was the following month in McLean, Virginia.

Birdie looked up from her tea. "Are you really thinking about going? Other family will be there."

Her father shrugged, her mother raised her brows, tilted her head. "Time, maybe, to show a little forgiveness. We're all getting along in years, who knows how much time anyone has."

Birdie met Victor's eyes across the table, looked away. She said, "You should take a lot of pictures, bring some back for me. I haven't seen them since I was a little girl, I have memories but they're hazy now."

"Jack used to carry you about on his shoulders," said her father. "You squealed with delight. Then, when I tried it, you squealed in terror." He laughed. "Something about Jack always inspired confidence."

Her mother smiled, said, "Jack was like that with everyone, very charismatic. Do you remember, Anton, the picnics we used to take with them along the James River in McLean. Caroline made such good tea cakes." She turned to Birdie. "You were a baby and went with us once, I have a picture somewhere . . ."

"I remember Aunt Caroline wore strong perfume, and great big coats," said Birdie. "She was always laughing. I wonder if she still does."

Her mother said to Victor, "Do you have anyone to remember your childhood with, Victor? Are there good memories?"

He said easily, "I have some good memories, sure. Picking piñon nuts on our hands and knees, the sound of coyotes singing in the night, the scent of roasting chiles wafting through the neighborhood. At Christmas, our family used to go skiing down around Albuquerque."

"Both your parents are still alive and well?" asked Fa.

Victor nodded, picked up his drink. "My mother paints, she did beautiful pictures of the New Mexico desert, now she paints Mexican landscapes."

"Speaking of art," said Birdie, "while we're in Palm Springs, I plan to look into the estate sales and auctions. What do you think, mother?"

Her mother was quick to respond. "You have a good eye, Bernadette. Why don't you focus on inventory, and I'll concentrate on the storefront and paperwork back here? We talked about a place south of Stickney Point Bridge so I'll keep my eyes open and see a realtor, maybe find out what the people at Elizabeth Lambie can do."

"What about a name for the place, have you thought about that yet?" asked Victor.

Birdie said, "I have no idea. Mother?"

Her mother smiled. "I had a couple in mind. I thought, maybe Authentique. But if not, maybe we could name the shop Yesterday's. How do you feel about that, Birdie?"

Birdie said, "Yesterday's has a nice sound, let's go with that."

Chapter Nine
March - May 1980

Birdie awoke to a dry sunny sky and a helicopter passing through, she could see the rotating blades as it flew low in the direction of Sunnylands. She stretched, looking at the clock. There was not another sound, no dogs barking, no cars driving past, no lawn maintenance crews, many residents had desertscapes. Their street was near the edge of the desert, no houses behind them.

"I'll make coffee," she announced, folding back the covers.

"Mmm," said the naked form next to her.

She smiled. She had fallen asleep listening to the faint sound of his typewriter pounding away late into the night, had no idea when he finally got to bed. Sometimes, when the words began to flow, he didn't stop and went on for hours, and even longer.

She went into the kitchen, started the coffee, showered, poured some and took it to him.

"It's nine o'clock, is it too early?" she asked.

He sat up, took the cup and drank. "Thank you, what about you?"

"I think I'll have tea, coffee doesn't appeal to me this morning. Would you like breakfast?"

He eyed her thoughtfully, drinking. "I'll wait a while, thanks. You're alright? No relapses, nothing like that?"

"No," she bent to kiss his head. "I'm going to check the paper, see if there are any auctions today."

She was still getting used to the geography of the city, kept a street map in the car and learned by getting lost. Once, looking for an auction, she made a wrong turn around Palm Canyon Drive and ended up winding along Highway 111, driving through the golf courses in Rancho Mirage.

There were no auctions, no places to get lost, she swam briefly in the pool then went inside for a cool drink and picked up her book, she was at the end of *Sophie's Choice*. When Victor came in the room to check on her, his expression changed.

"Birdie, what is it?"

She set the book aside and brushed her eyes. "So tragic, forced to choose between life and death for your children, how a mother could do it . . ."

He reached for her and kissed her hair. "Life is cruel sometimes, very cruel. I don't like to see you cry, Birdie, what can I do to cheer you up?"

She smiled against his side and sniffed. "Oh, I'm alright, just feeling a little weepy, I guess. How's the manuscript coming?"

"That's what I came to tell you. I'm at a stopping point, why don't we go out and do something? I need to breathe some fresh air, walk around and get energized."

She said, "I heard something about date palms, some sort of area around here where they make date shakes, it sounded different. Do you know anything about it?" She started to move out of the chair and he gave her a hand.

"I've heard something too, we'll find out," he said.

Half an hour later, the enormous highway sign rising before them, they turned off the road next to the shielded wooden centurion. For the next forty minutes they watched a film and toured the groves, learning about what was called 'the romance and sex life of the date,' which caused Birdie to giggle, but the film explained things in fascinating detail. The palms were very tall, about seventy feet, each fitted with a ladder so the date farmers could climb to the top and harvest the seeds of the male trees, which would afterward be sprinkled over the seeds of the female trees, another long climb up the ladder.

They left the building with date shakes in hand, returned to the car in the blinding afternoon sun.

"That was nice, but when we get home, I think I'll be back in the pool," she said. "It's hotter here than in Florida."

"Good idea, a swim will wake me up," he said.

It did, sort of. They swam a couple of lazy laps, stopped for a long kiss at the far end of the pool.

"All that talk about cross fertilization was kind of a turn-on," she said.

He kissed her neck. "Really. Maybe you're just easy."

She smiled. "Easier than a date palm in the Coachella Valley, that's for sure. You won't have to climb seventy feet to get to me."

He smiled, casually untied the strings of her bikini, then pulled down the bottom. The soft water flowing over her exposed skin felt cool and erotic. She removed his swim suit and let it float away, put her arms around his shoulders and her leg around his waist.

She caught his eye. "What would you like to do now?"

Her back was against the side of the pool, he kissed her mouth, gave a low laugh. "Pollinate you," he said.

She laughed, and he began the demonstration.

That evening, dinner at home, a simple meal that she prepared while listening to the Eagles' One of These Nights, she in the kitchen, Victor typing away in his study. When she called he came, groggy, frowning, running a hand through his hair, lost somewhere in the winter of 1939.

He complimented her linguini, picked at the salad, took the wine back with him into the study, the typewriter started again immediately. She smiled fondly, her husband, hard at work.

She phoned her parents after she was finished in the kitchen, they talked aimlessly for a few minutes, it was good just to hear their voices.

Then, her mother's voice, a little unsteady, "Bad news, I'm afraid. Bernadette, your Aunt Caroline passed suddenly . . ."

"What?"

Fa took the phone for a few minutes. "She had a stroke, daughter of mine. No one even knew she had a health condition. Your mother is very sad, we were going to see them you know, and delayed, we felt with the snow and ice it might not be the best time to try the cane."

"Oh, I'm so sorry, Fa. So very sorry."

Her mother was back on the line. "At least we talked to them a couple of weeks ago, at least . . . there's that."

"She knew how you felt about her," said Birdie, swallowing hard.

"Yes, there's that."

They went on to other things. The new help was doing well, her name was Antonella, she now came three days a week to do heavy housework, laundry, cook meals, her homemade pasta was very fine, and she was pleasant but not too familiar.

Birdie asked about a storefront for the business. They might have found one, they said, they would let her know when they were sure.

She relayed their greetings to Victor as they got ready for bed that night.

"I'm sorry about your aunt," he said.

"It was a missed opportunity to see her, I know my parents are regretful and will always regret it. Really, my parents are the only family I have, there are no aunts and uncles nearby, no brothers or sisters, I never had that growing up."

He put his arm around her. "You have me now. One day, we'll have a family of our own."

She pressed her ear against his chest, listened to his heart beating slow and strong. "I love you more every day," she said.

The next morning Victor told her he was going to Santa Fe. "Just a quick overnight trip, while I'm there I'll probably stop and see Amanda, make sure she hasn't burned anything down, then I'll be back," he said.

"Was this planned? I don't remember you mentioning—"

"The tax attorney called. He told me to make sure we don't do anything that would be construed as establishing residency in California, so we have to be careful and—"

"I don't understand, Victor, we're Florida residents."

"Yes, but the State of California is aggressive about taxes. If we do anything that gives an appearance of residency, next thing I know, I'll be paying the highest income tax in the country."

"What? That's crazy! We're both registered to vote in Florida, our cars are registered there, our home is there."

He nodded, "Yeah, but they make their own rules here. We have to document that our visits total less than six months a year, we shouldn't open bank accounts, and if we go somewhere for vacation we can't depart from here, they'd use those actions as supposed proof of residency. Owning this house is just a red flag to them. Anyway, I forgot to close out an old bank account in Santa Fe, I found it when I was going through our tax things for next month. I'm at a point in the manuscript where I need to get away for a day, rethink one of the characters. The trip will give me a chance to do that."

"Do you want me to go with you, Victor?"

He shook his head, "Sometimes I need the solitude, you don't mind, do you?"

She didn't like it but she understood. He flew out at nine forty-five, the return flight put him back in Palm Springs the following evening. She dropped him off at the airport, she had appointments of her own and an auction to attend. The day passed quickly and she arrived at the house late in the afternoon, phone ringing. She flew across the room, keys still in hand, to pick up before it stopped.

"Hello," she said breathlessly. It was the doctor's office.

Victor was back the next evening, he brought with him red and green chiles, said he had missed them.

She handed him his bourbon. "What do I do with them?" she asked.

He smiled. "I'll show you. There are dishes you make, you top them with the chiles. When the topping has both red and green chiles, it's called Christmas."

"Oh ho ho, very clever," she said. "Did you find what you needed, take care of the bank account?"

He looked down at his drink, "Yes, yes, everything's fine."

She hesitated. "Was Amanda around, were you able to see her?"

He lifted the glass, took a couple of swallows. "Yes, she was there, I stopped by her office on campus, she was in a hurry so I didn't stay long."

She was silent, watching his face. He blinked, looked away.

She rose and went to the cabinet, returned with a glass of wine.

He smiled. "Did I miss anything here?"

"Not really. Fa said they think they've found a storefront for the business, it's across from Crescent Beach Market, a very good location right by the Crescent Club. I had a good day yesterday, I went to an auction and bought some jewelry pieces at a great price."

He took a swallow of the drink, ice rattled in the glass. "It's starting to come together."

She nodded. "I worry about the timing, you know if things don't happen at just the right time, it can doom a project before it gets off the ground."

"Birdie, this is going to be good, better than good, you need to trust yourself. You know what you're doing, I've seen it in you."

She looked in his eyes, "You think so? I've never done anything like this, Victor. I know about the products, I know how to read people, but running a business is different."

"That's where your mother comes in, she helped to run your father's business, she'll teach you. You know, in the war, the soldiers, even the officers, didn't always have the proper training to know what to do beforehand. They knew about certain terrains, they knew human nature, had heard stories about other wars from their fathers, maybe they grew up hunting in the forests with older men in their families, that was battle preparation for some of them. Generals studied battle plans of their predecessors, what worked, what didn't."

He sipped more of the drink, set it on the table and leaned back.

"You're telling me that all of life is preparation."

"I guess I am, yes."

She smiled. "I never really wanted to be married, you know."

He grinned at her, "Looks like you took a wrong turn somewhere, Solnyshka."

She laughed. "I mean I didn't aspire to it. When I was growing up and my friends were playing with dolls and setting up little houses and things like that, I was off pretending to have adventures in the woods. While they were collecting pictures of wedding dresses, I was busy working my tail off."

"Are you . . .?"

"I'm not sorry about Nicholas, it prepared me for you. But you're truly the only one for me, Victor, and really, you taught me, oh . . ." her eyes watered unexpectedly and she dabbed at them with her sleeve.

He moved closer, said gently, "Hey, what's this?"

" . . . you taught me how to love in the long-term, for who we are now, for who we'll be in the future. Do you know what I mean?"

He raised her chin with his hand, kissed her mouth. "I think I do. I loved you the first time I saw you, and I can see who you're becoming. You've changed, Birdie, even in the last several months."

"That's good, Victor, because . . . because there's more of me to love now."

He kissed her again, "Well, you're very beautiful to me, especially lately."

She took his hand, pressed it to her abdomen. "Maybe I didn't say it as well as I should have."

He was very still. Their eyes met.

She smiled.

They kept it to themselves for a while. They hadn't made friends in their temporary city, lived just as anonymously as many of the other so-called snowbirds in Palm Springs, and they celebrated Birdie's announcement as an excuse for another honeymoon.

He took her to Don the Beachcomber's, the famous A-frame restaurant on Palm Canyon Drive with Tiki poles on both sides of the entrance. Inside, a Polynesian hodgepodge of flaming torches, tropical foliage, harpoons, grass matting, and paddles. She was delighted by the kitschiness of it all.

They had rumaki and crab puffs with their cocktails, she reminisced about a drink she'd been asked to make once, a request that came from the Beachcomber menu. "A Missionary's Downfall, I think it was called," she said, scrunching her brows. "Rum, fresh pineapple juice, lime, fresh mint, something else."

White uniformed waiters served them chicken almond, fried rice, mahi mahi, live piano music in the background. Fun, lots of laughter, clanging cutlery, people went there to be seen, a party kind of place.

Victor set the manuscript aside. One day they made a trip to the Salton Sea, where they picnicked near the shore. Another day they drove to Joshua Tree National Park, spent half a day hiking, took pictures of the tall ocotillo patches, the boulders piled high on the Mojave Desert, posed for smiling photos of each other, and saw a blacktailed jack rabbit as they were leaving the park near dusk.

He taught her to make green chili stew. They went to the market together and bought the pork and other ingredients, he roasted the chiles on the grill and they ate outdoors by the lap pool, watching the sun set. Afterward they went inside and Victor put an old Tony Bennett album on the turntable, they slow danced in the living room until she began to yawn and he led her off to bed.

"I'm not going to have these to myself much longer," he said, hands warming her breasts.

"It's only for a while," she said. "And I hear they get much bigger, you can pretend you're with Raquel Welch."

He said in the dark, "I don't want to be with her, she's not going to be the mother of my child."

She leaned closer and kissed his mouth long and slow, reached down and slipped off the last piece of his clothing. "I have a smart husband," she whispered, smiling.

He made reservations for dinner at Melvyn's one night, it wasn't too far from their house. He asked her to wear the chic black cocktail dress he had bought for her on their honeymoon.

She turned from the closet. "Are you sure?"

"Yes, I love that dress on you, do you mind?"

"Of course not, I love it too, I reminds me of Paris."

"There's another reason," he said. "I invited some people to join us."

She glanced over her shoulder. "We don't know anyone here, except for Sheryl the realtor."

"You'll see." He went to her, stood behind her and looked at their image in the mirror. "You are a beautiful woman."

She reached for the dress. "You're being mysterious. I kind of like it, it's like being in one of your novels."

She stepped into it, turned to be zipped. "Is the handsome diplomat going to step from behind the curtains and ask for help with asylum? Will the refugee ring our doorbell and beg for money to escape to Finland?"

He laughed, pulled upward on the zipper.

She brought out two pouches from the safe, produced necklaces and held them up. "Art Deco jade and diamond butterfly, or 65-carat oval jade link? I bought them for the store on Siesta Key. Which should I wear tonight?"

He pointed to the butterfly.

She added, "I hope this buying trip helps give credibility to our Florida residency."

He smiled. "Spoken like a true businesswoman."

They passed through the low white stone walls of the Ingleside Inn, gave their keys to the attendant, and entered the restaurant through the bar and lounge area. She watched him, his movements were hesitant, he had become very quiet.

"Victor, who are we meeting tonight?" she asked.

Their drinks arrived, she swallowed the liquid, it refreshed her dry throat. Here in the Sonoran Desert, it seemed her throat was always dry, or maybe it was the pregnancy.

He looked at her over the rim of his glass, took another swallow, placed the drink on the bar. "Pieces have been falling into place," he said. "Remember the raven that morning at the house in Santa Fe?"

She nodded, head tilted, meeting his eyes. He took her hand, kissed it, she looked up at a couple walking toward them.

"Oh my God," she said, a flush rose through her body. "That man is your father."

He looked over his shoulder, stood, and they were side by side, father and son, the older man had carefully combed thick silver hair, was tall, deeply tanned, had the same cool eyes as his son.

His mother was tall, too, her hair a beautiful white gold, worn long and secured back from her face with a large silver clasp at the nape of her neck. She was also very tanned, wore a blue and violet dress that accentuated the lean lines of her body.

They sat across from each other at dinner, a table lamp threw a warm puddle of light across their faces. Birdie listened while they talked softly, observed similarities in speech, gesture, articulation. There was a certain quiet formality to their demeanor, she wondered if it was good manners, or an unfinished component of their personal history which lay between them.

They talked in abstractions; weather, the terrain around central Mexico, the ease with which they had grown accustomed to living in the other country.

"Did it seem strange at first?" Birdie asked.

"It's a smaller, more rural area with fewer conveniences, but people are pretty much the same everywhere," said Madelyn, shrugging. "We just exchanged complexity for simplicity."

"Where is it, exactly?" asked Birdie.

"The nearest large city is Guadalajara, about 35 miles away," said Thomas. "Ajijic is on Lake Chapala, surrounded by the Sierra Madres."

"It's picturesque," added Madelyn. "Narrow cobblestone streets, painted houses, muraled buildings."

"It's very pleasant," said Thomas. "The temperature stays in the seventies, gets down to the fifties at night."

"Do you come back often to visit?" asked Birdie.

It was asked innocently enough. They both looked at their son.

"No," Thomas said finally, "I'm afraid we don't."

The tuxedoed waiter arrived, dinner was served and conversation resumed.

"I'm teaching her Southwestern style, but we're easing into it," said Victor.

"I love it, but it wasn't my tradition growing up," added Birdie.

"What was it then?" asked Thomas, slicing into the veal.

"Russian, my mother almost always cooked Russian dishes, so it's what I knew."

Victor looked at her, smiled. "Vareniki, syrniki, kotleti, and my favorite, blini with lots of sour cream."

She reached for her wine, they were in a low-ceilinged room near a fireplace, she could feel the heat doing a slow, uncomfortable spread through her limbs. She placed a hand to her cheek, then her neck. Victor's eyes followed her movements.

"That's a beautiful set you're wearing," she said to Madelyn, indicating the thick silver bracelet and earrings.

The woman smiled, "Thank you, they were a gift."

"Birdie is an expert on antique jewelry," said Victor.

Madelyn looked at her. "You know Mexican silver?"

"Slightly," said Birdie. She gestured. "I think those are Taxco silver, from south Mexico where most of it is mined."

"Yes, that's what I was told. The bracelet has a letter 'B' marking inside a circle, and a number beneath it."

Birdie took another swallow of wine, nodded. "Those are assay marks that tell who the artist was and the purity level of the metal. I think, but I'm not sure, that your artist was an American woman named Bernice Goodspeed. She was an anthropologist who settled in Taxco around the mid-thirties, she and her husband had a gallery where they sold pre-Columbian artifacts."

Victor signaled the waiter, he murmured a few words.

After the waiter left, Victor said, "Birdie is opening a gallery of her own when we return to Sarasota."

Thomas said, "Is that so? You certainly seem to know your stuff."

He turned to Victor, "Your books seem to be doing well, I see articles in the newspaper from time to time."

"Each book does a little better than the one before it. My editor wants me to produce a series, but it's not in my plans right now."

At Birdie's right side, a glass of ice water. She nodded her thanks, sipped gratefully.

"You get in any golf while you're here?"

Birdie looked up in surprise.

"No, I haven't played in years," said Victor easily. "What about you?"

His father shrugged. "I've started running, it's very freeing. Your mother's begun doing something called Tai Chi, with a group of friends."

"What is it?" asked Birdie.

"It's a series of thirty-seven movements performed like a slow dance, based on the Taoist principles of ying and yang, opposites."

"I've seen the group doing their meditation and it's remarkable, looks like a ballet," said Thomas.

"You still keep a garden?" asked Victor.

His parents exchanged a look. "We do," said his father.

Their waiter was removing plates and cutlery from the table. Madelyn turned to Birdie, smiled tolerantly. "We grow our own vegetables, and other herbs."

"I've started a garden, too," said Birdie.

Victor rolled his eyes. "They grow weed," he said to Birdie.

Madelyn said, "Actually, we've been experimenting with growing peyote as well."

His father cleared his throat. "Not much success, I'm afraid, we still have to go to Tamaulipas or Nuevo León to get it."

"What do you do with it?" asked Birdie.

"We take it for inspiration," said Madelyn.

Birdie smiled, amused.

Over coffee and dessert they described the effects of the hallucinogen. "Others add it to tea, but we've found that if we just chew the buttons with chocolate, the effects are so much faster," said Madelyn.

"What do they taste like?" asked Birdie.

"They're very bitter," said Thomas, "but five or six is all it takes. You have to eat them all at once. If you sample just a couple, you'll be too sick to your stomach to want to eat more. But after about half an hour, colors are brighter, sounds are sharper—"

"Everything is so much more profound and meaningful," said Madelyn, enthusiastically. "Really, it's an incredible ten hours, some of my best paintings were produced on mesc."

"Ten hours? That's a long trip," said Birdie.

She paused as a wave of dizziness swept over her, said, "Excuse me," and went in search of the powder room. She found it, entered and sat heavily on the lounge. After a few moments she rose, used the facilities, pressed cold water to her face with a towel and returned to the table.

Three faces looked up at her, Victor's hand reached out to hers.

"Sorry," she said. "I haven't been feeling quite myself, I don't know if Victor told you . . ." she looked at him, squeezed his hand.

"We're expecting our first child," he said.

His father immediately smiled, reached out to shake his hand. "That's wonderful news, congratulations to both of you."

His mother sat very still, then a small smile formed and she turned to Birdie. "This is a very special time for you. How kind of you to share it with us."

Later, at home, "A little forgiveness goes a long way," said Victor.

"I think that's true," said Birdie. "I forgive you for surprising me the way you did tonight."

He moved his arm, turned to face her. "I was getting ready to tell you when they got there, I had a little speech prepared. I'm sorry."

"I'll bet it was a good one."

"I called them when I was in Santa Fe. I'd been thinking about what your father said when we got engaged, how forgiveness and humility show what a person's made of. Then there were things I'd read when I was doing research for the book, about chaplains who were with the war criminals during the trials at Nuremberg."

"I didn't know about that," she said.

"I doubt most people do, it's one of the back stories that was never really told. It might have been too controversial at the time because it dealt with forgiveness." He paused. "It's a tricky question, where do you draw the line, how bad does someone have to be before you can say that what they've done is unforgivable?"

She said, "In our church, the priest has the power to forgive."

"Everyone seems to have different ideas about it." He shifted in the bed and continued. "But after the war, the U.S. followed the Geneva Convention and assigned a couple of army chaplains to tend to the religious needs of the Nazi criminals. I was astonished by that. If the concepts of grace and forgiveness could be extended to the worst of the worst, what about the situation between my parents . . ." he paused.

She reached up, touched his face with her hand.

"So I called, asked them to forgive me, and we spent a little time catching up on the last ten years," he said.

She turned in his arms, looked up at him. "You hadn't talked to them in all that time?"

He shook his head. "I don't think we intended it that way, but as time went on it just got easier to keep a sort of distance."

"Oh Victor, what a terrible thing, but you made it right."

"Not that they didn't do anything wrong, they did, but I wasn't blameless. Afterward, after we talked, something changed, I don't know exactly how. I remember a nun talking about a mystical feeling she had once after she prayed, and what she said stuck with me. I think . . . maybe it was like that for me." He stopped, was silent. "If I hadn't made the call, I wouldn't have been able to move into this next part of our lives with a good conscience."

"And your parents?"

"You saw them. Things will never be the same between us again, but maybe there can at least be peace."

She kissed his mouth. "I know it wasn't easy."

They were quiet for a time. She said, "I saw something like that when I was younger, my grandparents disinherited my mother because she married my father. There was a lot of anguish for her, on holidays she was lonely for them, I could sense it the way kids sense things. Since my father's family were left behind when he came here, he had no one, either. They became each other's family, they're everything to each other. Maybe that's why they're so close, maybe that's why you and I are so close, and why we take such care not to argue or to hurt. We're all we have in the world."

He tightened his arms around her. "Birdie, I'm happy about the baby and any other children to come, but you will always be more important to me, it will always be you first."

Her eyes became moist, she swallowed.

"They seem like lovely people, Victor. I'm sure they've missed you and were relieved to know how you are."

There was irony in his voice. "Oh, they already knew that, they've always stayed in touch with Amanda."

She closed her eyes, drew closer to him. "You will always come first for me," she said.

He went back to work on the manuscript, she attended auctions. One morning she got up, went immediately to the bathroom and threw up.

"I hope this is just a one-time thing," she said, returning to the bed after a short while.

"I love you," he replied, handing her ice water from the kitchen. "Maybe you'll laugh about it someday."

From her, a weak smile.

She began to nap for a while each afternoon, he began to wake her each day at four o'clock with tea, a new ritual for them. He sat next to her on the bed, they would talk about the day's progress on the book.

"What's today's history lesson?" she asked, leaning against him, drinking from her cup.

He paused, gathering his thoughts. "In March 1939, Slovakia became part of the German state and participated with Germany in the invasion of Poland. However, by summer 1944, the Slovaks were rebelling against the Nazis, and their government appealed to the Soviets for help. The Soviets had intelligence operatives in Slovakia who would coordinate the uprising and provide troop info. In fact, throughout 1943-44, the Soviets were already providing arms and leadership to them."

"The Nazis were aware of this?"

"Let's just say while the Soviets were drawing up battle plans, the Germans were using the time to fortify the region. Which brings us to the Carpathians."

He settled further against the headboard, set aside the tea. "Dukla Pass is in the Carpathian Mountains near the border of Poland and Slovakia, heavily forested, difficult terrain for tracked vehicles. The steep mountains meant communications had to be handled by radio and forward observers and not by wire. Artillery support was a problem because of concealment."

"If it was like that for the Soviets it must have been that way for the Germans, too," she said.

"The Nazis were already there," he said, "with their allies the Hungarians. The Soviets were going in with the Slovakians, moving quickly. They'd estimated an operation that would last only six days, but mountain and forest fighting is point blank, meaning hand to hand combat, high casualties. Instead of just six days, it took fifty days, at a cost of 70,000 men between them."

"What?"

"Nazi resistance was far better than anticipated, and they protected their flanks, a huge advantage. At one point in the fighting there was a hill that was taken and re-taken twenty times. It was the bloodiest battle of the Eastern Front. Military intelligence failed the Soviets, there were more and better trained troops than expected. The Soviets didn't ultimately succeed in aiding the rebels, the uprising had been quashed by the Nazis before they even arrived.”

She shook her head sadly. “Seventy thousand men. Each of those lives mattered to someone. Seventy thousand mourners.”

They left Palm Springs at the end of the month, arrived in Sarasota in the middle of a warm June downpour.

Birdie peered through the windshield, Osprey Avenue was flooding. Victor maneuvered the car to the stoplight, in a moment they would turn and cross the short bridge to Siesta Key. Even in a rainstorm the familiar landscape on the other side of the bridge was a welcome sight. She always thrilled at returning to the place that had captured her heart, and it skipped a beat when he turned right at their street sign.

The house was fresh, Georgette had taken good care of it while they were gone, no musty smells when they opened the door, no dust on the furniture. She had added a few grocery items to the refrigerator as well.

Birdie straightened and turned to Victor. “We’re good for tonight, no need to go out for anything.”

He said, “You want to drive down tomorrow?”

She nodded. “First thing in the morning.”

“I’m looking forward to it.”

She leaned into him. “So am I, it’s going to be a wonderful surprise for them. They’ve never been the type to pressure me. ‘When are you gonna get a job, when are you gonna get married, when are you gonna.’ And now that we’re going to give them a grandchild, I know they’re going to be overjoyed. It’ll be nice to see that look, you know?”

He kissed the top of her head. “We haven’t talked about names.”

“Why don’t we each make a list and compare them?”

“Anything off limits?”

She considered. “What’s your ex-wife’s name?”

He laughed. “Karen.”

“My daughter won’t be named Karen, and if it’s a son he won’t be Nicholas, how’s that?”

Chapter Ten

June - August 1980

Birdie was showing, but not as much as she thought she should. "Is this normal?" she asked her mother. "I've gained thirteen pounds, I should have gained more by now." She was taking vitamins, walking the beach several days a week, continued to nap every afternoon.

Her mother was reassuring. "Bernadette, you're just anxious, you'll gain more weight, you'll see. Your doctor hasn't said anything, has he?"

Well, no.

Birdie finished tying price tags to the new pieces, added them to the vertical display case and locked the door, tucking the keys into the desk behind the counter.

"Looks very nice," observed her mother.

"I'm glad we decided not to put all the new inventory out at once," said Birdie. "Better for customers to see different items each time they come in."

Birdie's mother had efficiently done the work required to turn the empty storefront into an attractive showplace. Location was prime, situated across from Crescent Beach among well-established entities, the Crescent Beach Market, Anna's Deli, Davidson's Drugs, and the Crescent Club. Kira and Birdie propped open the front and back doors and sat at the counter in the middle of the store, greeted customers as they walked through, chatted in a friendly way, asked where they came from.

Business was increasing, they instituted a three-month layaway plan for residents of the key. By the end of the sixth week, sales of furniture and jewelry were rising incrementally, aided by an ad in the Pelican Press.

At night, Victor massaged cocoa butter onto her belly and they made plans. If it was a boy, this, if it was a girl, that, if it was twins, well, it wouldn't be.

"Twins don't run in our family," said Victor. "Do they run in yours?"

"I don't think so, I'll have to ask mother and Fa. But Victor, the thing that's really worrying me is . . ."

His hand stopped moving, he looked up at her. "What."

She rubbed her forehead.

"Are you alright?" he asked.

"Just a slight headache, I think I got too much sun today," she said.

"You had a headache the other day, too," he observed.

She closed her eyes. "I don't remember. Anyway, I've been thinking about all the pain that's going to come. You know how I am, I could barely stand that iron shot they gave me, how am I going to handle childbirth?"

"In fairness, that was a monstrous needle. I felt sorry for you when I saw them do it. That bruise on your beautiful behind is going to be there for months."

"Victor, I think I'd like to be on drugs when the time comes. I know it's a big deal to have natural childbirth, but I just don't think I'm strong enough for it, I'm sorry."

He took her chin in his hand. "What are you apologizing for? I wish I could spare you the pain, but I'll do whatever I can to help relieve you of some of it."

"Thank you for understanding."

"Although, I've heard women in other countries just stoop in the fields to deliver and then continue with their farming as if nothing happened. I don't know why I couldn't have married someone like that instead of such a delicate little flower—"

"Victor!"

He laughed, kissed her mouth.

Finally she was gaining more weight, four pounds since a week ago.

Kiki and Georgette took her to lunch at the Greenhouse. After their waitress left they commented on the changes.

"You've very glow-y," said Georgette.

"That's a tan, silly," said Birdie. "I've been walking the beach a lot."

Kiki's eyes went over her. "I've heard you should remove your rings around this time, darling. Saves them the trouble of cutting them off if your fingers get too swollen."

Birdie placed her napkin in her lap, said crankily, "Well, I've gained a few pounds. I'm supposed to, I'm pregnant."

Kiki and Georgette exchanged a look across the table.

"Of course, darling," said Kiki smoothly. "And your hair looks beautiful. Who's cutting it for you these days?"

Conversation during lunch centered around Georgette's new boyfriend, a man she'd met while jogging through her neighborhood one day.

"Jogging? I didn't even know you did that," said Birdie.

"It's a recent thing," said Georgette, spearing a shrimp from her salad. "It relaxes me."

"Why do you need jogging to relax you when you have Eric?" said Kiki.

Georgette smiled. "Eric is what keeps me in shape, which helps my jogging."

Kiki laughed. "Touché."

"Tell me about him," said Birdie. "Is he from around here?"

"No, he came from Jacksonville a few months ago. He retired from the navy, now he's looking for a small boat to charter out of the marina downtown."

"He's gorgeous. Tell her, Georgie," said Kiki.

Georgette looked at Birdie and took a sip of water, winked. "Perfect age," she said. "Forty-four. Medium height, wide shoulders tapering off to a small and perfect ass—"

"Georgette, I'm not—"

". . . and an angelic face. Blond hair, green eyes that look at you like he's never done a bad thing in his life."

"Does he make you laugh, Georgie?"

"He sure does, Birdie."

"Well, that's a good start," said Birdie as the waiter began removing plates. "But how can he be only forty-something and retired? That doesn't sound right."

"He told me that's how they do it in the military. After you've done it for twenty years, you can retire. That's why he wants to start a charter business."

"You ever follow up on finding a way to work with animals?" Birdie asked her.

There was a long pause.

"Oh, that was just me talking," said Georgette. "Just dreaming."

Birdie gave her a skeptical look.

"Dreams have a funny way of happening," Kiki said, "if you work at them."

Birdie rose and excused herself to use the powder room, a wave of dizziness swept over her and she sat again, waited for the feeling to subside.

Georgette went with her. "I don't want to be responsible to Victor if anything happens to you," she said as they made their way to the lounge.

"How are you doing lately with the . . . I'm sorry, I've forgotten the name."

"Crohn's." Georgette leaned against the counter washing her hands. "Most of the time I'm okay. And then one day, surprise, I'm in pain and have to cancel plans or miss work because I need to be near a bathroom. It's a bummer."

"You seem okay now, I'm glad."

"Yeah, I try to be good about what I eat. I'm better off if I stay away from certain vegetables, tea, spices, and booze. I really hate that last one." She made a face.

Birdie nodded sympathetically. "You look thinner."

Georgette smiled briefly. "Well, there's the jogging, but when I have an episode of the disease I get tired, lose my appetite, get dehydrated, and there's weight loss."

"I'm really sorry, Georgie, it's been a tough year for you."

"Well, you know, Eric seems to understand, so maybe things are looking up."

Birdie looked in the mirror to check her eye makeup, there were smudges underneath her eyes. As soon as she got home she would take a nice, long nap.

As soon as she got home she threw up, went to bed but couldn't sleep. When Victor reached home he found her curled with her hands pressed to her side, flushed and in pain.

"Birdie, how long have you been here like this?" he exclaimed, sitting beside her.

She shook her head, grimacing. He picked up the phone and dialed the doctor's office, spoke sharply, listened.

They went to the hospital, the doctor met them in the emergency room, examined her and ordered tests before meeting with Victor and Birdie back at the bedside.

"Preeclampsia," he said, without preamble.

There was a short silence. Finally, from Victor, "What is it, and what can be done about it?"

"Blood pressure's 156 over 94. You said you've been having headaches," he said to Birdie.

She nodded weakly.

"That's the reason, high blood pressure will cause headaches. I noticed your weight, you said you gained four pounds since last week, it's likely fluid retention." He looked down at the chart in his hands. "There's a high level of protein, low platelet count, all the signs are there."

He looked up, set aside the chart and removed his glasses. "We don't know why this happens, but you haven't done anything wrong," he summarized. "The problem occurs around the third trimester, usually after week twenty-five or so and here you are, week twenty-nine, right on schedule."

Birdie reached for Victor. "Is this going to stop?" she asked in a small voice.

Dr. Farley smiled briefly. "We can control it, you need to be very careful. You're not far enough along yet to deliver so here's what I'm going to do. We just gave you the IV of mag sulfate to lower your blood pressure, I'm going to follow that up with a prescription medication that I want you to take every morning so we can get it back to normal. If you still get an occasional headache, you can take aspirin but nothing else."

He reached for the chart and began writing while he talked. "Watch your salt intake, and no alcohol, none. I also want you on bed rest, no spring cleaning, no exercise programs."

The pen stopped, he looked up. "Last, I want to see you in my office twice a week. This is serious, we're going to get you through it by being cautious. What are your questions?"

Victor said, "What . . ." and stopped short.

The doctor waited, said gently, "This is not what you expected, I understand. It's your first child, right? I remember our first child, the same thing happened for us." He laid a hand on Victor's shoulder. "Make your plans, Mr. Babel, this is a joyous time. We'll go through this together."

He pushed aside the curtain, called for a nurse as he walked toward the nurse's station.

Birdie swallowed and looked at Victor. "You know this was all part of a plot to make you my servant, don't you?" she said. "Every time I want a drink, or a massage, or the window opened or closed—"

He smiled, sat on the bed and kissed her hand. "I'm already your servant," he said lightly. "Now, let's get out of here." He looked around. "Where's that nurse."

She removed her rings, explained to Victor that Kiki's suggestion made sense, she didn't want to risk damaging her most valued possessions. She wore them on a chain around her neck, looked forward to placing them back on her finger after the baby was born.

Her parents were in Michigan, they visited the following week. Her mother came into the bedroom, gathered her in her arms, held her silently against her cheek. After a moment she drew back, put her hand to Birdie's chin, said, "You are stronger than you know, darling. You always have been."

"I'm a little scared, mother."

"I was, too, when I was pregnant with you, at all the things that could go wrong. Some things did go wrong, Bernadette, but it's part of life, the part that makes you stronger. Do what Dr. Farley tells you to do and say your prayers, you can't do more than that."

"Mother, if anything should happen—"

"Oh, now, Birdie—"

"Please, if anything happens, he hasn't had an easy life. You and Fa mean so much to him. You'll—"

"That's enough," her mother said firmly. "What is this? All you have is a little high blood pressure."

"I have a bad feeling, mother, a premonition. There was a dream—"

"I'm going to go and make breakfast, I'll send Victor to let you know when it's ready." She left the room abruptly and Birdie lay, feeling alone and distraught, until Victor appeared after a while, smiling, tender.

"Time for breakfast, Solnyshka." He placed his hand on her abdomen, looked at her.

"Does it hurt when it kicks?" he asked.

"Not really, it feels like something swishing inside," she said, and smiled.

Her father broke into a wide grin, greeted her with open arms when she entered the living room.

"Our beautiful gardener," he said. "I have just been telling your mother how proud I am of your tomatoes."

"A little neglected lately, I'm afraid," said Birdie. "Victor takes care of them for me, but he doesn't enjoy digging around in the soil like I do."

"It's true, your vegetables miss you, Solnyshka," said Victor.

"I'll put a little fertilizer around them before we leave, that's all they need."

"Thank you, Fa."

"In another seven weeks or so, you'll be back in your garden, Birdie, pulling up strawberries and wishing the sun wasn't so strong," said her mother, passing the blintzes.

"I miss walking the beach," said Birdie, "and I miss bicycling."

"You'll miss sleeping, after the baby is born," said her mother.

"Have you decided what my grandchild is going to be called?" asked her father.

Birdie sipped her tea and looked at Victor, smiled.

Victor cleared his throat. "We don't know what it's going to be, of course," he began, "but if it's a girl, we think, Johanna. And we like Anton for a boy."

Her father was silent, then he swallowed. "That would be an honor," he said simply. His eyes filled and he dabbed at them with his sleeve. "A great honor."

Birdie was half asleep a week later when the doorbell rang. She glanced at the clock but it was blurry, rose on an elbow, heard murmured voices and the soft thud of the door as it shut. An engine started. She waited, but there were only the sounds of the birds outside the open windows, the red-bellied woodpeckers picking in the trees.

A while later Victor entered with tea, smiled when he saw she was awake.

"Are you hungry, my sun? I went to the French Hearth and picked up the apple pastries you like. Maybe some strawberries?" He bent to kiss her.

"That sounds fine, Victor, thank you. Who was at the door?"

He was helping her out of bed. "The door? Oh, some legal docs for me." He held up her wrap. "I'll be back with breakfast when you're ready."

She bathed and changed, felt refreshed, he was waiting for her when she returned.

"Kiki is going to try and visit this afternoon," he said. "A rare day off and she wants to see how you're doing."

"I feel like I haven't seen her in years," said Birdie. She broke off the tip of the turnover, warm apple filling flooded her mouth.

He smiled. "This will all be over soon."

She smiled back at him. "I know. I'm glad we took care of the baby's things when we did, before I was so confined."

He nodded. "Nothing left to do now except make sure you stay well."

She set the tea down suddenly, leaned back on the pillows. "I feel so helpless, Victor, all I do is sit around. I've always been active and independent, and—"

"And you will be again," he said. He left the chair and sat beside her on the bed, took her hands. "This is an adjustment, a reminder that that some of the best things in life come with a struggle. But we'll get through this, Birdie, we're good at being there for each other."

She closed her eyes, fought to control her emotions. "I know," she said. "I know, I guess I just need to be reminded lately, I'm sorry."

He kissed her mouth. "A treat tonight, I nearly forgot to mention it, your mother's bringing dinner. She said she's not staying, she has to get back to your father."

She smiled. "You were right about bringing my mother into the shop, she's perfect for it."

"She's in her element. I stopped by a couple of days ago and it looked good. There were a couple of serious buyers so I didn't stay."

"She was the backbone of Fa's business, ran it for over twenty years."

"I believe it," he said. "When the time is right and you're ready to step back in, I think you're going to want to name the shop after her."

She laughed. "Kira's Attic. Sure, why not?"

Kiki was offhanded and cheerful, full of gossip and chatter later that afternoon.

"Oh darling, you look awful!" she exclaimed as she entered the room. "What has Victor been feeding you? Well, never mind, after the birth you'll be back to your usual lissome self, and if nothing else, the baby will get you running and back in shape."

"Kiki, I've been having a little trouble sleeping, and you're not used to seeing me with an extra twenty pounds. Umm, aren't you here to cheer me up?"

"You've always been a funny sort of girl. Remember John, tall, blond, I think I saw you flirting with him once at a party."

"Well of course I remember, you went to London with him."

"He's gotten himself *engaged*! Can you believe it? To some girl from Oklahoma whose father owns a cattle ranch out in the middle of Nowheresville

Birdie smiled. "He's not going out there to live, is he?"

"I have no idea, he was practically swooning with happiness last time I saw him, the big goof."

"You want your friends to be happy, don't you, Kiki?"

"Well, of course I do, Birdie, but I'd rather be the reason."

"How's Gene?" Birdie said, not-so-subtly.

Kiki smiled. "Wonderful. You know, he's been hinting around lately."

She couldn't sleep, felt restless, her back was aching so badly she rose awkwardly from the mattress, went to the chair at the foot of the bed, found no comfort there. She glanced at Victor's sleeping form, walked out of the bedroom down the hall to the living room and stood at the window looking out in front of the house. All was still, silent.

The porch light was on at the house across the street, its warm glow met the tranquil black of the surrounding night, obliterating the stars overhead. She let the drapes fall back in place, massaged her back and turned. Tea, she would make some tea.

While she waited for the brew to steep, she wandered the house. Many of Victor's Hawaiian pieces had been replaced with antique furniture from her condo, now the house had a subtle Asian look. She punched down pillows, peeked in his study, switched on the lamp and sat in the chair behind his desk, swiveled around. She picked up a framed photo that had been taken at the museum a year ago, the wind ruffling the waters of Sarasota Bay behind them, scattering her hair, Victor laughing. It was a good picture and she smiled fondly.

She remembered her tea and hurriedly replaced the picture, in her haste swept a sheaf of papers to the floor. She got up, went slowly to her hands and knees to retrieve them, a large legal envelope caught her eye and she stopped. A mixture of curiosity and dread began to creep through her body, a dull hum that began in her spine and made its way up to her ears.

By the time she finished reading, tea forgotten, backache raging again, light was creeping through the edges of the curtains at the windows. She lifted her head, listened as his footsteps grew louder.

"Birdie?" Victor stood in the doorway, his eyes scanned the desk.

"I couldn't sleep," she said. "I . . ."

He was motionless, staring at her hands. His gaze rose to hers.

"What is this, Victor?" she said. "What is this lawsuit from California?"

He swallowed. "I'm going to make tea," he said, and disappeared.

They sat together on the bed, he had fussed at her for disobeying doctor's orders but her mind wasn't on what the doctor wanted. The tea rested on the table beside her but she wasn't thirsty for tea, she thirsted for the truth.

She put a hand to her head, still sleepy but restless, said wearily, "Victor, if I can't trust you, I haven't got anything." She didn't look at him as she spoke.

"Birdie, you don't mean that." He took her chin in his hand and turned her face toward his. "I didn't want to upset you, it's been a difficult time and I didn't want to make things worse."

"What could be worse than finding your husband's cheated on you?"

He stared at her. "That's what you think? Oh God, Birdie, that's not true. That's not what happened."

She closed her eyes and rubbed her head. "Then why don't you explain it, my eyes are a little blurry and I . . . nothing's making sense—"

He grasped her shoulders. "Birdie, look at me, are you feeling alright?"

She tilted her head back. "I'm tired, Victor, and I don't understand."

"Did you take your medicine this morning?"

"Uh, I don't think, is it time . . ."

He got up and got the medicine for her and after he had watched her take it, said gently, "Solnyshka, you know I have never been unfaithful. That document is . . . it pains me to say it. My ex-wife, the one from college. She apparently read about me and figured out I made a good life for myself after we divorced. It also seems she got pregnant during the time we were together but didn't tell me. She's suing me for child support, going all the way back to his delivery expenses."

Birdie tilted her head, looked at him. "What?" she asked, finally. Incredulously.

His eyes roamed her face. "There's a thirteen year-old boy."

She said slowly, "Is the child yours, Victor?"

He didn't respond right away. "It's my blood type," he said after a moment. "I lied to you about the trip to Santa Fe, Birdie. I also went to Los Angeles. To see him. I'm sorry."

She closed her eyes momentarily, took a deep breath. "What exactly do they want?"

He shrugged. "She wants money, a lot of it, but I have a good attorney. I didn't want you to know because you have enough on your mind, we have our child to look forward to."

"You already have a child, Victor. With someone else!"

He took her arms, gripped them hard. "Listen to me, Birdie, and listen well. I have no connection to them other than the tissue I donated. I was responsible and I'll pay, but he made it clear that he's not interested in having me around and it's also clear that she's using him. I wasn't informed thirteen years ago, and the only reason I'm being informed now is for the most sordid reason, money."

"Does she have anything valid against you?"

"No," said emphatically. "When I realized her true nature back then I divorced her. I told you that before."

She looked at him. "Is that who called when you were away? Casey?"

He scowled. "Her name is Karen Carpenter but she uses her initials, KC. I don't know how she learned our number but I told my attorney if she contacted me again, she should be served with an injunction."

She leaned back against the pillows. "Victor, I didn't mean what I said earlier, I'm sorry. And I'm sorry they hurt you with this. You have a son, it's something that should be celebrated, not fought over in court."

He hesitated, in his eyes there was sorrow. "On the way there, I was asking myself some pretty hard questions." He shrugged. "I couldn't have lived with myself if I hadn't gone to meet him. Maybe one day we'll have a son and it will be the way things should be, not like this."

"Please don't leave me in the dark from now on, Victor."

He kissed her mouth. "The doctor said it's bad for you to be worried or upset. Forgive me, I did it because I wanted to protect you."

"I love you," she said.

He took her hand, she blanched.

"What," he said.

She felt a tremor, put a hand to her abdomen.

"Is the baby kicking?" His voice was quiet, tentative.

She didn't respond, she saw his mouth move but couldn't hear him.

"Birdie?"

She clawed at his hand and cried out as the first convulsion seized her body.

He reached across her for the phone. His hand was shaking.

The delivery room lights were too bright, the gurney railings cold, the padding not thick enough, she wanted time, more of it, she wasn't prepared. She was surrounded by people in masks talking loudly to one another. The same people spoke to her in warm, measured tones. *Where was Victor?*

A crippling, contorting pain spasmed through her and she screamed his name.

He was there at last, leaning above her in the room, smoothing the hair back from her face. He smiled, said, "Hello."

She was drowsy, all the pushing and breathing and the pain. "Victor." She groped for his hand. She wanted him to climb up on the bed with her but knew somehow that he wouldn't be allowed. She remained silent.

"She's beautiful. Johanna."

She smiled weakly. "Um-hmm, I love you."

"Thank you for going through all that for me," he said. "I love you, Birdie, you're going to be alright now."

"She's alright, isn't she?"

He brushed her cheek, kissed her mouth. "She's fine, Solnyshka, small but perfect. They'll bring her back in a few minutes, I think. You were a little out of it, they wanted to give you time to rest. How are you feeling now?"

She swallowed. "Tired. Please don't leave me, I felt so alone back there."

He hesitated, lowered the railing, sat on the bed with her and put his hands on her arms. "Is this better?"

She smiled, sat forward gingerly, leaned into him. "Thank you, you knew what I needed."

"Your parents are on the way, Birdie, I called them just before I came in."

"Okay. You told them it's a girl?"

"I did, I got caught up in the excitement."

"Victor, it's alright. You're her father, you're entitled."

He held her away from him, looked in her face. "And you're a mother. You're going to be great at this."

She smiled up at him. "With you, I—"

There was a brief knock on the door as it swung open, a nurse stepped in carrying a small tray. She looked at the two of them as she made her approach.

"Mr. Babel, I'm afraid we can't have that," she said firmly. "Those railings must be kept up."

Victor slipped off the bed, smiled guiltily at Birdie.

"First things first, I need to take your blood pressure," said the nurse. She attached the cuff around Birdie's arm and placed the stethoscope inside, pumped and listened. When she was finished, she frowned, said, "How are you feeling, Mrs. Babel?"

"Okay."

"I'm going to give you your meds, just like you were taking at home, and shortly they'll be bringing your daughter in. Congratulations, by the way."

Birdie smiled, drew a breath, paused.

The nurse studied her face, reached for her wrist. "Mrs. Babel?"

Her face began to twitch. "I . . . I . . ."

"Bernadette!" The nurse's voice was clipped.

She tried to look toward Victor, jerked involuntarily, felt a strange, warm panic take over her body. She wanted to cry out but couldn't form the words, her mouth was producing too much saliva and it was salty and it leaked down her chin.

The nurse reached above her head and pulled down an oxygen mask, clamped it over Birdie's face. She picked up the phone. "Code white!" she cried loudly.

She dreamed she was at the gulf, the water was crystal clear when she looked down, it lapped at her feet and felt warm and soothing. She walked the shoreline alone, the sun was bright, so bright that it hurt her eyes, where were her sunglasses? She must have left them behind in her bag.

She turned back and saw Claire sitting on the towel, waving to her, looking like her old self, eyes clear and untroubled, Birdie knew without being told that this was before. There was a child at her side, she was playing with the seashells, turning them over in her hands the way Victor had done that first magical night they were together. Her head was bent, when she looked up Birdie could see the blue-green eyes framed by light hair, she laughed a delighted child's laugh. Birdie tried to walk closer but couldn't make progress, the air in front of her was dense, like an invisible wall.

And then, nothing. Gliding on a whisper.

"She's aware of what's going on around her, so speak normally," said Dr. Farley. "She can hear you, she just can't respond."

"Do you know how long this will go on?" asked Kira.

"No, unfortunately, we do not. We're monitoring her brain activity, we know in cases like this, which are rare, incidentally, that coma is not usually long, usually a few hours."

"You've handled this sort of thing before?" asked Anton.

"Yes, I have, and I know it's not easy. Never easy."

"But it's been two days."

"I know, Mr. Babel, I wish I could give you something more definitive but I cannot. She does not appear to have suffered brain damage or trauma to her vital organs. We're giving her medication to prevent further seizures. She delivered a healthy baby. Those are very good signs indeed. If this goes beyond another few days we'll move her from ICU to a private room. In the meanwhile, continue to spend time with her. She's young, and beyond the blood pressure issue, is in good health, so hang in there."

Pain hovered in the air, danced around her bed, ghosts whispered in her ear; Tommy from the Crescent Club in his faded khakis, Aunt Caroline in her big coat blowing down from the north, Claire with her dripping wrists. She sighed and moaned, her back ached, a familiar voice called to her from a distance, "Miz Birdie, you're too kind fer that." She felt a detached sadness for the times she had not, would never respond. She told the ghosts no, they faded away, then an onrush of memories; the owl that flew overhead the night she lost her virginity, the way her science teacher looked at her when she didn't have the answer, the clink-plop when her car keys fell into the sewer drain, the bitter taste of wine at communion, the feel of his hand in her hair.

First, silence, infinite and deep. After a while, voices.
Victor's was worried. She had never known him to worry.
"Birdie, I know you can hear me. Our daughter is fine but they're keeping her here for a few days for her lungs. Birdie please wake up, I miss you and I need you to come home with me. Solnyshka . . ." Warm mouth that lingered on hers, trembled on her cheek.
"Birdie? This is Georgie, I . . . hope you can hear me. Listen, Birdie, this is all a big shock, you know? I mean, who goes into a coma after having a baby. Your parents, they look a little stunned, but Victor, oh geez, Birdie, he's wrecked. I don't think he's slept a wink, your mother's making him eat right now. Listen, I miss you, but if I had someone like that waiting for me, I wouldn't waste a minute, know what I mean? And Birdie, she's beautiful, you did good."
"Can you hear me, Bernadette, are you . . . are you listening? Darling, she's the perfect combination of you and Victor. You must be strong for your daughter now, she needs her mother. Do you remember that day long ago when we first came here, and you said you loved the sun and the water so much you would never leave? Well, you did better than that, Birdie, you married a wonderful man who gave you a world of love. Birdie, you have to be strong now, you hear? Because he needs you too, very much."
"Anton, say something, she should hear her father's voice."
"Daughter of mine . . ." And something she had never heard before, the broken sound of her father weeping.
"Anton, my dear, please, we need to keep her spirits up."
"She's still my little girl."
"Come now, Anton, we have to be brave for her."

The silence that followed their departure was cold, like a frost. Birdie had never liked cold, even when wrapped in long, fur-collared coats in Michigan.

". . . miracle, Lord, that's what I'm askin', not for me but for those who depend on her now. The gift of time, Lord, a lifetime of memories, the chance for that baby girl to get to know her mother. Reach down from heaven and return his wife to him, and return our . . . our cherished friend to us. Not for my sake, but for . . . but for his. Please."

A kiss, light as a sigh, on her forehead.

A door opened and closed.

"Nicholas." *Nicholas?*

"Victor. I'm so sorry about all of this."

"Thanks for coming by."

"I hope you . . . well, when her parents told me . . ."

"No, of course not, she'd like knowing you were here for her."

"Well, thank you, Victor, I appreciate that. I'll be goin' now but if you need me, I'll do anything. Anything. You take care, you hear?"

Nicky?

The olive and eucalyptus trees. She saw the spreading branches in the back yard of their home, could smell them even where she was, between the sky and the desert floor. She breathed deeply and tried to touch them, wanted to feel the hard texture of the thick leaves between her fingers, but was hovering too high overhead, too far from the pool where they had once made love with such joyous abandon. Had she been pregnant then? She couldn't remember, it was a lifetime ago.

"Birdie," a voice in her ear from far away. "Free-as-a-bird, our daughter is here, I wanted her to know her mother. We need to spend some time getting to know each other, so here we all are."

A warm pressure against her side, an unfamiliar little bundle that made mewing noises.

"You're going to be the best kind of mother, Solnyshka, I know because you're the best kind of wife. I knew it the morning we talked on your lanai. I had come to you the night before, remember? I had something to tell you but I had to have a few drinks to get up the courage, and I overdid it and lost my nerve. You didn't turn me away, you took me in. You know what day that turned out to be? You'd remember this, Birdie," a short laugh. "John Paul II was elected the same day."

"We talked the next morning about touch, do you remember? Did I ever tell you how I missed you when I was away on the tour, physically ached for you? How I yearned for you those months when we broke up? Please come back to me, oh God, Birdie, I miss you so . . . so badly."

She wanted to reach out and touch him but could not. Instead, she touched him inside, spoke to him from where she lay, pleaded with him to give her time, she was so tired, she needed rest, had been through so much and loved him more than anyone or anything she had ever known. She lay on the bed and thought it and willed it and loved him, and gave her thoughts wings.

Day seven. The nurse turned her from her side to her back, fluffed the pillows and smoothed the sheets. She checked her vitals and notated them on the chart.

Victor rose from the chair at the corner of the room. "Any change?" he asked.

"No, but there hasn't been any deterioration, so that's good," she said, giving him a glance. "Have you been downstairs for breakfast yet, sir?"

"I have, thank you."

"I'll be going then, call me if you need anything."

She left without a backward glance and he stepped up to the bed, took Birdie's hand, leaned down and kissed her mouth. "Good morning," he said.

Her mouth twitched.

His eyes carefully scanned her face. "Birdie," he said in a low voice.

"Mmm."

A short silence.

"Birdie, wake up," he said, "time for breakfast."

" 'Kay," she whispered faintly. Her eyelids fluttered.

He bent forward, laid his head on her chest, and began to cry.

Chapter Eleven
September – November 1980

Sunday breakfast after the christening was bittersweet for Birdie. She sat and watched the others talking, held Johanna in her lap and knew that Sunday mornings would never be the same again.

Her father laughed as he told a story about his early days in Detroit, the challenges of learning construction in a new culture, the various people and languages and misunderstandings.

That's me, that's what I'm going through right now. Foreign territory.

She looked across the table, her mother was watching her. She smiled and passed the child to her mother's waiting arms. In exchange, her mother would pass on to her the wisdom she had accumulated from the years spent raising her. It would be like this from now on, she knew. Life coming full circle.

Her mother smiled, held the baby over her shoulder. "This brings back memories, doesn't it, Anton?"

He laughed. "It's been a journey, twenty-nine years."

Birdie said, "Nothing like the journey you made from Europe to here, Fa. After that, everything else must seem easy."

Victor said, "I've never had to experience anything like that, a new country, taking on a new language, new ways, it took a great deal of courage. What made you do it?"

Her parents shared a long look across the table.

"He's one of us, Anton," said Kira. "You really should tell him."

Her father turned to Victor, shrugged. "So maybe it's time," he said. He poured more vodka into their glasses and leaned back, looked at the younger man, nodded.

"My name is not Anton. It is Andreyan Baranovsky," he said.

Victor's brows went up. "Are you a wanted man?" he asked.

The older man laughed. "No, son, I don't think so." He picked up his glass and drank from it.

Birdie placed her hands on the table, said, "Fa." *Enough*.

Her father leaned forward, elbows on the table, said, "In the last days of World War Two, there was Red Army Intelligence created by Stalin, he called it Smert' Shpionam, it meant Death to Spies. They interviewed soldiers, Cossacks, and refugees returning to the Soviet Union. Many people, you understand, did not want to return."

"The agreement between the allies at Yalta," said Victor. "Forced repatriations."

Anton nodded, paused.

"We had all lost . . . well, you can imagine, the losses were terrible. Family members, friends, homes, people shared what they had, but they lived day to day, you know. At the end, I knew I had nothing to go back to."

He drank from his glass, went on. "I was serving in Berlin at the end of the war and got to know some of the American Forces there, they were allies, after all. I liked them, they were a friendly bunch. I had some English, we drank together, shared stories, there was a major who took a liking to me." He shrugged. "You know how it goes, maybe he missed a son back home, I didn't know where my father was, we talked about our interests."

Victor said, "How did you learn English, Anton?"

The man grinned. "One of the nuns who taught at my parish school when I was a boy. She received her education in England and wanted someone to practice with so she wouldn't forget. It fell to me, for a half hour each day, to learn a little English."

Victor and Birdie exchanged a look, she lifted her cup, drank her tea.

The narrative continued. "This major, you see, was very interested in the buildings, was heartbroken over the history that was being blown to pieces. I shared with him what I knew about building in the Soviet Union, I had worked on projects under my father who was an architect. Major Campbell, it turned out, owned a construction company."

Victor began to smile, swallowed some vodka, held onto the glass.

Birdie added tea to her cup, no vodka for her until her next checkup. She glanced at her mother, Johanna resting peacefully against her mother's shoulder.

Her father uncapped the bottle, poured, continued.

"He worked in military intelligence, Major Campbell," he said. "He obtained documents for me, identity papers, told me what to do. When the time came, I hid, I . . . deserted. It wasn't so unusual, there were others. I spent the next two years waiting for the right time, hiding, avoiding. Europe was a mess of displaced persons, camps, refugees, stateless people, resettled people, people fleeing repatriation, struggling to survive, starving. There were various agencies everywhere, barbed wire everywhere, unexploded munitions. Germany was cordoned off but I learned where to go, moved around between where the American third and seventh armies were patrolling."

Anton stopped to take a drink, the others remained silent.

"Finally, I saw my chance. The American Congress passed a displaced persons act that allowed Russians from the American zone in Berlin to immigrate into the United States. Major Campbell kept his word, he gave me a job, and I kept my new name."

Victor set his glass on the table. "What happened to your family, Anton? Is there anyone—"

Her father leaned forward. "My family is here in this room," he said intently. "Just like for you."

Johanna shifted and began to fuss. Birdie rose and lifted her from her mother's shoulder, cradled her in her arms, looked at Victor. She wanted to nurse her at home, it was time to go.

In the car, driving up Tamiami Trail, Victor had questions. "Did your mother know from the beginning, Birdie? Did they . . . when did they sit down and tell you?"

She stroked Johanna's back. "They told me when we came to Florida. I was going out on my own, they felt I was mature enough to understand. Fa told mother the day he proposed, he wanted her to know what she was getting into. She told him she didn't care."

He nodded. "His whole family gone, what a tragedy, do you know where they came from?"

"It's called St. Petersburg now, but it was Petrograd when he was born. Later it was called Leningrad. He had one older brother who was killed fighting in Poland. His mother died of cholera around the time the war broke out. His father died in a Nazi prison camp. I don't know about extended family. He has no pictures, which is so sad to me, so sad not to have a single photo of the ones you loved."

"What about the man in Detroit who took him in?"

"The major? He died seven years later. He left the business to Fa, his own son was killed in France during the war."

They arrived home, she carried the baby into the house, sat and lowered the shoulder of her dress and began to breastfeed. Victor sat on the chair opposite, watching.

She looked up at him.

"Beautiful," he said, went to her and kissed her head, drew a finger around the curve of her breast. "The doctor will clear you in a couple of weeks," he said.

She smiled.

Victor was on the telephone with his attorney, Birdie was out in the garden with Johanna, on her hands and knees pulling up weeds. It had rained earlier, she was taking advantage of the softer ground and cooler air.

She tilted her hat back, looked up at Victor as he walked toward them across the grass. His body language was neutral.

He hunched down so they were at the same eye level. "Okay, we're gonna take a hit, but she'll be out of our lives forever in five years."

She met his gaze.

"Child support until he reaches age eighteen, I wasn't opposed to that. The problem is, the state of California where she resides uses a different fee schedule than the state of Florida, and they've been doing a little investigative accounting so they know what my earnings and assets are, I didn't try to hide them."

She nodded. "What's the damage?"

"Twelve hundred a month. She lost on the retroactive support and she has a gag order, which means she can't disclose the case or the terms. Further, if she ever tries to contact me again without going through the attorney, she knows we'll take legal action."

She nodded, looked at Johanna and reached over to pull the blanket higher.

"Birdie . . ."

"Victor, I was just thinking about that poor boy, having a mother like that. When you were in college, what was her major, her degree? Does she have a good home for him?"

He laughed and stood upright. "Child psychology. Don't worry, he's not starving."

She awoke to firm hands on her shoulders, fingers digging skillfully into the muscles, moving lazily down, kneading the lower back, drifting between her legs.

Her eyes came open.

The clock showed one thirty-five, the house was peaceful, their room flooded in moonlight, she had forgotten again to lower the shade.

"Mmm," she said, stretching against him.

He kissed her neck, slid an arm around her waist.

"Birdie," he whispered.

She turned around, faced him.

He kissed her mouth a long time, warm and slow. "I miss you," he said.

She felt the familiar stirring, felt his hardness against her. She opened her mouth to him and brushed her tongue against his, moved around until she was sitting on top of him. "You don't have to miss me, I'm right here," smiled at him in the moonlight and leaned forward until her breasts were touching his chest.

He sat up, smiled softly, eased inside of her.

It was like a joyful homecoming after being away on a long trip.

They went to the house in Palm Springs. Victor made a case for needing a getaway from the uncertainties and agonies of the past months, he wanted to erase the remaining shadows of the illness, the tensions and annoyances of the lawsuit. A vacation, he said, to a place where only good memories had happened.

"Can you understand that, Birdie?"

She had looked in his eyes, seen his need for recuperation, and nodded. Victor was an introvert, would always seek solitude when the capriciousness of life became too painful or intrusive.

So here they were, the month of October stretched out before them like a laughing mistress. They shopped for baby things, set up the room for Johanna, talked and dreamed into the night while their child slept in her little room with the skylight in the ceiling.

He told her by the pool one night that it was Nicholas who had brought her back to him.

This surprised her. "Nicholas? What do you mean?"

He turned over on his stomach, rested his body across hers. "He came to see you when you were . . . when you were in the hospital." He never referred directly to her coma.

"Nicky was there?" She thought hard, she had not been able to identify any part of the week-long ordeal. For her, it had been a series of half-remembered dreams followed by a frightened and bewildered awakening.

He reached up, touched her face. "We were afraid, you know, that it might be the last time . . ."

"Oh Victor . . ."

"And when he came, he prayed over you."

She received this information in shocked silence, closed her eyes. "Poor Nicky."

"I don't think he's so poor. He seems to have a special connection with the Almighty that works. He told me that he does it every day, no rosary, no blessed virgin, he doesn't even go to confession, just talks directly to God. Nicholas said he asked him to wake you up and next thing we knew, there you were."

She didn't know what to say, there were tears in her eyes. She touched his cheek.

"I owe him, Birdie."

"Victor, you owe God, not Nicholas, but I'm glad you became friends."

Victor had a long phone conversation with Scott one afternoon. He was between books, mulling over ideas for the next, said it hadn't fully taken shape in his mind.

"Do you know who your protagonist is?" she asked him that night. He always worked from his main character, the plot, the location, everything else radiated from there.

He smiled, kissed her fingers one by one, turned her hand over in his. "I think so." Like her hand, he was turning over ideas, fitting them this way and that.

She shifted in the bed so she could fit her body against his, warm, firm, masculine. He swept his hand down her back, halted.

"Did you hear that?" he said.

She sighed, rolled away. "Yes."

Johanna.

He pushed aside the covers. It was his daughter, too.

They went to Tahquitz Canyon late the following morning, it was a short hike, the day hot and clear. A bighorn sheep greeted them when they turned a corner and stepped onto a plateau. Three others stood just beyond, gazing placidly at the human interlopers.

Victor looked over his shoulder at Birdie, grinned. "We're trespassing."

She glanced at Johanna, enfolded in the knapsack on his back like an oversized burrito. "Is it safe, should we turn around?"

"No, we'll go on, there's room out here for everyone."

Further ahead, the waterfall. It was their reward for the forty-minute walk in 84-degree heat.

He went to an auction with her one afternoon, inspected the rows of items with her, stood at her elbow as she asked questions, read her notations next to the catalog descriptions. He sat at her side with his hands in his lap, laughed aloud when they left with their prizes.

"You were great," he said.

She smiled. "My idea of fun."

"Your face is your weapon, you know."

She looked at him, raised a brow.

"You look so young, they don't take you seriously until it's too late."

She laughed, shrugged. "When I get back to the shop next month, these pieces will be the stars of the display case."

"Your mother'll sell them in no time, I'm sure."

Other days they read by the pool. Victor liked classic novelists, Dostoevsky, F. Scott Fitzgerald, she liked contemporary writers, P.D. James, Ian McEwan.

They made dinner together, green chile chicken, stuffed poblanos, beef tacos using the hot hatch chilis from Santa Fe, sometimes dancing to ZZ Top or Bonnie Raitt while they cooked. Neither of them cared for the disco music on the radio.

She watched him sometimes, when he was chopping chili peppers, walking arroyos, arranging furniture, changing his crying daughter. Without a book plot to keep him focused he seemed pensive, withdrawn.

One morning he went to her, she was taking pictures of Johanna by the fireplace, told her it was time to leave.

"What?" she said.

"It's our anniversary tomorrow."

"Yes, I know." She kissed his mouth. "Happy Anniversary."

He took the camera from her hands and led her to the sofa.

"Birdie, my solnyshka, we need to go home, I miss the gulf."

She looked in his eyes, saw what she needed to see, nodded.

Their flight arrived in Sarasota in early afternoon, they called her parents and asked them to take Johanna for the evening.

They went to Siesta Market and put together a picnic, drove over to Crescent Beach, sat and talked and made plans.

"A book a year," he said. "Just like I've been doing. It's not a bad pace, I like it, it keeps me focused. Maybe even a series like the publisher suggested. I'll think about it."

"My mother loves that shop," she said. "I haven't done much with it yet, but it's evolved from her helping out to a fifty-fifty proposition. I think it's better that way, gives me more flexibility."

She finished the last of the pear, wiped the juices from her hands and set aside the napkin.

"The sun will set in fifteen or twenty minutes," she said. "Maybe we'll catch that flash of green this time."

He nodded, looked out at the water, back at her. "It's been the best year of my life," he said. "A couple of rough patches but there was always you, you make everything worthwhile."

She put her arms around his waist. "I love being married to you, Victor."

"You ever wonder about the chain of events that brings people together, Birdie?" He turned and looked at her. "You know, those ordinary and not so ordinary things."

"You mean, destiny?"

He smiled, took her hand. "I've been thinking about the next novel, wondering which part of the war I should focus on. So much of what we are goes back to that war. When we think about the past, why things happen the way they do, it's often a mystery. But sometimes, if we wait long enough, we see things more clearly."

She nodded, squeezed his hand.

He shook his head. "Years ago, I was a little bitter about the divorce until I started thinking about it as part of a bigger picture. It actually made me more open to my uncle's suggestion to work for him, and that gave me the knowledge for a lifetime of investing, which gave me money to live on when I started writing, which meant I could live anywhere I wanted while I wrote, which meant I could come here to live when when Dana invited me. Later, when she died, I didn't understand why my heart had to be broken, didn't see where it could be leading."

He brushed the bangs from her face. "It led me to you."

She smiled softly.

He went on. "But long before all that, in another part of the world, there was a man whose parents sent him to a school where he would learn English."

She sat very still, watching him talk.

He kissed her hand, said gently. "That man from Russia has a story about the war that needs to be told, and I've been searching for such a story. He was a soldier, he had a destiny. He went through an historic time, a turbulent time, but he had courage and foresight. Now I have my main character, Birdie."

She stared at him.

He smiled. "Later, he came to Florida and built a life. He had a beautiful daughter, she married someone but they weren't a good match. But on just the right night, there was a party, and the writer with the broken heart went, and he met the beautiful girl who was no longer married to the wrong man. The two met and fell in love, and now they have a beautiful girl of their own. Now it all makes sense, pieces have fallen into place."

"Victor, are you sure?" she whispered.

He saw the tears in her eyes, leaned closer and kissed her mouth.

"Destiny playing out, Solnyshka," he said. "The soldier with a story and a beautiful daughter, and the writer who needed a story to tell. I love you, my sun, Happy Anniversary."

"Happy Anniversary," she said, leaning against him.

They watched the sun set, packed up their picnic things and drove home. They hadn't caught the flash of green this time, rain clouds had gathered and it was sprinkling. By the time they reached the car, they were damp.

When they arrived home they put away the rest of the food and Birdie looked for the wine.

"It must still be in the car," she said. "I'll be right back."

The door was locked when she ran back to the house. She rang the bell, rain fell lightly from the roof in a steady stream behind her.

No answer.

She rang again, a subtle sense of Déjà-vu whispered something to her memory.

After a minute the door opened, he stood dressed in his jeans and washed out tee-shirt, looked down at her and drew her inside.

"What are you doing here, Birdie?" he said.

She leaned against the door, looked at him curiously. Something . . .

It had rained the first night they spent together. She had gone to him.

She was very still. After a moment she said, slowly, "I was wondering if you wanted company. Tonight."

He took her hand, led her down the hall to his room, sat her on the edge of the bed.

"I wasn't expecting anyone, wait here," he said.

She did as she was told, sat and waited, looked around. It was a good room, dimly lit by a standing lamp behind a leather chair in the corner, with pictures on the walls, silent candles perched on a ledge above the bed. She was aware of a taut stillness inside her, a warmth and expectancy wound tightly. She knew what he would be like, had known from the first touch. She kicked her flip flops aside, waited.

He returned with a towel. "You're wet, let's get these things off you," he said, and he knelt on the floor in front of her and kissed her mouth. Their eyes met, he kissed her again.

"I remember," she whispered.

He smiled. "Do you remember what happened next?"

She nodded.

"Solnyshka, why don't you show me?"

She slid off the edge of the bed, and she showed him.

ABOUT THE AUTHOR

Jaime R. Forth spent most of her professional career writing about travel, public health, and politics before turning to contemporary fiction. Her first novel, *Midnight Pass,* was published in 2019. Her third novel, which also takes place on Siesta Key, is due to be published in summer 2021. She lives in Southwest Florida.

www.ingramcontent.com/pod-product-compliance
Lightning Source LLC
Chambersburg PA
CBHW020913160726
47993CB00005B/1958